A Hero for Ellie

A Hero for Ellie

Willow Wood Brides: Book 5

by

Teresa Slack

Other Titles

Willow Wood Brides:

A Promise for Josie: A Willow Wood Prequel
(Available to Newsletter Subscribers)
A Lawman for Lisette
A Love Letter for Jessa
A Dream for Harper
A Wedding for Felicity
A Hero for Ellie
A Cowboy for Meggan

Nine Brides for Cowboy Creek

Rennie
Eliza
Carrie
Bridget
Katie
Marianne
Scarlett
Rachael
Amelia

Jenna's Creek Series:

Streams of Mercy
Redemption's Song
Evidence of Grace
A Jenna's Creek Wedding-
(A Christmas Novella)
Legacy of Faith

Tender Blessings Series:

Love Begins
A Little Goodbye

Sterling Family Tree

Cheater, Cheater
The Money Tree
Carla Comes Around

The Ultimate Guide to Darcy Carter
Runaway Heart
Joy Redefined

What Readers are Saying about the Willow Wood Brides Series

"From stagecoaches and sheriffs to outlaws and saloons, your cowboy loving heart will be satisfied. Add a new lady doctor in town (when lady docs weren't exactly the norm --that's an understatement) and a romance, and you've got a great cozy read to hunker down with." –Linore Rose Burkard, award winning romance author, *Forever Lately*

"Teresa Slack hits one out of the ballpark again." Reader review

"Great romance & suspense read. …will keep you turning the pages and won't let you put the book down. Highly recommended." –Reader review

"Incredible characters that touch your heart! …Hooked from the first page. The author keeps the reader engrossed with mystery, romance and a longing for healing. Outstanding series that has me binge reading!" – Reader review

"…Fun characters and a great setting with a nice pacing made this book a true escape. Historical fans, you'll want to read this one. –Reader review

"…Loved this book by Teresa Slack. Her characters are both interesting and real. This book hooked me with in 4 pages. I could not put it down. I can hardly wait until the next book comes out." –Reader review

"...Suspense, intense action, and tender moments to warm your heart. Well written...and the ending wrapped everything up nicely. I highly recommend reading it." – Reader review

"Once I started reading I had such a hard time putting it down! It's one of those books that makes you feel good while you're reading it, and after you're through! I'm so ready for the next one in this series!" –Reader review

"A good balance of action, life in the West, danger and romance. The characters were well developed, and the settings described so well that the reader feels right there." –Reader review

"Another wonderful read... These kinds of stories keep you intrigued, wondering how the love story is going to pan out." –Reader review

"Rating this book a 5! ...Teresa's work never fails to keep me on my toes from beginning to end. I would love to read the next book in the series, or even one of the author's previous series. I am never disappointed with any of her work." –Reader review

"Love this new book! I love the descriptive writing and the fact that it is so different from her other books! I hope she will have more installments of this one." –Reader review

Dedication

For my beautiful sisters in Christ, Linda Warnock,
Becky Norman, and Angie Williams. Your support of
my writing and enthusiasm for the books is so
appreciated and means the world to me.

Chapter One

March, 1892

The ground shifted under the horse's feet. Ellie Lundy stiffened in the saddle and tightened her legs around the horse's body as if the pressure would keep the animal upright.

She shouldn't have chosen this trail. The last few weeks had been unseasonably wet. That, coupled with winter thaw from the last few months' snow accumulation, had made a painting excursion into the mountains this morning reckless at best. At worst, she may have gravely injured herself or the horse.

Saturn had whinnied and reared his head less than a heartbeat before the mountain's vibration traveled through the horse's legs and into the saddle. Ellie was halfway to the ridge that provided the easiest route back to the hotel where a livery hand would see to the mount while she went over her work. Her feet were cold inside her muddy boots, and her eyes burned from squinting into the rising sun as she captured the glorious sunrise over the lake. But she was too excited about painting again after a long, dreary winter to think about rest and sleep.

All thoughts of the productive morning flew out of her head as the strange vibration turned to a rumble. A rushing, crashing, ground-shaking rumble that seemed to echo through every sinew and fiber in her limbs.

The rumble roared over her like a tidal wave. Dust rose into the air, stinging her nostrils and lungs and obscuring her view.

Panic and fear forced her to act without conscious thought. She leaned over the pommel until she was nearly flat against the terrified horse's neck and buried her fists in its mane. She urged it off the trail to her left and away from the avalanche's heaving epicenter.

The horse leaped off the trail just as the ground disappeared under its hooves. A rock about the size of a melon glanced off Saturn's shoulder and barely missed Ellie's chest.

The heart-pounding roar continued as the horse leaped farther away from the trail. Through the dirt and debris, Ellie saw the vegetation beneath the horse's hooves had been laid flat from the winter's thaw. Fresh panic rose within her as the horse fought for traction on the slick slope. Saturn whinnied in fear and alarm. His hooves lost purchase. Ellie ripped her feet free from the stirrups and pushed her body as hard as she could away from the direction of the falling horse. Her teeth clacked together when she hit the ground hard. She tasted blood. Ignoring the pain in her mouth and her right shoulder which took the brunt of the fall, she rolled to avoid the horse. Its massive body hit the ground not four feet from her, its hooves a blur as they rushed at her face.

She flinched and squeezed her eyes shut, but the blow didn't come. Saturn leaped to his feet and charged into the brush.

Ellie hugged the mountain beneath her. Ragged breath pounded in her ears. Blood ran over her lips and dripped off her chin. Gingerly, she ran her tongue around the inside of her mouth. No broken teeth, thank goodness. She poked her tongue between her lips and winced as she found the source of the blood. Her upper lip was already swelling under her probing tongue.

She started to lift her hand to find the wound. Fresh pain exploded through her right shoulder. She warily opened her eyes to survey the damage. From the degree of agony, she half expected to find a tree limb impaled through her shoulder or her arm hanging by a tendon.

Both shoulder and arm were intact and whole. She exhaled and nearly burst into tears. "Thank you, God."

The sound of her voice, muffled around her swollen lip, seemed to echo in the earth's sudden stillness.

No crashing rocks. No falling trees. No panicked panting from the horse. All was completely still.

She remained flat against the ground and caught her breath. Not far from her head, a bird landed in the brush. A breeze whispered through the thin branches over her head. Somewhere below, a deer or other cautious animal moved into the open. The world was already restoring order upon itself.

Ellie needed to do the same. She rolled onto her left side—which thankfully did not scream out in pain—and carefully inventoried her injuries.

Her right shoulder and wrist had taken the brunt of her fall. She wiggled her toes inside her boots and shifted her legs. Her right hip hurt nearly as much as her wrist and shoulder, but she was able to pull her legs toward her chest and maneuver into a seated position. She lifted her left hand to her face. Her eyes were still in their sockets, and her ears remained where they'd been her whole life. Her nose smarted, but she could inhale without difficulty. She found the source of blood on her top lip. She reached under her skirt and tore off a length of her shift and held it against her lip.

As she waited for the blood to clot, she looked around. Saturn was nowhere in sight. The horse had either run over the ridge or back down the hill toward the stream. She wondered if he would come if she whistled. Whether he would or not was moot since she couldn't fit her lips together to produce a decent whistle.

She couldn't see the top of the ridge from where she sat, but she had been nearly there when the earth began to move under Saturn's hooves. She was at least three miles from Scottstown. In all her trips through the area, she had never seen a farm or cabin between the ridge and the tiny settlement where she spent the night when she went into the mountains to paint. If Saturn wasn't waiting for her on the ridge, it would be a long hike back to the hotel, especially with her hip and shoulder complaining with every step.

She struggled to her feet and straightened as best she could on the steep incline. She groaned in dismay at the damage around her. Most of the trail had been obliterated by the rockslide. Huge boulders balanced precariously against each other. Navigating the mountainside would be dangerous and nearly impossible unless she could find the trail the horse had taken. She reached for a tree root to hoist herself past the first rock.

Something called out. Loud. In pain. And close.

Ellie froze in her tracks. On the hillside it was impossible to tell from which direction the sound had come. She trained her ears and listened. Silence. Had it been her imagination? Or from farther away, and her pain and fear amplified the sound?

Before she could take another step, the sound came again. Her heart froze. It sounded like a horse or other animal in pain and distress. Saturn may have gotten spooked and run into the avalanche. If so, there wasn't a thing she could do for him. She couldn't leave her faithful mount hurting and alone either.

She picked her way through the rocks and debris until she came to a spot that provided a clear view to the top of the ridge and the open sky beyond. She was tempted to forget the injured horse and begin the climb. Her body ached from head to toe. Once she arrived in Scottstown, she would send someone back to see to the injured animal.

Immediately, she realized that was out of the question. It would take at least three hours for her to reach help and another three—at least—for rescuers to find this spot. By then, it would be too late for whatever lay broken among the rocks.

She turned in the direction of the sound and continued her trek around the face of the mountain. She had only made about fifty feet of progress when she heard the sound again. Louder and more distinct.

It wasn't Saturn. Whatever was out there had been caught in the epicenter of the avalanche. Whether a horse or mountain cat or bear, something was dying on the other side of the hill.

She pulled herself along, grasping at exposed tree roots and flat spots and refusing to think of hibernating snakes that had been awakened by the rockslide. When she was a girl a father of one of the boys at school had killed a rattlesnake in the mountains. The boy brought the decapitated snake to school to show off to his friends and terrify the girls. Ellie had bad dreams for a month after.

After ten minutes of carefully stepping from one rock to the next, she realized she hadn't heard the sound again. Perhaps whatever it was had succumbed to its injuries, and she was wasting precious daylight and energy searching for it. She climbed onto a large boulder to catch her breath. If she didn't hear anything in the next sixty seconds she was going back.

Not six feet in front of her, she saw it. If she had continued around the boulder in her original path she would've nearly stepped on the magnificent creature's head.

A horse's broken body was angled up the hill toward her. Huge, terrified eyes stared at her. The animal's sides heaved from pain and exertion.

"Oh, no," Ellie cried out in dismay at its suffering. She knew horses and recognized the large bay was as big and powerful as any of the horses Papa kept in the stables at home.

"You poor thing," she said in a soothing voice. The horse looked nearly delirious, but she didn't want to alarm it further. Forgetting her own pain, she crouched on the rock to crawl closer. There wasn't a thing she could do but try to soothe the proud animal and keep it company as it died.

Then she saw the saddle cinched around the horse's heaving side, and she groaned again. An empty saddle.

She stood and looked over the horse. "Hello?" she called softly. She didn't want to panic the horse more than it already was. She also didn't want to trigger another avalanche.

"Anyone there?"

She listened but didn't hear anything over the horse's labored breathing. "Hello?" she called out louder. She didn't expect a reply. If the horse was this bad off, she could only imagine the state of the rider.

The least she could do was find the body and take note of the location to make it easier for men from Scottstown to recover the remains.

She picked her way down the mountainside to circle the horse. The bay either heard her or sensed her presence. It gathered what was left of its strength and struggled against the pile of rocks that pinned it.

Ellie's heart sank at the horse's distress, but she kept going. The animal was beyond help. As she scanned the hillside, she nearly wished she wouldn't find whoever had occupied the saddle. Last summer Papa had been thrown from a horse and killed. She had been the first to reach him that night. The sight of his blood mingling with the rain and running like a river into the gutter still jerked her from sleep most every night.

Frustration and weariness washed over her. "Where are you?" she cried, forgetting for a moment the risk of another rockslide. "Answer me. You're not dead. I'm here. I'm coming."

Twenty feet past the horse, she spotted the man nearly concealed under the rocks. He wasn't moving.

Chapter Two

C lementine was dead. Or dying.

Zach Walsh couldn't tell which from his position where he'd landed when the avalanche struck. He hadn't heard the horse panting or moving around for a while. It could already be over.

"Please, Lord, don't make her suffer more than she has to," he whispered.

The only thing worse than hearing the life ebb out of his beautiful friend was knowing her death was his fault.

A sob lodged in his throat. Over the last five years, Clementine had become an extension of himself. She was a solid, sturdy mount who read his movements as if she understood every word he spoke. He loved her and would miss her nearly as much as he would his own right arm. She deserved better than a slow, painful death on this mountainside because of his carelessness.

It was only fair that his own precarious situation wasn't any better than Clementine's. Fireballs of pain lit up all over his body. With his head pointed down the hill and his legs pointed up, all he could see past his chest was his right boot. The top of his head throbbed with every heartbeat. Blood plastered his hair to his forehead and pooled in his ears and on his neck. He had explored the area enough with his fingers to know the blood wasn't coming from his face, ears, or neck. But when he tried to touch the top of his head, fear prevented much of an examination. His hair was sticky from blood and his head felt like it belonged on someone else's body. He knew he wouldn't last long before the blood loss or swelling under his skull did him in.

He wasn't sure what had become of his left leg and foot. A jumble of rocks covered the left half of his body. It was probably just as well that he couldn't see what was going on, considering he couldn't feel anything below his belt buckle.

He was going to die on this mountain alongside the horse, and no one would ever know.

That was probably just as well, too. Ma was the only one who would care, and she was gone. Abigail had written him last summer to tell him their mother had passed away. Zach had almost been relieved to know her suffering and shame had finally reached its end. Her spirit rested in the arms of Jesus now, free from the disgrace her son had brought upon her.

Zach didn't believe shame or remorse existed in Heaven, but he planned to apologize to her once he got there, nonetheless. And to Pa. They had done their best to raise him right, but he had flung their teaching back in their faces.

He laid his head against the rocks and closed his eyes to the treetops overhead. "Lord, give me strength." He thought he spoke the words aloud, but he couldn't be sure over the pounding of blood in his head.

This morning when he left the cabin, he had known the ground was too soft for travel. Winter thaw had loosened the rocks at the top of the ridge. But he had to see to the traps he had set out along the stream two days ago. If he left them unattended for long, the captured pelts could be buried under a late snow or stolen by scavengers. He needed the money from the pelts for seed for the coming spring planting.

This was the first clear day he'd seen in weeks. The vivid blue sky had reflected off the creek as he collected a good supply of pelts. When he finished, he considered following the stream north to where it circled around the mountain, but it would've added five miles and several hours to the trip. He didn't have the hours to spare. A never-ending list of chores demanded his attention. He couldn't allow one errand to turn into an all-day job.

Now the chore had cost him Clementine and possibly his own life. Caesar, his other horse, and the cattle in the field would manage well enough without him. They'd eventually tire of waiting for him to come home and drift onto another rancher's spread. The chickens and the goose would get along just fine. The only one that worried him—besides his own fool self—was Bossie the milk cow. She'd be powerful miserable in a few hours if he didn't get home to milk her, to say nothing of tomorrow and the next day. More needless suffering inflicted upon an innocent because of his poor choices. He had a history of that.

He needed to get off this mountain.

He turned his eyes as far as he could without moving his aching head to gage his position. If he shifted to try to move some of the rocks from his body, he was likely to slide the rest of the way down the mountain. He closed his eyes and took a deep breath to quell the rising panic. He had to keep his head if he was going to make it out of this fix alive.

The instant before the rocks let go of the ridge above Clementine, Zach thought he heard a sound, like the cry of alarm from a small animal. It had reminded him of a woman, but that couldn't be. He'd lived out here nearly five years and had never encountered a woman. He barely saw anyone at all. There wasn't another homestead between here and Scottstown. The only time he heard a woman's voice was when he went into town to sell his pelts and crops for food and supplies he couldn't raise on the farm.

He had attended church a time or two since moving here from Catahoula Parish, Louisiana. Each time, he found himself on the receiving end of appraising glances and welcoming smiles from every unmarried woman and her mother in attendance. He didn't encourage attention from the women of Scottstown. There was no place in his life for a woman. It wasn't that he didn't want one. But a wife deserved better than a husband who'd done the things he'd done and then skipped town to flee the whispers and judgmental stares.

Even though he knew he could never have a woman in his life, he sure wished one waited for him today back at the farm. In a few hours, she'd realize something was wrong and come looking for him. A woman couldn't do much to free him from the rocks and debris that pinned him to the side of the mountain, but he wouldn't have to die alone.

He wanted to call out for help. Scream. Beg. Cry. Anything to release the frustration, and yes, the fear. But calling for help would only waste what remained of his strength. He was two miles from home. Scottstown was three and a half in the opposite direction. No one with any good sense was on this mountain. And if they were, they were in no better shape than he was.

If he managed to get out from under this pile of rubble, he'd never make it to the top of the ridge and back to the ranch without Clementine. His head was split open, and his left leg was busted in who knew how many pieces. He couldn't even tell if it was still attached to his body. It sure didn't feel like it.

He trained his eyes back on the sky. After all these years, God had orchestrated a bitter justice for what he'd done. One might escape retribution from a small town sheriff, but he couldn't expect to outrun God.

Zach wondered how long it would take the pain or blood loss or exposure to finish him off. Though he had no right to seek mercy, he prayed it would happen quickly before scavengers came, attracted by Clementine's death throes or the smell of his own blood. His rifle was in the scabbard strapped to the bay. His sidearm was within reach, but that would only hold them off a short time.

Through the pain-addled fog, he thought he heard something approach on the other side of Clementine. A wolf maybe or a mountain cat. If he had to be torn apart and dragged out from under the rocks, he hoped God would hold the animals off until he was dead.

The noise came again. He put his hand to the butt of his gun. His gun belt was full of ammunition, but he was so weak he doubted his shaking hands could reload fast enough to protect himself or Clementine.

Whatever the animal was, it was getting closer. Then he heard a voice. A woman's voice. Zach's eyes widened. Impossible. His brain was playing tricks on him. Or he was dreaming, though he was pretty sure he was awake. He tried to lift his head, but it felt as heavy as a bucket of coal. He was better off remaining still and conserving his strength until the thing got within gun range. Though he hoped death would take him quickly, he knew he would fight it with every fiber of his being.

Clementine thrashed against the rocks again. Zach groaned in dismay. She wasn't dead. She was suffering. She made an easy target for whatever was skulking along the hillside. He prayed whatever it was would kill him first so he wouldn't have to listen while his beloved horse was torn apart.

The sound came again. A voice. Unmistakable this time. He had no idea how, but it was human. And a woman at that.

It sounded like the voice was talking, but he couldn't make out the words. He tried to look in that direction, but his head wouldn't cooperate. Then she stepped into view.

An angel.

The most beautiful creature he'd ever seen glided across the rocks toward him.

"Am I dead?" he tried to ask, but he couldn't get his lips to move.

Zach allowed the angel's voice to lull him to sleep. In his dream, peace washed over him as the angel gazed down at him, love and compassion in her dark eyes. She had come to take him home. He would wake up in Heaven with no headache and no mangled leg. He hoped Clementine would be there too. He would leap into the saddle, and the two of them would ride like the wind across an endless prairie where neither would ever tire.

No mocking voices to him of how he had failed Pa, shamed Ma, and killed Clementine.

Zach focused on the angel. He hoped he would see her in Heaven. Long dark hair swirled around her slim shoulders. Gentleness shone from her smoldering dark eyes. Zach sank into the rocks as if they were a feather bed beneath him. His pain was nearly over. God had truly forgiven him for the evil he'd done, and He was taking him to heaven.

The angel finally reached his side. She tried to speak. Something was wrong with her mouth. Her lips were blue and swollen. Zach couldn't understand what she was trying to say, but it was the loveliest sound he'd ever heard. The rocks fell away as if they weighed nothing, and he sat up. He reached out to the angel. She smiled sweetly.

Sheer joy washed over him. "Did you come to take me home?" he asked.

"I'm so glad I found you, Zach." Her voice was as sweet as honey. "You knew we wouldn't stop looking for you."

Dread rose in his gut. It was a trap. She wasn't here to save him. She had come to condemn him.

"Hurry, Zach. Stand up. Face your accusers like a man."

He blinked. There they were. The whole gang. He recognized each one of his old friends. Standing on the rocks above him, some laughing, others sneering.

Justice. God had forgiven him, but these men never would. He couldn't even forgive himself.

Zach tried to stand. His left leg exploded in pain. He looked again. The men were gone. Only the angel remained. Rocks covered the lower half of his body again. The angel knelt at his feet trying to move them aside, but they were too heavy. There were too many. He tried to tell her to stop. It hurt too much. He couldn't speak.

As if reading his thoughts, she crawled along his body, moving carefully on the uneven rocks. She stopped at his gun belt and put her hand on his sidearm.

He exhaled in relief. The angel was going to shoot him. A quick and just end. He hoped she'd shoot Clementine, too. The horse didn't deserve the circumstances he'd put her in.

He closed his eyes. While he welcomed the end to his misery, he didn't want to see it coming.

Like a butterfly's wings, the angel's cool fingers settled on his throat. Zach hadn't felt anything so soft in years. He tried to move against them. The smell of lilacs filled his nose. He breathed deeply, relishing the scent. What were lilacs doing on the mountain this time of year? Maybe this was what Heaven smelled like.

His eyes fluttered open. The angel's face was suspended a few inches above his. Her swollen, battered lips were so close. He parted his own lips to receive her kiss. The angel's eyes widened, and her sumptuous mouth sprang open. She emitted a blood-curdling scream. Zach jerked away. His head thudded against the rocks. White hot pain burst out of the top of his head. Everything went black.

Chapter Three

Ellie screamed and jumped away from the stricken man, nearly losing her footing on the uneven pile of rocks. She had kept her eyes on him the entire time she circled the horse to reach him. He hadn't moved as much as a muscle. From the way he lay twisted and half-buried among the rocks, she knew he couldn't have survived the fall from the horse. His left leg appeared to be partially under him and under the rocks. It may have even been severed in the fall. She wouldn't be surprised if his back was broken as well. It was probably a good thing he would never know.

A pool of blood had collected on the rocks above his head. She had nearly burst into tears at the sight of it as it stirred memories of Papa's gruesome death. She wanted to scurry back up the hill and leave the man and the horse to the mercy of the mountain. There was nothing she could do for either of them anyway. She was only one person. The man was already dead. The horse would be, too, in a matter of minutes. She needed to start thinking of her own precarious circumstances.

She forced her feet to stand still. "Think about someone other than yourself for once, Ellie Lundy," she scolded aloud. "You can't leave a fellow human being on this mountain to be torn apart by animals. Aren't you tired of being selfish? Aren't you tired of being *afraid*?"

She *was* tired. Sick and tired of the cowardly woman she'd been most of her life. She didn't want to be that woman anymore.

Even though she couldn't help the man, she owed it to his family or whoever was waiting for him to find out who he was. When she reached his body, she knelt at his feet to determine the damage to his left leg. She removed a few rocks and was relieved to see the leg hadn't been severed, not that it mattered at this point.

She slowly moved up his body and paused at his gun belt. Many frontier men carried distinctive guns. The sidearm could help identify him when she got back to Scottstown. She didn't see any descriptive marks or initials, but she took note of the gun anyway before continuing toward the man's head.

Up close, his color looked better than she had expected for a dead man. She stared down at his chiseled features, his broad forehead and angular jaw. Who was he? How had he ended up on this mountainside alone? She estimated him at about her age. Twenty-six or thereabouts. It was always hard to tell with men who spent their time exposed to the elements. She was a bit surprised to find him cleanshaven. Most frontier men didn't put much effort into hygiene. This one apparently did. Though his clothes were ripped and covered with dust from the rockslide, they were in good condition and free from stains. That indicated a woman waiting for him in a cabin somewhere. A woman who would never know what became of her husband if Ellie didn't do something.

Ellie imagined a wife in a plain dress and apron, standing at the cabin door, her gaze sweeping the mountain peaks, watching for movement, for a horse to take shape out of the pines, bringing her man home. Sadness for this unknown woman washed over Ellie. She knew loss. She had waited for two and a half years for Matthew Dunleavy to come back to her. Long before she knew what happened to him, her heart had known he was gone. She hadn't been able to face the truth, so she continued to wait. Continued to hope for the sound of his feet at her door, his voice calling to her.

She couldn't let another woman suffer the same pain and not knowing.

She laid her fingertips against the man's throat. She hadn't expected his skin to be cool since dust from the avalanche still hung in the air, but she hadn't expected the degree of warmth on his throat either.

Was it possible he had survived the avalanche?

She moved her fingers around his broad neck, more for her own assurance than for his sake. If she found Saturn waiting at the top of the hill, it would still take a good hour to reach Scottstown considering the trail conditions following the avalanche. If she had to walk, she wouldn't reach the settlement before dark. It would be too late to send anyone back to retrieve his remains. By morning who knew what would be left of him.

She shuddered. She couldn't leave until she confirmed he was dead, and completely so.

Beneath her fingertips she thought she felt a flutter. A pulse. No, it couldn't be. She leaned closer and angled her cheek toward his nose and mouth. She heard a slight intake of air. She jerked her gaze back to the man, her face only a few inches from his.

Vivid blue eyes sprang open and looked up at her. The man stiffened, as much in shock as she was. Though Ellie had been hoping for this very thing, she screamed. The once-dead man jerked away from her. His head bounced off the rock where he lay. His eyes closed again.

She flinched at the sound. "Oh, no. I'm so sorry." She patted his cheek, just beginning to bristle from a morning shave. "Mister, are you all right? I didn't mean to scare you. Are you hurt?"

She winced. Of course he was hurt. It was nothing short of a miracle he wasn't dead. She had probably just finished him off.

"I'm so sorry," she repeated, gentler this time. "Mister, can you hear me? Please open your eyes. Please don't be dead."

The man's eyes fluttered open. Ellie exhaled. She would've hugged him if not for fear she'd kill him good and proper this time. "Oh, thank goodness. You're alive."

He didn't seem to hear. His gaze swept her face and stopped at her split lip. In the last few minutes, she had forgotten her own injuries. She must look a sight. Her cheek was scraped. Her hair was tangled and full of dust and twigs. She could barely close her mouth around her swollen lips.

"Are you an angel?" he asked.

She laughed at the absurdity of the question. "No. I'm not."

His brow furrowed in doubt. He raised his right hand and touched her face. She winced as his thumb gently brushed a rising knot on her cheekbone. She hadn't felt a man's calloused hand on her skin since—since Matthew. Despite everything, it was nice.

"You are real," he announced.

"Very much so." She took hold of his wrist and lowered it to his side. She took a deep breath as the warmth from his touch subsided.

"I'm Ellie. Who are you?"

He squeezed his eyes shut against a spasm of pain.

"Zach Walsh," he said through gritted teeth.

"Well, Zach Walsh, everything is going to be all right. I'm going to get you off this mountain."

As soon as the words slipped past her tongue, she wondered how she planned to do it. Zach was big; at least six feet tall. He outweighed her by no less than sixty pounds. She couldn't assist him to his feet, let alone help him to the top of the mountain where her horse may or may not be waiting, and then all the way to Scottstown. But if she didn't do something, and do it fast, he was going to die right in front of her.

He glanced past her, probably hoping she wasn't alone. Disappointment darkened his features. Ellie didn't have time to salve his worries.

First things first.

She needed to elevate his head to staunch the bleeding and access his wounds. Then she needed to get the rocks off him. If nothing else, it would make him more comfortable while she saw to his head.

She glanced around for something to prop him up so his head would be higher than the rest of him, or at least not pointing directly downhill.

A few feet on the other side of him she spotted a tree limb that had been severed in the rockslide. She scurried around him and snatched it up.

"I'm so sorry but I have to elevate your head and shoulders. This isn't going to be comfortable."

She snaked her arm under his shoulders and tried to lift. He barely budged. She gasped from the effort. "You're going to have to help me, Mr. Walsh." She shifted a few rocks off him and put her arm back in place. "I'll lift, and you raise your shoulders as far off the ground as you can. We've got to slow the blood loss from your head before we worry about the rest of you."

She still hadn't looked too closely at the wound. For all she knew, his skull was split wide open. She managed not to gag. His thick, wheat-colored hair was slick with blood. That was enough to tell her it was more than a scratch. She had no idea what she would do once she determined the extent of the damage. She'd worry about that when the time came. All she could hope for was someone else—anyone but her—would come along and take over.

She wedged her shoulder as close to the center of his back as she could reach and braced her feet against the rocks.

"Are you ready, Mr. Walsh? I'll push as hard as I can while you lift."

"Take—take it slow," he murmured. "I think—I'm going to black out again."

"Please don't do that. We've got to get you elevated so I can look at your head."

Ellie shifted her feet among the rocks to get a better grip. "All right. Are you ready? Let's go."

As slowly and as gently as she could, she pushed her shoulder into the man's back. She knew it hurt, but they had no choice. Every minute put him closer to bleeding to death. He was surprisingly strong considering what he'd gone through. He managed to raise up enough for her to shove the branch under his shoulders. His head still wasn't higher than his heart, but at least it was no longer pointed down the hill.

He grimaced as he leaned against the limb. Ellie stood and looked around again. She needed something to make him more comfortable so he could maintain the position while she examined the top of his head.

If her horse was here, she could use her saddle and cover him with her bedroll. She always carried emergency supplies into the mountains. Water, a blanket, a little food. Getting lost, stranded, or injured was always a consideration, even in the best of circumstances.

Her horse was nowhere in sight but his was. She looked at the animal, exhausted, sweating and panting among the rocks.

"We need your saddle." Even as she said it, she had no idea how she would ungird it from around the massive animal and drag it to him.

He followed her gaze. He slumped against the tree limb. His face was ravaged with pain. And now grief.

"She's dying," he said. "You have to do it."

Ellie's breath lodged in her throat. "Do what?" she squeaked out.

"End it."

The blood drained from her face. "I—I can't."

He clamped his hand around her wrist, surprising her at his strength. "She's suffering. Don't you have a heart?"

Ellie tried to pull free. "Yes, but I—I can't." Her heart ached at the thought of the beautiful horse suffering on the rocks, but she wasn't the one to take action. She got squeamish when she had to squash a spider. Wasn't it enough that she was trying to save *him*?

He held fast to her wrist. "My rifle." He looked past her to the scabbard hanging from his saddle. "Please." He released her wrist and slumped back against the limb.

He was right; she had no choice. The longer she took to put the horse out of its misery, the worse Zach's condition would become. On shaky legs, she stood and faced the horse. Blocking what she was about to do from her mind, she climbed across the rocks to reach the scabbard. Fortunately, the horse had fallen on its side opposite the scabbard. Perhaps if it hadn't, the rifle would've discharged, saving her the task of shooting it.

Ellie pulled the rifle free and broke it open. As expected, it was fully loaded.

She looked back at Zach. He watched her, his face a grim mask of determination.

She dried her sweating hands, one at a time, on her skirt. She climbed onto a rock above the horse and looked down at it. The mare's chest continued to rise and fall, but its breathing was shallower than before. It was too weak to even look at her.

Ellie squeezed her eyes shut to gather her nerve. What if she missed, though it was unlikely at such close range? What if her bullet grazed the animal and only added to its suffering? What if the bullet ricocheted off a rock and hit her or Zach?

She opened her eyes. Zach had leaned forward a few inches, his body rigid. His face was tight with pain. Whether for himself or the horse, she couldn't tell.

She had to act. Now. Each labored breath from the horse tore at her heart. She couldn't let it suffer another moment. She knew how to use a firearm. Growing up in Willow Wood, a frontier town where men outnumbered women four to one, Papa made sure she could protect herself. One carefully aimed shot would do the job. But target shooting bottles off a fence was a different matter than shooting and killing a living, breathing thing.

"Stop being a coward, Ellie," she whispered aloud. "Do what needs done."

She swung the rifle onto her shoulder. She winced at the stiffness where she had landed when she fell off the horse. She gritted her teeth and stared down the barrel. She blinked away the sweat in her eyes and took a steadying breath.

A gun exploded beside her. A wheezing gasp escaped from the horse, and the animal went quiet. Ellie lowered the rifle and spun around to face Zach, still holding a smoking sidearm.

"What are you doing? You could've hit a rock. Or me."

"You were taking too long," he growled. "I couldn't watch her suffer another second."

Ellie wanted to defend herself. She had been about to pull the trigger. But could she have gone through with it? She wasn't sure.

She carefully laid the rifle on a level spot on the rocks. Shooting the horse had taken the last of Zach's strength. He stared through the tree limbs over his head. She didn't have time to chastise her cowardice. Her inability to end the horse's misery was another example of her many weaknesses. And now, here she stood, wholly responsible for another human being. If there was a God in heaven, He had a wry sense of humor.

Chapter Four

Ellie picked her way across the expanse of rocks and churned earth until she reached Zach's side. "I need your knife." She indicated the long blade strapped to his belt.

He looked past her to the horse and back again. A good saddle was as valuable to a frontier man as a good horse. To allow someone to cut the cinch strap and render the saddle useless was sacrilege, even in a life or death situation.

Ellie held out her hand. Whether he realized it or not, there was no time to delay or discuss alternative plans. Wearily, he loosened the fob that held the knife in the leather sheath. Ellie carefully took the long blade from him and hurried back to the horse as quickly as she could. Her right shoulder was so sore it took some effort to saw through the thick leather, even though the knife was razor sharp. When she completed that task, she sat on the boulders, braced her feet against another to leverage herself, and pulled the saddle free. She had handled saddles before. This one probably weighed forty pounds. Her injured right arm made it feel like eighty.

Ignoring the pain as best she could, she dragged the intricately tooled saddle across the rocks. Zach pulled himself forward with his right hand while she positioned the saddled over the tree limb. He sank gratefully into it. He may never use the saddle again, but she could see the relief in his face as it took the pressure off his back against the tree limb. His head was now elevated another ten inches, which would surely help staunch the blood flow.

Ellie went back to the horse and pulled the saddlebags free. She dropped them next to Zach and opened the first one as she asked; "Do you have a sewing kit in here?"

She always carried one when riding alone. If he hadn't thought to bring one, he was in for a world of hurt.

He squeezed his eyes shut against another spasm of pain. "I don't think so."

She stopped rummaging. It was just as well. She had no way to sterilize a needle or thread, and she wasn't sure how well regular fabric thread would work to stitch a man's head together.

She noticed the canteen strap around his chest She followed the strap to where a canteen lay partly under him. She pulled it free. She uncapped the canteen and tipped it over his mouth. She wanted a drink as well to remove the dust and grit from between her teeth, but she might need the water to clean his wound. If she had to, she could climb down the hill to the creek. It would take a long time to get there and back. Hopefully his wound wasn't as bad as it looked. He was still alert and talking.

That was a good sign. If he was going to die from the head wound, he would at least be in shock by now.

"Mr. Walsh, do you have any whiskey?"

"Please, call me Zach. The only people who call me Mr. Walsh are bankers and lawyers, and I don't have much use for either of them."

Ellie was heartened that he had retained a bit of a sense of humor. "My apologies. Zach, do you have any whiskey?"

"Why? Do you need some to steady your hands?" More humor. She smiled in reply. He must be quite a man to make jokes at a time like this.

"Not for me," she said. "For you. I need to look at your head, and I'm sure it will be quite unpleasant."

"It's already unpleasant, and no, I don't have any whiskey."

Ellie wasn't sure if his lack of imbibement was a good thing or bad. Most men traveled with a flask of some kind. She felt safer in his presence knowing he didn't have any with him. He probably wasn't a bandit or a ne'er-do-well. And there was almost certainly a wife waiting for him at home.

"All right, then. I'm going to move my hands around a little on your head to see if you cracked your skull. Hopefully all you've done is broken the skin."

She swallowed hard. Even the most skilled physician could only do so much for a head wound. If the damage went deeper than the skin, he probably wasn't long for this world. He seemed cognizant enough, but he could keel over at any moment.

Don't let me see brains. Don't let me see brains, she chanted to herself as she moved behind him. She grimaced as she parted his blood-soaked hair. She should've gone to the creek first, though she had nothing to bring water back in except the canteen and it wouldn't hold enough to clean his hair.

Her hands hovered over what seemed to be the source of the bleeding. She took a deep breath to steady her hands. She had a nice pair of leather gloves in her saddlebag. Leather gloves weren't good for accessing a head wound but wearing them would surely be better than touching a stranger's disgusting bloody head with her bare hands. In Willow Wood, there was a lady doctor, Lisette Dutton. Ellie knew her quite well since Dr. Dutton had visited Ellie every week for nearly a year. Ellie knew her quite well since Dr. Dutton had visited Ellie every week for nearly a year to treat her melancholy after her fiance's disappearance. Since Ellie wasn't sick anywhere but in her heart, there was nothing the lady doctor could do for her. Except listen and help Ellie take her mind off herself.

The visits had helped, and Ellie had great faith in the doctor's abilities. What she wouldn't give to see Dr. Dutton ride over the hill about now on her gray dun mare, Damsel. But there was no doctor. No leather gloves. No needle and thread. No way to sterilize anything. And no choice but to find out just how much damage had been done to Mr. Walsh's—Zach's—head.

"All right, Zach. Here we go."

On the crown of his head, slightly left of center, she saw an angry goose egg rising through the hair. She carefully parted the hair above the swelling to begin her examination. The metallic smell of warm blood assailed her nose so strong she could taste it. She turned her face away and gagged silently. She couldn't have her patient knowing she had a weak stomach. Fortunately, she hadn't eaten since breakfast or she may have discarded it on his shoulder. So far, it was only blood. She could handle blood—she hoped—as long as wasn't knuckle deep in his brains.

She swallowed back the nausea and continued her examination. She kept her face turned away so the smell wasn't so bad and let her fingers examine the damage. Despite her gentle ministrations, he stiffened beneath her.

"I'm sorry," she said. "Almost done. There's a cut on your skull. It's a couple of inches long going down your head toward your ear. But I don't think it's very deep."

"Thank God," Zach mumbled through clenched teeth.

"Yes, indeed." Ellie was thankful, too. But she couldn't help wondering why God had chosen to put both of them on this mountain just as the avalanche let loose. She would've been more thankful if she was on her way back to Scottstown about now.

She noticed the corner of a faded bandana sticking out of the corner of his pocket. Before she could question taking a personal article of clothing from a stranger, she grabbed the corner and yanked it free. It looked relatively clean if not a little dusty. She snapped it in the air to remove the dust and folded it into a square. She grimaced at the smears of blood her fingers left, but there was nothing to be done about that. She pressed it gently to his head and slowly applied pressure.

His shoulders lifted in pain, but she kept the pressure on. Blood immediately soaked through the cloth. She needed another handkerchief. Or a hundred of them.

She folded the cloth over on itself and reapplied. "Please, stop bleeding," she whispered to the back of his head. She glanced at his other pockets, but nothing else revealed itself.

She had nothing on her to use. When painting at home, she wore a painter's smock. That would've worked perfectly. She could've used the smock for a poultice and tied the strings under his chin to keep it in place. But today she wore no smock under her duster. She had known it would be too cold to remove the duster, so she hadn't worried about protecting her clothes.

Blood showed through the last layer of cloth against her fingers, but not as heavy as before, and the spot didn't spread. Ellie looked around for something to tie the rag in place.

She could tear another strip of cloth from her slip, but how could she do that with this strange man sitting right here? Yes, he faced away from her, but he would know immediately what she was doing as soon as he heard the ripping sound. Oh, it was too much. She needed another solution.

Her eyes landed on the bedroll laying near the horse along with the cinch strap she had cut from the saddle. Of course.

"Zach, I need you to hold this bandana in place over your wound. Can you do that?"

Without waiting for an answer, since she thought he was only half conscious, she took his wrist and guided his hand into place.

"Keep the pressure here. I'll be right back."

She stood and took a moment to rotate her sore shoulder. She hurried across the rocks and grabbed the bedroll. She shook it out. It was faded and worn thin in places but clean, just as she expected.

"Hallelujah," she said aloud, mimicking her cousin Harper's favorite phrase every time something went in her favor. Harper meant it as a prayer. Ellie wasn't sure God deserved thanks right now since He was the one who put her on this particular section of mountain this morning. Okay, maybe she had put herself here, but He could've sent a thunderstorm or bee swarm or other natural phenomena to prevent her from leaving the hotel this morning.

She carried the blanket back to Zach. She wished she had her bedroll, too, so she could throw it over him. She was pretty sure she needed to keep him warm to prevent shock, but she could only handle one problem at a time.

"I'm going to tear a few bandages out of your blanket. We have to make sure the bleeding stops before you can move."

Zach pinned her with those penetrating blue eyes. He looked as doubtful as she felt. Stopping the bleeding wasn't going to put him much closer to the top of the ridge.

She couldn't think about the next step in the process. She just needed to focus on this one.

She gripped the edges of the blanket and yanked with all her strength. Her sore shoulder popped in complaint. The fabric didn't budge.

Though his face was tight with pain, Zach managed a chuckle. Ellie's stomach did an inappropriate flutter. Despite the circumstances, he was downright handsome when he smiled like that, though she had no right to notice.

She snapped the blanket like a sheet on a line. "I suppose you could do better." She couldn't help but smile down at him.

He held up his free hand. "Can you bring me my knife, Miss... What'd you say your name was?"

"Ellie."

"Ellie what?"

She paused barely a breath. "Ellie Dixon."

Ellie turned and hurried back to the where she'd left his knife on the rock. She didn't want him to see her lie.

What possessed her to give him Harper's last name instead of her own? Maybe because he was the first man she found attractive since Matthew. But a handsome face was no excuse to lie. She should tell him right now she had misspoken. Her name wasn't Dixon. It was Lundy. She was Ellie Lundy, one of the richest women in Idaho. Maybe the richest.

Then she'd stand back and wait for realization to cross his face. She had seen that look on faces her entire life when people realized she was the heiress to the Lundy railroad and mining dynasty.

Calculating and scheming looks as the bearer considered what she might be able to do for them. Matthew had been the only man who hadn't seemed to care that she was rich, and Papa was powerful.

In hindsight, she wondered if Matthew *had* cared. Papa said her money was the only reason Matthew gave her the time of day. Her friends believed the same. Maybe they were right, and she was a fool. Maybe money was the only thing she had to offer anyone.

She handed Zach the knife and the blanket without a word. She needn't worry herself over one little lie. A lie between them was better than the judgmental look that was sure to follow.

"Cut a couple good-sized squares out of the corner," she instructed.

"Yes, boss."

She jerked her eyes back at him. Had he figured out who she was? She saw the teasing lift at the corner of his mouth. He didn't know. If she had her way, he never would.

She knelt back over his saddlebags. "Do you have another handkerchief or something I can use to tie the rags in place under your chin."

"I don't know."

She watched him warily. He was in bad shape. He looked close to losing consciousness. She wished he had a little whiskey or something to take the edge of his pain. Somewhere in the back of her mind she remembered that liquor could make a person bleed more freely. It was probably better that he didn't.

In the depths of the saddlebag she found another bandana and a few leather thongs. She pocketed the leather strips. She was sure she'd need them later.

She folded one of the rags from the blanket and removed the bloody handkerchief from his head. It was sodden with blood, but the wound looked to have clotted. Only a little red showed around the edges of the wound. She tossed the dirty bandana aside and carefully set the clean cloth in place. She tied the clean handkerchief around his chin to secure it in place.

She sat back on her heels to survey her handiwork. Though ashen from lack of blood and dark circles under his eyes, she found ridiculous humor in the handkerchief tied under his chin. She burst out a laugh and then pressed her sore lips together to squelch it.

"What?" he asked, feigning indignation.

"Nothing. It's just…" The bubble of laughter threatened again. She had no right to laugh. He was in misery. He could even die. But he looked so funny. And if she didn't laugh, she might just cry.

"You look like somebody's grandma with that handkerchief tied around your head."

He lifted his chin. "I didn't come here to be mocked."

Ellie burst out laughing until tears filled her eyes. "I'm so sorry," she said as she gulped for air between guffaws. "I don't mean to laugh at your predicament. I'm just so tired. My arm hurts. My face hurts. I have gravel in my hair." She pulled out a few small rocks to prove her point.

The laughter subsided as worry and self-pity took its place.

"And I still have to figure out how to get you to Scottstown."

"I can't make it to Scottstown."

"You have to. Someone needs to sew up your head. You've lost a lot of blood, and I don't know how long..." The words tapered off. He didn't look stupid. He must realize the gravity of the situation without her spelling it out.

"Have you seen my leg?" he asked.

"What?"

"My leg. It's buried. I can't feel it. I can't stand up. There's no way I can make it over the ridge and all the way to Scottstown."

Ellie looked down the length of his long, muscled body to where his left side lay concealed under a small mountain of rubble. She had been so relieved his brain wasn't spilling out of his skull, she forgot all about the way he lay twisted on the rocks, his left side nearly buried.

She blinked back fresh tears of worry and exhaustion and forced her voice to remain steady. "That's what you have me for," she said with a bravado she didn't feel.

She half walked, half crawled along the rocky surface to the lower half of his body. At least moving the rough rocks from his body would clean the worst of his blood off her hands. "No use worrying until after we see how bad it is."

It took several minutes of digging before she was able to get a clearer view of his left leg. Her hands stilled, and bile rose again in her throat. The leg wasn't severed from his body, but it may as well have been. His left knee was bent outward at nearly thirty degrees. A huge ball on the side of his leg strained against the fabric of his pants. Gingerly, Ellie ran her trembling fingertips along the protrusion. Just as she feared. It was his kneecap.

She swallowed hard before looking at him. He stared into her eyes as if waiting for an answer. He said he couldn't feel his leg. She had a feeling that was about to change. Her mind reeled. She had to do something; she just had no idea what. Her gaze landed on the canteen strap over his shoulder.

She handed him the canteen. "Take a drink."

Without taking his eyes off hers, he obeyed. She took a drink herself and then recapped it. She slid the canteen strap off his neck.

"Bite down on this. The next few minutes are going to be very unpleasant. I can't have you fighting against me."

His eyes bored into hers. Ellie didn't break contact. She couldn't let him see she was nearly as afraid of what was about to happen as he was.

He took the strap between his teeth. Ellie held his gaze a moment longer, hoping to give him strength while gathering her own.

"Your knee is dislocated. Broken, I'm sure. We have to get your kneecap back where it belongs and splint it if we're going to have any hope of getting you off this mountain."

His pupils dilated, but he didn't speak. He gave a brief nod and turned his gaze toward the sky. Ellie wondered if he was praying. She would, too, if she thought it would do any good.

Moving quickly before she lost her nerve, she put her hands on either side of his knee. She took a deep breath to rally her strength and squeezed the sides of his knees together as straight as she could while wrenching his kneecap into place.

She shuddered at the grinding, popping sound of tendons and sinew and who knew what else snapping into alignment. Zach's upper body stiffened, and a deep guttural sound around clenched teeth were the only indications of his suffering. When she was done, the knee looked more like a knee should, but she could only imagine the damage her ministrations had done.

She wanted to apologize. She wanted to cry for him since he obviously wasn't going to do it himself. She instinctively knew neither would be appreciated by this mountain man. He looked like the kind who accepted the risks of living on the frontier and willingly paid the price when he lost a battle against nature.

She took the strap from between his teeth and offered the canteen for another drink. He drank deeply before falling back against his blood-stained saddle.

Ellie allowed herself a sip. She should probably climb down the mountain to refill the canteen in the creek, but it would take too long. Who knew what the condition of the trail was like after the avalanche. The sun was sinking below the mountains. The temperature had already dropped several degrees. She shivered inside her duster. They needed to reach help, even if he thought it was impossible.

Zach covered her hand over the neck of the canteen. "Why are you here, Ellie?"

The contact startled her, making her realize how vulnerable she was out here in the middle of nowhere with a strange man. Gravely injured, yes, but she could see the strength in his hands. Should those hands turn on her, he could snap her in half before she could jump out of reach.

She looked down into his deep blue eyes. Any concern for her safety flew out of her head. He had every right to wonder why she was here. No reasonable person would be on the mountain alone with the weather as unpredictable as it had been, especially a woman. But she didn't want to tell him too much about herself.

"I came out here from Scottstown."

"I thought you were an angel."

She sniffed. "Not hardly. What are doing you here?"

He looked toward his horse. Several strings of pelts lay near the mare's body. "I came to check my traps. I needed to collect the pelts before they got buried under a foot of snow."

Ellie glanced uneasily at the sky. "Snow? Isn't it too late in the year for measurable snowfall?"

"Not in these mountains. We've got a few hours before we're caught in the thick of a storm. No more than twelve, at best. With the condition of the trails and me slowing you down, we can't risk a three-mile trek to town. Our only choice is to get to my cabin before we're buried."

Chapter Five

Ellie scrambled to her feet as the gravity of Zach's words sank in. Could she trust his judgment? He looked like he'd lived up here long enough to recognize an impending snowstorm. But maybe he'd been alone so long, he had turned to overreacting and scaring women for entertainment.

Just to be safe, she scanned the ground on the other side of the rocks for some straight sticks to fashion into a splint. He would also need a crutch. She couldn't support him herself. Since the avalanche had broken limbs out of trees and completely leveled others, she quickly found several large, suitable branches. She tested a few with her own weight before selecting one she believed would support him best.

"Cut the rest of your blanket into strips. I'll secure them around the splint with these." She showed him the leather strips she had found in his saddlebags.

While Zach worked with his long knife, Ellie arranged the lengths of wood on either side of his knee.

"I know everybody in Scottstown," he said, watching her as he worked, "but I don't know you."

Ellie didn't like the accusation in his voice. "I said I came here from Scottstown. I didn't say I was *from* Scottstown."

She took the strips of the blanket and tied the splints to his knee as tight as she could pull. She hoped she wouldn't have to tell him she was from Willow Wood. She didn't want him to figure out her identity. Now that the lie had been told, she liked the idea of being plain old Ellie Dixon, not Ellie Lundy, heiress to the *Lundy List* empire.

"What about you?" She turned the discussion on him. She had noticed his lilting accent that reminded her of her cousin's. "You don't sound like you're from around here either."

His face tightened in pain. "Louisiana."

"Louisiana? How'd you end up in Idaho?"

A shadow crossed his features, making them look nearly black instead of blue. "The same way as most folks. I rode."

It looked like she wouldn't get much more information. It was only fair. She hadn't been forthcoming either.

After she secured the splint on either side of his knee, she shuffled back across the rocks to his head. She checked the dressing. Satisfied the bleeding was still in check, she positioned the large stick next to him. "We're going to have to climb that mountain, so I need you on your feet. You'll have to lean on me, but I can't support you on my own. We'll take our time standing up so you don't pass out on me."

"You don't need to worry about that. It hurts too much."

"I imagine so."

Ellie stuck the remaining rags he had cut from the blanket into the sleeve of her duster in case he started bleeding again, then put her arm around him and helped him into a seated position. While she waited for his apparent dizziness to pass, Ellie collected her own breath. Zach was a big man. Bigger even than he had looked when lying down. She rethought her assurance that she could get him up the hill. She didn't really have a choice though. A blizzard was coming. The man had a serious headwound and a busted-up knee that would not allow him to get up the mountain on his own. If he stayed where he was, he would be dead in a few hours.

She may not be responsible for his current situation, but his blood would be on her hands if she turned and climbed to the ridge with only a promise to go for help.

She put the crutch under his right arm and positioned herself under his left. "All right, Zach, about thirty yards back, the trail isn't as steep. The climbing will be easier there."

She knelt at his legs. Through his pants, she could see his knee had already swollen around the splint. She looked away.

"Are you ready?"

Instead of answering, he adjusted the crutch under his right arm and shifted most of his weight to that side to ease the burden on her.

Ellie braced her feet against a boulder, and they rose together. She had been too distracted to think about her own injuries. Supporting much of Zach's weight, she nearly cried out in pain. Even though he did much of the work, she was sweating from exertion by the time they were on their feet.

Zach swayed dangerously. Ellie tightened her arm around his waist. Fully standing, the top of her head came up to his ear. Broad shoulders dwarfed hers. If they fell, there'd be no getting him up again.

"You still with me, Zach?" she asked breathlessly.

It took a few minutes before he could answer. "Don't forget my pelts," he said in a weak voice barely above a whisper. "I came all this way, I can't leave them behind."

"Of course not." She led him a few halting steps to a large boulder where he could lean. She looped his saddlebag over her left shoulder, the only part of her body that didn't yet ache. She slid the rifle back into the scabbard and took up the strings of pelts. There was no way she could carry it all.

Zach held out his free hand. "I can do it."

Ellie looked doubtfully at the gravely injured man in front of her. They both knew she had no choice. She handed them over, and he looped the line of pelts and rifle scabbard over his right shoulder. With her sore shoulder under his left side, they began their limping progress to the trail. As they passed the downed horse, Zach lowered his gaze in reverence. Ellie kept her eyes fixed on the rocks in front of them. She didn't want to see the horse whose suffering she had been too much of a coward to end. She wanted to put as much of this miserable episode behind her as quickly as possible.

When they reached the spot where the trail leveled off, they stopped at a fallen tree to catch their breath. Ellie slid the saddlebag to the ground and rotated her sore shoulder.

"I didn't even ask if you were hurt," Zach said.

"I wrenched my shoulder when I jumped off my horse. It's nothing."

It didn't feel like nothing. If she was at home, she would call for one of the maids to massage it and then run her a hot bath. How much difference a few hours could make in one's life.

The avalanche had cleared the hillside. Some of the trees had been sheered out of the way, and the larger rocks were now at the bottom of the mountain. Nevertheless, it was a long arduous journey to the top. Ellie's heart surged at the sight of her horse munching on the short grass.

"Saturn," she cried. "I knew you'd wait." If she wasn't about to collapse from exhaustion, she would throw her arms around the horse's neck.

Zach seemed to perk up, too. The steed was big enough to carry both of them to Scottstown with no trouble. But with Zach's injured leg, Ellie couldn't ride behind him without jostling him more than he could bear. She would have to walk, which meant Zach was right and they wouldn't make it to the settlement before dark.

The immediate problem was getting him into the saddle.

Zach sagged against a tree as Ellie slung his saddlebags across the horse atop her own saddlebags and looped the string of pelts and the rifle scabbard over the pommel. At least that was less she'd have to pack.

Zach's eyes had closed. Sweat plastered his blood-streaked hair to his head. Still, he was handsome despite his clenched appearance and the ridiculous bandana tied under his chin. His tan shirt was taut across broad shoulders, and his ripped pants hung low on his hips. Ellie wondered briefly about what brought this man from Louisiana. The fact that he was short on details heightened her curiosity. Meeting someone from another part of the young nation wasn't an odd occurrence. The person's hesitancy to share why they headed west usually meant they were hiding something. Or hiding *from* something.

Zach opened his eyes as if he sensed her watching him.

She indicated a fallen log. "If you can climb onto that log, I'll help you into the saddle."

"Can you ride behind me?"

She shook her head. "I'll have to walk and try to take some of the weight off your knee."

He studied the horse and then her. "I can't take your mount. I'll walk. My cabin's little more than a mile that way." He jerked his thumb in the opposite direction from Scottstown.

Ellie nearly laughed out loud. "You can't walk a mile on that leg." She thought of the permanent damage she had probably already done setting his knee. A mile walk would cripple him for life. "If you're right and a snowstorm is coming, we have to get you home as soon as possible."

Though she spoke firmly, it took all her resolve not to burst into tears. Her shoulder ached. Her feet hurt inside her pointed-toe boots. Her own cuts and scrapes chafed under her dress. Now that she thought about it, she was hungry. She had only eaten a few bites of sweet rolls while she painted this morning, her mind focused on capturing the sunrise instead of feeding her body. She would like nothing more than to prop him against the tree, cover him with her own bedroll, and ride to Scottstown for help. Chances were good she could get to the village and send help before the snowstorm arrived.

As soon as she entertained the notion, she knew she couldn't leave him. She wouldn't leave an animal here in his condition. The sun had already slid over the mountains. It would be full dark by the time she reached Scottstown—if she didn't run into trouble or a blocked road or washed out bridge along the way. Most rescuers wouldn't be willing to travel back this way at night with a snowstorm threatening. They would insist on waiting until morning.

By then...

Ellie shook away the image. She went to Zach and positioned her sore shoulder under him to help him to the log. It took some maneuvering to get him onto the log. He clung to the pommel while Ellie stood behind him on the log and lifted his left leg over the saddle so he could hoist himself up. She tried not to think about wrapping her arms around a strange man's hard-muscled leg or the way his hip brushed her head as she pushed him into the saddle.

After he was settled, she leaned against the horse to catch her breath. She had never worked this hard in her life. She hurt all over. Her hands were crusted with dirt and blood. And she still had a mile walk ahead of her.

"Let's hope it's easier getting you out of the saddle than in it," she quipped with a tired smile. She looked at his left leg hanging limp against the side of the horse. "Give me your belt."

His eyes widened. "Pardon?"

She held out her hand. "I need to make a sling for your leg. You can't have it hanging down like that. We need to relieve the pressure on the joint as much as possible."

He straightened and slid the narrow leather belt out of the loops. Ellie threaded the belt onto itself to make a loop at the buckled end. She slid the loop over his boot and then handed him the other end. "Wrap this around the horn and then hang onto it. I'll take the rest of the weight off as best I can."

"I guess it's better than walking."

Ellie bit back a smile. He sure looked funny with his left leg sticking out in front of him at a nearly ninety-degree angle and a bandana tied under his chin. Her fatigue and the pain all over her body almost made her break into another fit of hysterical giggles.

She looked toward the barely discernible trail that led off through the trees. "Point the way, captain. We're burning daylight."

"Head west," he said from his perch. "Just follow the trail. When you get to the Y, bear left and follow the stream. There's nothing else out here. You can't miss it."

Ellie walked in silence. Occasionally she lifted Zach's leg and set it on her shoulder to give him a rest from holding onto the belt. Within less than ten steps, though, his leg got too heavy for her sore shoulder and she had to put the brunt of the weight back on him.

She couldn't believe she was in this position. Last night she had eaten porkchops and roasted vegetables in the hotel dining room before going upstairs to sleep on soft sheets washed by someone else. The tiny inn in Scottstown only had three rooms for rent, and she was often the only guest. She paid Mr. and Mrs. Meeks well to keep her favorite foods on hand whenever she was expected. The village didn't have a bakery, so she paid the preacher's wife, an excellent baker, to send delicate pastries to the hotel for her breakfast the following morning. Mr. Meeks always had her horse saddled and ready when she walked out the door to head into the mountains to paint. Everywhere she went, she was treated like royalty. She had never lived any other way.

She looked over her shoulder to make sure Zach hadn't passed out, though she figured his pain would keep him conscious. While she didn't think he could sleep, she worried he might go into shock. She didn't exactly know what shock was, but she knew if it happened he could die.

"Where were you when the avalanche hit?" Zach asked after about ten minutes of slow travel.

His voice startled her. "On the east side of the hill. I got Saturn off the trail just as it overtook us." She shuddered as she remembered how the mountain had thundered through her hands on the pommel, her chest, her ears. She could still taste the rising dust and debris in her throat. "I've never been through anything like it. I don't imagine I'll ever forget it."

One corner of his mouth lifted. "I expect not."

"What about you?" She hoped the conversation would take their minds off their mutual discomfort.

"I came over the mountain in hopes of getting home before the snow hit. The avalanche shouldn't have been a surprise considering all the rain and snow we've had." He looked into the distance for a moment. "I knew better. Clementine…"

"You couldn't have known you'd get stuck in the middle of it."

He didn't look mollified. "I was in a hurry. Thinking of my own convenience."

Ellie looked back at the skies. The clouds hung lower than when they first reached the ridge. Mrs. Meeks at the inn would wonder why she hadn't returned from her painting excursion by now, but the innkeeper wouldn't worry overly much. She would assume Ellie had noticed the weather and headed home to Willow Wood instead of going back to the inn. When Ellie didn't return tonight, she would clean the room and leave Ellie's things in place. If she needed to rent the room before Ellie returned, she would move Ellie's belongings to her private quarters until Ellie returned for them.

It suddenly occurred to her she wasn't going home tonight. It would be nearly dark by the time they reached Zach's cabin. After that, she would have to get him settled, stitch the cut on the top of his head (yuck!), fix him something to eat, and see to whatever other needs he had before she left. According to Zach, it was nearly five miles from his cabin to Scottstown. A five-mile hike in the dark. With an aching shoulder and sore feet. In unfamiliar territory. With snow coming, no less.

"Is anyone waiting for you at home?" she asked hopefully.

Someone with supper on the table.

"Just another horse, a cow, a goose, and some chickens. The rest of my stock are grazing in a canyon east of my cabin."

Her heart sank all the way down to her blistered feet. No wife? No one? She wanted to cry. Even if the snow held off and she knew the trail as well as the back of her hand, she couldn't leave him alone in a remote cabin with a head injury and a busted leg.

"Miss Dixon, I want to thank you."

She almost asked who he was talking to. Then she remembered he was talking to her. She should tell him she had lied. Her name wasn't Dixon. She was Ellie *Lundy.* Unskilled at absolutely everything but telling her household staff what she wanted for dinner and mixing colors to get just the right shade of chartreuse. He deserved to know his life was now in the least qualified hands in all of Idaho.

"I thank God He put you there when He did. If not, I would've died on that mountain next to Clementine."

God? Ellie thought.

She had been blaming Him for putting her in this fix while Zach thanked Him for sending her. As usual, she had only been thinking of herself. But if God was truly in charge of the situation, He would've sent someone else. Someone more qualified and compassionate and less self-serving.

Ellie paid people to see to *her* needs. Now she was supposed to see to someone else's?

Zach wasn't finished. "I would've either froze to death or bled to death or been torn apart by animals. I'll never know how it worked out, but without you I'd be buzzard mea by nowt."

She grimaced at the image. She needed to tell him he had it all wrong. Would it change his perception of here to know she'd been inwardly complaining and feeling sorry for herself the whole time? He looked close to falling off the horse. He wouldn't understand if she tried to explain how much of a fraud she was and how she didn't deserve his gratitude. What was the point? He'd figure it out soon enough.

She faced forward and watched the sun slip out of sight beyond the horizon.

Chapter Six

In less than thirty minutes they reached the Y in the road. Zach seemed to have dozed off. Ellie turned the horse left without disturbing him. As long as he stayed in the saddle, she'd let him rest. A few minutes later, a neat, well-developed barnyard came into view. A large barn with a lean-to, a shed, a chicken coop, and a small, square cabin with a narrow porch that ran its length, were laid out in a convenient grid.

Ellie's feet ached inside her boots. Her knees wobbled. She hadn't walked this long or this far since she was a kid, if then. The sounds and smells of home roused Zach. He straightened in the saddle while Ellie led the horse as close to the porch as possible. She helped him slide out of the saddle onto the raised planks. He landed awkwardly on his right foot and fell against her sore shoulder. She nearly snapped at him. Didn't he realize she was hurting too? She managed to clamp down the outburst. She had no right to complain considering what he was going through.

"I'm sorry," he mumbled. He looked half out of his mind with pain. Ellie doubted he knew what he was saying. She kicked herself again for her impatience. With him leaning heavily into her, Ellie jiggled the door handle until it released. She pushed open the door. She hadn't known what to expect from an unmarried frontiersman's cabin, but she was pleasantly surprised. The interior was tidy and well-kept, though smaller than she thought possible. In fact, the entire cabin could easily fit inside her bedroom at home, including the porch, and there'd still be room for the chicken coop and the shed.

The cabin consisted of one room with an alcove directly across from the door that served as Zach's sleeping quarters. The space was dominated by the bed covered with a patchwork quilt of no discernible pattern. She wondered if it had been a gift. She couldn't picture Zach sewing it himself.

The cabin's pale pine floorboards had been sanded smooth. A rag rug just inside the door matched another in front of the black cookstove that appeared to be the cabin's only heat source. The fire was out, and it was nearly as cold inside the cabin as out. Getting a fire going was Ellie's first priority.

Two stools flanked a narrow table. The sink stood under the only window with a small sideboard attached. The table was cleared of dishes and spare food. In the corner opposite the stove was a wooden chair with a wide back and a cushion on the seat. Next to the chair stood a small table barely bigger than the stools on which sat a Bible, a tablet, and a dull pencil. The Bible's leather cover was curled at the edges and the lettering faded. Ellie didn't often read the Bible herself, but she felt safer knowing Zach did. Not that he was in any condition to take liberties or get out of hand.

She looked around for a second bed. Naturally, there wasn't one. There wasn't much floor space either. If she had to spend the night—and it certainly looked like she would—she didn't see a space big enough for her to even stretch out. Her back, hips, and sore shoulder ached at the thought.

She started to steer Zach across the cabin's main room to the alcove. He stiffened and pulled to a halt. "I can't go to bed. I have chores."

"I'll see to them. You need to lie down."

His gaze swept her thin frame. For the briefest moment he looked like he might laugh out loud. Not that Ellie would blame him. She'd always been slender. After the last few years of worry and heartache over losing her true love, she was downright waifish. Fortunately, Zach was too weak to resist. When they reached the bed, he collapsed into it before she had a chance to pull back the blankets.

Blood had seeped through the wrap around his head. Ellie couldn't do anything about it right now. He'd have to stay where he was until she got the fire going and heated water to clean his wounds. If snow was coming, she needed to get Saturn settled in the safety of the barn before it got here.

She opened the stove lid and poked the ashes. Glowing embers winked up at her. She exhaled in relief. There was also a good supply of kindling and paper. It was a good thing. She had never built a fire from scratch and only seldom added fuel to one. Her mansion staff saw to such details without a passing thought from her.

Ellie quickly built up the fire and set a pot of water on to heat. She went outside and led her horse to the barn.

It was tight and warm from the livestock's body heat and as well constructed as the cabin. After securing Saturn in the empty stall that looked like it had housed Zach's felled horse, she removed the saddle and fed and watered all the animals.

In one side of her saddlebag, she found the simple sewing kit and slipped it into her pocket. The cabin was decidedly warmer when she got back inside. No black smoke hung in the air, which meant she had obviously vented the stove correctly. She removed her duster and began searching for supplies to clean Zach's head. In the alcove, Zach hadn't moved. His soft breathing was proof his pain was manageable enough that he could rest and that he had not succumbed to his injuries.

Ellie poured boiling water into a bowl and sterilized a needle, thread, and the only scissors she had with her. Zach probably had a more suitable pair, but she didn't have time to search for them. She laid everything out on a towel she found on the sideboard that looked and smelled clean. She kept her hands busy so she wouldn't have to think about what she was about to do.

Oh, why had she left the hotel this morning? Rockslides and flooding were common occurrences this time of year. She had been foolish. Foolish and reckless. She should've waited another week. She should've...

A moan came from the bed, reminding her that if she had waited Zach might be dead now.

She set one of the stools next to the bed and laid out her supplies on it. She didn't know what she was doing. She hadn't threaded a needle since she was a girl and Mrs. Philips forced her to practice embroidery. How was she supposed to sew up a human being? What if she made matters worse? What if his skull was cracked, and he was beyond the help of a few stitches? What if he never walked again after what she'd done to his knee? What if he died and she was stranded here alone with a snowstorm coming?

Zach moaned again.

"Stop thinking of yourself, Ellie Lundy," she said under her breath. "This man needs you."

She gently rapped her knuckles against the bottom of his right boot. "Zach, I need to get your boots off. Then you can sit up so I can clean your head and see how many stitches you're going to need."

He mumbled something into the straw mattress.

"Let's get this over with while the water's hot," she said in reply.

Without waiting for an answer, she gripped his right boot. "Hold yourself still while I pull." She waited until he grabbed hold of the corner of the mattress. She'd never removed boots from anyone other than herself. It was harder than it looked. Removing the right boot, though, was a piece of cake compared to the left. She worked the left boot back and forth, trying to minimize moving his ankle, which would in turn, move his knee. He grimaced aloud as she finally pulled it free and dropped it to the floor next to the right.

"Can you roll over on your own while I go wash my hands?"

He put his hands on either side of him and attempted to rise. He lifted his upper body, but his left leg lay still like a dead weight.

Ellie looked down at the man's long, lean body, the muscles across his back rippling under his shirt as he struggled to move. She'd never seen a man stretched out on a bed. This job would be a lot easier if every breath he took didn't remind her of his raw masculinity.

She quickly looked away. "Let me help. I'll hold your leg as still as possible while you roll."

She wrapped her arm around his leg, above and below the clumsy splint, and tried not to think about what she was doing. It wasn't a man's leg, she told herself. It was a log in a stream. A carpet roll. A bolt of cloth.

She supported the weight as best she could while he turned on the mattress. By the time, he was flat on his back, they were both red-faced and breathing heavily. Ellie wanted to collapse onto the floor in exhaustion and exasperation. Zach stared at the ceiling, looking as uncomfortable as she felt.

"Is there any whiskey in the house?" she asked.

His eyes moved to her face.

"Do you have any whiskey? You're going to need something for the pain."

"I don't have anything."

She groaned inwardly. What kind of mountain man didn't keep a little whiskey on hand? Or a lot?

"I guess I'll have to work as fast as I can."

"Don't worry about me. I'm numb all over."

"Do you at least have something I can use to clean your head?"

"There's carbolic acid in the larder I keep to treat the animals."

She helped pull him into a sitting position, another major feat of strength. She untied the bandana under his chin and lifted the dressing she had put there. As expected, the fabric stuck to the dried blood on his head. He didn't flinch as she pulled it free. His hair was wet with blood, but she didn't see fresh bleeding. It had clotted, which probably meant his skull wasn't cracked. If it had been, she wouldn't need to bother stitching him up. She'd just read to him and keep him company until he died.

Her hands began to shake at the thought of it. "I'll have to cut some of your hair away from the wound. I must warn you I have no experience as a barber."

He tried to smile. She quickly crossed the cabin floor and put more water on to heat. She would need a lot of hot water before the night was over.

Back at the bed, she began clipping away great hunks of blood-soaked hair. She tried not to gag as she dropped them onto the floor. She hadn't thought to bring a bucket or piece of paper to put them on. Now she'd have to gather them up later. How did doctors do this every day?

After she cut enough hair away to see the extent of the damage, she went to the larder to find the carbolic acid. She set it on the stool next to her other supplies and then scrubbed her hands. She took a deep breath to steel herself and carefully parted Zach's hair.

"The cut isn't that deep," she said more to reassure herself than him, "but it's quite swollen. You probably got whacked on the head with a flying rock. One almost hit me before I jumped off my horse."

"I wish I'd ducked," he said between clenched teeth.

"Me too. I don't know much about swelling, but it could mean your brain is swelling. The only thing I know to do is sew you up and make sure you lay still and get plenty of rest."

"I'm not going anywhere."

Neither am I, she thought dismally.

With trembling fingers, she cleaned the wound as best she could with soap and water. She soaked a clean rag in carbolic acid and dabbed around the edges of the wound. She didn't know if she was doing too much or not enough. This man needed a doctor. Or a midwife. Or a seamstress. Anyone but her.

"Tell me about Louisiana," she said to distract them both.

"There's not a lot to tell, Miss Dixon."

Ellie's conscience nudged at her. She shouldn't have given him the wrong name, but she didn't have the time or the energy to set him straight. "Please, call me Ellie."

"The area where I grew up was ravaged by the War," he began. "My pa died eight years ago. Without him, it wasn't as hard for me to leave home."

Ellie thought of her own papa, dead now eight months. The pain of losing him—and the pain from the revelations of the night he died—was as raw as if it had happened this morning. She wondered how long it would take before she could speak of his death without the threat of tears.

"Do you have brothers and sisters?"

"A sister."

When he didn't say more, she took over. "I always wanted to be part of a big family. All my friends had several brothers and sisters. I was so envious of them."

She licked away the sweat on her upper lip. She was an artist; she had a steady hand. She could do this. She pinched together the skin on either side of the gash and started to sew.

"This reminds me of embroidery," she said after a few stitches. "I did a lot of it when I was a girl. Not that I had a choice. My housekeeper said all young ladies should be adept with a needle and thread."

"Housekeeper?"

Ellie gave herself an inward kick. Few people in Willow Wood hired household staff. Admitting that she did indicated she had means.

"My mother died when I was eleven," she explained. "Papa hired Mrs. Philips to take care of the house. And of me. She practically raised me."

"I'm sorry," he said, his voice barely a whisper.

Ellie kept her gaze on the line of tiny stitches. She seldom thought of Mama or growing up without a mother. It was another thing that made her envious of the other girls. She knew she missed out on a lot, but it was the way things were.

"Mrs. Philips had old fashioned ideas of what young ladies should and shouldn't do. I liked to paint like my mother. Mrs. Philips said it was too messy a pastime. She said I should stay inside and pursue clean and ladylike endeavors if I ever hoped to snare a rich husband. You can thank her for this exemplary sewing job."

"Did you?" he asked.

She paused her stitches. "Did I what?"

"Did you marry a rich man?"

Her needle missed a stitch at the bittersweet image of Matthew Dunleavy, the closest she'd come to marriage. She realized now Matthew wasn't the marrying kind. He liked fun and adventure too much to settle down. Everyone in Willow Wood knew it but her.

"I was in love once, but not to a rich man." The words slipped out effortlessly. It was easy talking to the back of someone's head. It helped that Zach was semi-conscious and probably wouldn't remember anything she said by morning.

"Papa didn't approve. He agreed with Mrs. Philips. He wanted me to marry a man of means like him. Not like the one I chose. Maybe they were right. He was more interested in playing cards than being a husband. Or becoming rich."

She pressed her lips together. She was saying too much. Even if Zach didn't remember the conversation, she would. Thinking about Matthew and the last three years of her life was painful. It was easier to put it all out of her mind and focus on other things. Like her art. Or Zach and why he lived here alone.

At the last stitch, she tied off the thread and clipped it close to his skull. "What about you? Why isn't there a Mrs. Zach around here? It would certainly help me out. She could cook us a fine dinner while I finish up with this."

She didn't add that he was handsome enough to attract a wife. The farm was small, but it looked prosperous. He could support a wife and children. He wouldn't have a bit of trouble lassoing a wife from the bevvy of pretty young women in Scottstown and hauling her home if he put the least bit of effort into the process.

For a reason she refused to take the time to examine, she was strangely pleased that he hadn't.

He didn't move as she applied a fresh dressing. "Sometimes it's not easy to find a woman who wants the same thing as you."

"What do you want, Zach?"

"To be left alone."

Chapter Seven

Ellie stared at the cow. The cow stared back. Her head ached. Her shoulder hurt ten times worse than it had yesterday when she jumped off the horse. She had spent the night on a thin pallet on the floor in front of the stove. She lost count of how many times she tried to roll, only to bang her knee or elbow or hip against the stove or a table leg, depending on which direction she moved. She was unaccustomed to anything under her body but a luxurious mattress and cotton sheets. She couldn't wait to sleep in her own bed tonight.

After Zach told her he wanted to be left alone, she didn't speak another word except for the few times she checked on him during the night to make sure he was still alive.

His terse response probably had nothing to do with her. He was half out of his mind with pain. His brain may have swollen inside his head, which could lead to all sorts of problems she couldn't begin to fathom. Still, she didn't appreciate someone snapping at her, especially when she was only trying to help.

At the first strains of daylight through the window, Ellie had untangled herself from the blankets, unlatched the door, and gazed anxiously into the dooryard. The snow Zach predicted hadn't arrived. She couldn't decide if she was happy or annoyed that he talked her out of going to Scottstown when they reached the ridge instead of coming here. He probably couldn't have endured a longer ride than what they'd taken, but if they had tried, he'd be under a doctor's care right now, and she would be soaking in a hot tub at the inn.

All that aside, she had survived.

A sense of pride swelled in her bosom. She had survived an avalanche and saved a man's life! Who would have thought she—Ellie Lundy—could do such a thing. What a story she'd have to tell. her cousin and the rest of the household when she got back to Willow Wood in a few hours.

While a maid rubbed her sore shoulder with liniment and another brushed the dust and gravel out of her hair, she would make everyone laugh with every sordid detail of her day and night on the mountain.

Of course, she wouldn't leave Zach here to his own devices. She'd send a buckboard from Scottstown to transport him to Dr. Dutton's office in Willow Wood. He'd get the care he needed, and she could go back to the painting she had begun on the mountain yesterday.

Ellie exhaled wearily. But first, she had to figure out what to do with this cow. She didn't know much about bovine, but even she knew they became miserable when their udders were full. Besides the pain, it was unhealthy. Ellie wouldn't let another animal suffer needlessly the way she had Zach's horse on the mountain.

Two cats mewed impatiently in the corner, depending on her too. The cow regarded her suspiciously through lowered lashes with the same distrust and apprehension Ellie felt toward it.

She had never been this close to a cow. The beast was huge. It took up the entire barn stall. And it looked annoyed that Ellie hadn't yet eased its misery.

If only Harper were here. Her cousin was from a small farm in Kentucky, where they surely had cows and chickens and pigs and all manner of species Ellie had never encountered in person. Harper would relieve her fear and remind her cows were docile creatures. She'd never known of one maiming or mutilating a person. There was no need to worry.

She set her trembling hand on the cow's massive hip. It was warm and oddly comforting. "Easy there, girl. It's all right. We'll get through this." She stroked the cow's side as she spoke, hoping to build a camaraderie that might make the milk flow faster.

The cats crowded closer and wound around her ankles. She wasn't afraid of cats, but these two were getting on her nerves. "Give me a minute."

She pushed them aside with her foot and pulled the stool alongside the cow. The cats weren't easily dissuaded. Ellie swallowed her irritation. The only way to get the cats from around her ankles and the baleful look out of the cow's eyes was to finish the job ahead of her.

She balanced on the stool and positioned the pail she'd brought from the house under the cow's udder. She looked at the pale, bulging udder and cringed, as much for the cow's discomfort as her own. It couldn't be that hard. She had seen pictures of little children milking cows. Surely, she could figure it out.

"Pardon me, girl," she told the cow. "Be patient and this'll be over in a few minutes."

She rested her head against the cow's warm side and took a teat in each hand. She squeezed. Nothing. Not even a dribble. She tried again, one at a time, squeezing as she pulled. There was probably a method to the process; she just had to figure it out. She worked both hands rhythmically.

Nothing happened.

The cats studied the teats and then Ellie, clearly wondering where Zach had found this incompetent woman. The cow swung her head around to glare at Ellie. She stamped her foot, narrowly missing the pail.

"Hey," Ellie said. "I'm doing the best I can. Mr. Tatum delivers our milk to the house."

She glanced at the barn door, willing the little milkman to walk in. He didn't. It looked like it was up to her. She could do this. She flexed her fingers and worked the tension out of her sore shoulder. Maybe the cow knew she was nervous. That's why the milk wouldn't come. She stuck her tongue out of the side of her mouth and tried again, mimicking movements she hoped would get results.

Tears of frustration welled in her eyes. She was nearly five miles from Scottstown. Ten miles from Willow Wood. No one knew where she was. An injured man inside the cabin depended on her. Yesterday, she hadn't been able to shoot a horse to put it out of its misery. Today, she couldn't make milk come out of a cow, something tiny children had been doing since the dawn of time.

"Come on, Ellie, it can't be that hard," she said aloud. "Just relax and squeeze and fill that bucket."

She squeezed and pulled and was rewarded with a weak trickle. The cats crowded closer at the sound of milk hitting the bottom of the pail. "Don't get excited," she told them. "We have a long way to go."

She shook the tension out of her fingers and tried again. She was about to give up and pour the residue of milk out to the cats when a solid stream of milk flowed into the bucket. She squealed. "We did it," she told the cow.

The cow bellowed in reply, clearly not impressed.

At least there was only one cow. If Zach Walsh had been a dairy farmer, she would jump on her horse right now, ride over the ridge, and never look back.

The sun was well over the hills by the time she exited the barn with barely a quarter of a pail of milk. A skiff of snow had fallen while she was in the barn. She warily eyed the heavy gray clouds hanging low in the sky.

"Mr. Sun," she called to the sky. "Where are you? Show your face already. I have to get to Willow Wood this morning."

She picked up her pace. If a storm was coming, she was sure she and Saturn could beat it. All she had to do was fry up some bacon and eggs for breakfast—even she could handle bacon and eggs—change Zach's dressing, stoke the fire, and saddle Saturn and ride.

Inside the house, she set the milk pail on the table with a satisfied plunk. She looked toward the alcove where Zach slept. She wanted to tell someone, anyone, of her accomplishment. She—Ellie Lundy, spoiled daughter of Hugh Lundy—had milked a real live cow. But there was no one to tell. No one cared. Only the cow and the cats, and they nearly could've done better themselves.

She looked around the cramped cabin. She had lit the stove before she went outside, but no breakfast sizzled in the skillet. For the fiftieth time since the avalanche, she was reminded of how much of her comfort came from the labor of others. Someone else baked her bread, churned her butter, brewed her coffee, and heated water for her bath. Sadly, none of those people were in the cabin right now. If she was going to satisfy her growling stomach, she needed to get to it. And quickly, if she hoped to beat the snow.

First, there were eggs to gather. At least that was a chore she could handle. How much trouble could a couple of setting hens be?

Ten minutes later, Ellie slammed the pen door, nearly taking off the head of a squawking, hissing goose, bent on biting her legs, fingers, and anything else it could get its nasty beak around. she gazed forlornly into the basket. So much work for four measly eggs.

How did pioneer women do it? She was exhausted. And starving. Her shoulder throbbed. Her hands already had blisters—how did that happen? She had discovered a scraped place on her hip that chafed inside her clothing. Before going outside this morning, she had attempted to tame her thick dark hair with her fingers and fashion it into a braid. Much of the hair had come loose from the braid and swirled around her face. It would take a week of combing for her maid to get the knots out.

Refusing to give in to the self-pity welling up inside her, she headed toward the small shed she noticed yesterday. It looked like a smokehouse where she hoped to find a hunk of bacon for their breakfast.

The way her morning was going, she didn't hold out much hope.

She soon discovered the smokehouse door was as stubborn as the goose. It wouldn't open.

Ellie glared at it. "Why is everything around here so hard?" she demanded of the door. It didn't reply.

With an angry huff, she set down the basket containing the four eggs and yanked on the handle. It didn't budge. She yanked again. She got nothing for her efforts but a shooting pain through her shoulder. She stepped back and gave the door an angry kick.

"Open, I tell you."

Her gaze traveled to the top corner of the door where she noticed a bent nail holding the door closed. She would laugh if the situation weren't so pitiful. The nail kept the corner secured against high winds and hungry predators. Ellie twisted the nail. The door opened effortlessly. She glanced at the cabin door. It was still closed. At least Zach hadn't witnessed her tantrum. The cats and the goose were probably mocking her from their lairs. She was too tired to care.

•••

Zach jerked awake when the door slammed. Again. The first time it happened, he nearly went for his long gun until the pain emanating from every pore of his body reminded him he wasn't alone in the cabin.

The woman—Ellie, he thought she called herself— had managed to set his leg, bring him home, and sew up his head, which felt like it had swollen to twice its size. All of yesterday was a pain-riddled blur. But each time the door slammed the memories rushed back into focus.

For the life of him, Zach couldn't figure out how a reed of a woman—so slender he could wrap both hands around her and they'd meet at the small of her back— could make as much racket as a team of oxen stomping around his cabin. She'd been in and out the door half a dozen times, letting the door bang shut behind her each time.

She'd slammed the stove lid, clanged his milk bucket on the table like it weighed a hundred pounds, and banged the pots and pans louder than a child using them for drums. Somehow, she even made a ruckus rummaging through the larder, and it didn't have a door to slam.

Craziest of all, she talked to herself. A lot. Despite the pounding at the top of his head that amplified each sound into a shotgun blast, Zach found he didn't mind the talking as much as he thought he would. It was kind of nice hearing a woman's voice in the cabin, even if it made him wonder if she was a little tetched in the head.

At least she'd gone outside again. He wished his body would cooperate and give him a few minutes of rest before she slammed her way back inside. A spasm of agony shot through his knee. Every nerve ending on his body throbbed and refused to be ignored. His knees and elbows were skinned raw. His ribcage ached with each breath. Even his ears hurt. The dried blood in his hair scratched at his neck. He hoped the woman wouldn't notice or she'd try to wash it out and drown him in his own bed.

Zach checked his irritation. He had no right to complain, no matter what she did or how loud she did it. If she hadn't been on the mountain yesterday when the avalanche struck, he wouldn't be in this bed today. He would've frozen to death or died an agonizing death as scavengers ripped him apart. No matter how much her wrenching his kneecap back into place had added to his misery, he owed his life to her.

He turned his gaze toward the ceiling. "Thank you, God," he whispered around his dry throat, "for the beautiful angel you sent. Even if she is clumsy and noisy, and seeing her coming at me is a little bit terrifying."

An image of her huge coffee brown eyes and dark hair with the copper-colored streaks crowded to the front of Zach's pain-clouded mind. He couldn't remember much about yesterday, but he remembered her warm breath on his face as she examined his wounds and scent of lilacs distracting him from the pull of thread in and out of his head.

He supported his head with one hand and eased into a sitting position. The ensuing dizziness and nausea helped dispel his wandering thoughts. He wouldn't spare one moment of time or ounce of energy thinking about a woman. He had more important matters to consider. Like the worrisome pain in his ribs.

He couldn't risk developing a respiratory ailment by spending too much time on his backside, no matter how severe his injuries. Ten cows in the fields were ready to calve within the next two months. They needed to be moved closer to the barn. He had spent most of the wet winter repairing fences. There were still countless slats to cut and place. One of the outbuildings had lost part of the roof in last week's high winds. Most pressing of all, the spring planting season stared him in the face. He wouldn't allow a headache, bum knee, or busted ribs to keep him from what needed done.

Or a houseguest with a lyrical voice and two left feet.

He pushed his left arm into his ribcage to alleviate the pain and took as deep a breath as he could manage. He touched the spot below the dressing on his head. His fingers came away wet. He grabbed one of rags Ellie left next to the bed and held it against his head. After a time, he pulled it away. The blood was bright red. He sniffed the rag but thankfully didn't detect infection.

"Well, Zach, you got quite a predicament here. Lay down and you'll take tuberculosis. Move around and you'll cripple yourself or bleed to death."

He chuckled. The woman had been in his cabin less than a day and he was already talking to himself.

After a few moments he felt like he could move without heaving or falling over. He looked around the room, careful not to move his head too fast. The crude crutch he had used to get off the mountain leaned against the wall under the window. Ten feet away. It may as well have been a mile. One thing was sure, it wasn't going to walk over to him. He'd have to go after it.

Zach took hold of his left leg to lower it to the floor. He was weaker than he thought, and his foot hit the floor with a thud. Pain radiated through his knee, up his ribcage, and out the gash on top of his head. He cried out, biting his tongue in the process. He wiped sweat from his forehead with a sleeve crusted with dirt from the mountain.

A few more deep breaths, and he was ready to stand. The whole process took more time and effort than he wanted to admit. He abhorred weakness, especially in himself. His stupid decision to take Clementine over the ridge to collect his pelts had killed his horse and rendered him as weak and helpless as a kitten. He wouldn't let it take his entire ranch.

He gripped the edge of the bed and pulled himself up onto his right foot. He braced his right arm on the wall and drug himself to the alcove doorway. Each step sent a jarring pain through the left side of his body. His head swam. Blood trickled down the back of his head.

This was a bad idea. What if he tore the stitches loose? But what choice did he have? He needed to use the outhouse. He was halfway to the crutch. No point in turning back.

The door burst open and banged against the wall. A cold blast of air rushed across the room, drying the perspiration all over his body.

Ellie stood in the doorway. Her face was flushed, either from the cold or the unexpected sight of him on his feet. Coppery brown curls had escaped the messy braid over her shoulder and framed her face. Her gray duster hung open, revealing a rumpled dress that clung to feminine curves. Zach momentarily forget about the pain.

Yesterday, he had mistaken her for an angel. Today, he couldn't deny she was all woman.

She pulled his egg basket against her middle as if shielding herself with it. "What are you..." Her voice cracked. She licked her full lips. Zach watched the simple movement in fascination. "What are you doing out of bed?" The quaver in her voice was unmistakable.

He nearly smiled. She appeared as unsettled at the sight of him as he was at seeing her. He straightened against the wall. He didn't know why, but he didn't want to look frail and helpless in front of her. "I have to go out."

Her pert little chin lifted into the air. Rich brown eyes smoldered. "You don't have to go anywhere. Whatever you need I'll do for you."

He would've liked to laugh at the comment, but he hurt too much. "I'm afraid this is one thing you can't do. I have to go to the outhouse."

A flush rose in her cheeks, two splashes of color against her porcelain skin. Zach's fingertips tingled with a nearly irresistible desire to reach out and touch her face.

She swallowed as she regained her composure. "I don't know what to tell you. You can't walk that far."

"Well, then, you better come up with a plan quick or we're going to have a serious problem here."

Chapter Eight

Ellie had nearly dropped the egg basket when she walked in the cabin and saw Zach in the alcove doorway. Despite the dressing on his head, his wrinkled clothes, and his eyes shadowed with pain, he still managed to look... Virile. Powerful.

Her gaze barely took note of his swollen left knee in the crude splint. Instead, all she noticed was his right arm braced against the wall and how his stance expanded his chest and made his broad shoulders look as if they nearly filled the room. She imagined he could tote a half-grown calf across those shoulders.

What was wrong with her? He was a mess. He was nearly dead, and all she could think of was the long-dormant feelings he stirred inside her.

So she yelled at him.

When her gaze finally made its way to his face, she saw his blue eyes sparkling with humor. His too-long wheat-blond hair stood up in disarray. A light shadow of scruff darkened his jaw. The entire masculine effect made her nearly forget what she was doing in his cabin clutching an egg basket as if her life depended on it.

The immediacy of his need snapped her to action.

"I—uh—I'm sorry I should've—I didn't foresee this issue. Do you have a—a—" She didn't want to finish the question. Never in her life had she imagined the need to discuss this topic with a perfect stranger. A man, no less.

"A chamber pot," she forced out.

Mischief managed to shine under the pain in his eyes. "A what?" He could no longer hold back the ghost of a smile. "You mean a slop jar?"

Ellie pursed her lips. He was enjoying her unease way too much. "Yes, that's what I mean."

He wagged his chin toward the door behind her. "It's under the lean to. Haven't used it since—well, that's where you'll find it."

Blood pounded in her face. "I'll get it. Let me help you back to bed first."

"It's all right. I—" Zach reached for the crutch and swayed dangerously. His reach missed and the crutch crashed to the floor.

Ellie set the basket on the table and rushed across the cabin floor. She wrapped her arms around him just as he fell into her. She stiffened to support his weight. He grunted in pain as her arms tightened around his middle. He grabbed again for the wall and managed to keep both of them on their feet.

"I…I'm sorry," he mumbled against her cheek. "Got a little light-headed there."

"That's why you shouldn't get out of bed without me," she scolded.

A lecture was not warranted. He had no other choice. She just couldn't think straight with his body against hers. "I mean, the next time you need something, you should call for me."

As soon as she helped him onto the bed, he slumped onto his right shoulder. He kept his left arm clenched against his ribcage. She positioned the pillow under his head.

"Are you having a hard time breathing? I should've thought to ask last night."

She dreaded his answer. A rib injury could mean death, the same as infection to the gash on his head and the poor way she had set his knee. She wanted nothing more than to feed him and climb on her horse and ride out of here. But was it safe to leave him alone for half a day? What if she couldn't find anyone in Scottstown to come out to tend to him while she went the rest of the way to Willow Wood for the doctor? What if another rockslide blocked the road? Any number of catastrophes could keep her from reaching help. What would happen then?

She couldn't think on that now. He had more urgent needs. "Don't move," she said, though it didn't look like he was considering it. "I'll go get the—um—"

She practically fled out the cabin door, her entire body atremble. What if he was dead by the time she got back inside? A rib may have punctured something important, and neither of them had any way of knowing. If it had, there was nothing anyone could do for him, not even the doctor.

"Don't borrow trouble," she said aloud. "All you can do now is make him comfortable. That means finding a chamber pot."

She nearly laughed at the ludicrousness of the situation. A chamber pot. Ellie Lundy was supposed to be back at the hotel in Scottstown working on a masterpiece for the Denver businessman. Not cleaning out a slop jar for a cowboy with mesmerizing blue eyes and a teasing smile that melted her insides.

•••

After delivering the chamber pot, she went outside to the woodpile and found several flat-edged boards to fashion into a splint to replace the knobby sticks she'd taken from the mountain. She chose several of the correct length and laid them on the porch. Then she took the water bucket and headed to the well. She had never been inside a house without an indoor pump. Why hadn't Zach taken the time to install one? It sure would make his life easier. A few daily trips to the well were a fair exchange for avoiding the work of installing a pump. He had plenty of other jobs demanding his time. She doubted he'd bother without a wife around to badger him into it.

A wife.

Zach's brusque response to her inquiry yesterday had only raised more questions. Had he been jilted? Was he a widower? Was he a mean crank that turned off the fairer sex once they got to know him?

It had to be one of those reasons. He wasn't homely or morally repugnant. He didn't drink. He certainly wasn't physically lacking. If Ellie had more time, she'd think of a few more explanations, but she was on her way back to Willow Wood and civilization. Let one of the girls in Scottstown peel the onion that was Zach Walsh.

A mournful low sounded from the barn.

Not the cow again. What did she want now?

It had only been an hour since Ellie had milked her. Ellie hadn't turned the animals into the paddock. Maybe that's what the cow wanted. She went to the barn and opened the side doors to allow the animals into the corral. She wouldn't turn them into the field. She was pretty sure domesticated animals stayed close to their barns, but she wasn't about to take the chance. If they ran off, she'd never round them up again.

The cow didn't follow the horses into the paddock. She stood there glaring at Ellie as if she were personally responsible for whatever was ailing her. Ellie didn't have time to decipher what that baleful expression suggested. She wasn't a veterinarian. She had more important things on her mind.

Even with muddy roads and an occasional blocked trail, she would make it to Scottstown in under an hour. That was plenty of time to hire someone to fetch Zach. Best of all, she'd be back in Willow Wood by late afternoon. She couldn't think about his head injury or possible broken ribs. Despite the extent of his injuries, he would be better off under someone else's care.

She decided she'd been outside long enough for Zach to take care of what he needed to do inside. She left the paddock door open so the cow could go out when she was ready, and the horses could go back inside when they decided to.

Halfway across the yard, large fat flakes began to lazily drift toward the ground. Not snow. Not now. She needed to get out of here. She needed to get help for Zach. She needed to get home. She needed a bath. She needed a decent meal. The last thing she needed was to spend another night on that hard floor.

Her shoulders drooped. She was so tired she couldn't even muster a tear. She wanted to drop onto the ground and throw a good old-fashioned temper tantrum, but then she'd have to wash the mud out of her already dirty dress.

A gust of wind whistled down the valley and grabbed the tail of her duster. The garment wasn't warm enough for riding into a snowstorm. Maybe Zach had something she could borrow. Whoever she found to look after him could return it for her.

She swallowed her self-pity and trudged toward the cabin. A few more hours. That's all she had to endure, and then she'd be soaking in a hot bath while someone fixed her a decent meal. For now, she needed to do what she could to make Zach comfortable before she rode over the mountain back to where she belonged.

At the edge of the yard three young willow trees grew in a straight line. Zach must've planted them there. Willow trees were slow growers, and these obviously hadn't been there long. A long-forgotten memory pushed to the front of her mind. Tea from the bark of young willow trees was good for something. Croup? Indigestion?

No, not indigestion. Pain! She nearly whooped aloud in victory. Willow bark tea relieved pain and inflammation. Finally, something real she could do for Zach before she left.

Mrs. Philips had once told her a story about the time her pa climbed a tree to trim some dead branches and fell out. Her ma had brewed willow bark tea for the pain. Her pa never walked straight again, but anytime the pain and swollen joints flared up, the tea helped him through it.

Ellie ran back to the barn and straight to her saddlebag. She quickly found the small knife she always carried. She hurried across the spongy ground to the trees. Buds hadn't yet sprouted on the willow trees, but the bark was young and green. She inserted the tip of the knife into a slim branch and sliced off a strip. She didn't know how much bark it took to brew tea strong enough to relieve pain. From the look of Zach, it was probably a lot. She cut three strips off the same tree. In case she cut too deeply and killed the tree, she didn't want to kill all of them.

By the time she reached the porch, her duster was coated with snow. The flakes had gotten larger and were falling faster with each passing minute. Ellie stamped her feet on the porch floor to remove the snow and mud as well as alert Zach of her approach in case he wasn't finished with whatever he needed to do.

She set the tree bark and bucket of water on the table. "It's snowing," she announced unnecessarily as she brushed snow from her hair.

Across the room, Zach's tension was palpable. "How long?"

"It just started. But it looks like it could really pile up."

He didn't answer. She poured part of the water into the larger pot to heat for his wounds and a little more into a small pan for the tea. Zach didn't seem to own a teakettle, but even she knew all tea needed was boiling water. She stepped back outside to gather the lengths of wood for his splint.

"As soon as the water's hot enough, I'll clean your stitches and reset your knee. If you're up to it."

She wanted to add she needed to hurry so she and Saturn could leave before the snow hit in earnest. No need to bother him with the particulars. She'd fix his knee, wrap his ribcage, and look at his stitches. Then she'd feed him and leave enough prepared food to last a day or two in case real help was delayed.

Zach mumbled a reply she couldn't understand. It sounded like weary acquiescence, so she went to work.

She had no idea how to make willow bark tea, but it couldn't be much different than any other tea. The brew smelled terrible, and probably tasted worse, but what choice did he have? His knee looked like a swollen sausage inside his denim trousers. She didn't know much about the lasting effects of extreme swelling, but Zach couldn't run his farm if he couldn't get out of bed.

As the tea steeped, she sawed the bacon into chunks and dropped them into a hot skillet. She sliced two potatoes and an onion and added to the bacon. The skillet was too hot, and the potato immediately began to char. Ellie thought about asking Zach how to control the heat, but he appeared to be asleep. They'd just have to eat burnt potatoes.

She poured the tea into the only tin cup she could find. She found a jar of honey in the larder and stirred in a large dollop. She pushed the skillet to the back of the stove to slow down the destruction of their breakfast. She wrapped a towel around the cup and lifted it to her nose. Dreadful. She hoped he could choke down a few sips.

"Mrs. Philips says willow bark tea is good for inflammation," she said as she set the cup on the stool next to the bed. "I hope you don't mind, but I sliced some bark off one of your trees."

"You can cut them all down if it'll ease this pain."

Ellie bit back a sound of disgust at the sight of his knee up close. The swelling was worse than she thought. Had she tied the splints too tightly? Had her ministrations impeded the blood flow, and now he'd lose his leg? She needed to remove his sock and look at his foot. Discoloration below the knee was a bad sign, not that she knew what she could do about it.

This man needed a doctor.

She helped him sit up to drink the tea. "Drink this while I finish cooking breakfast. Hopefully it'll ease the swelling a little before I reset it with some pieces of wood from the woodpile. They should make you more comfortable."

"Whatever you think."

He could barely keep his eyes open. His handsome face was lined with fatigue and pain. He didn't look like he'd slept a wink. Ellie's conscience pricked at her. Was it a good idea to leave him? What if something happened to her or Saturn on the way to Scottstown? What if the snow got worse and prevented anyone from coming back?

She couldn't worry about that now. He would be much better off with anyone other than her as nursemaid.

His lip curled in distaste at the first sip of the tea. "I hope it's strong enough," she said as she went back to the stove.

"It tastes bad enough to be good for me."

"I'll add more honey next time," she said, though she knew there wouldn't be a next time for her to do anything in this cabin.

She went back to the stove and stirred the contents in the skillet. She had scrambled two of the eggs with some milk in hopes they'd go farther. There wouldn't be more eggs until tomorrow, so she knew to save some. The eggs had congealed around the bacon that she hadn't sliced thin enough. The onion was burnt, but she hoped the taste would overpower the char on the potatoes. Despite the less than appetizing presentation, her stomach growled in anticipation. She had been too tired last night to think about food, and Zach had been nearly delirious from pain to notice. This morning, though, she knew he must be as hungry as she was.

She scraped the food onto two plates in two unappealing piles. She carried the plate with the bigger pile to the bed where he was slouched over his tin cup, nearly asleep.

"Is the tea making you sleepy already?" Secretly, she hoped she hadn't made it too strong. Could willow bark poison a person? She should've thought of that sooner.

"I dunno," he said groggily.

Hoping she hadn't just killed the man, she took the tin cup and handed him the plate and a fork.

"I'm sorry it doesn't look very good. I don't spend much time in the kitchen."

A more obvious statement had never been uttered.

Zach lifted the fork and then set it back on the plate. He bowed his head and mumbled something over the food. Ellie hoped he remembered to pray he'd live until lunch.

Ellie went back to the table for her own plate. She turned on the stool so she could watch him while he ate in case he keeled over. She cut into the egg and took a small bite. It was overdone and rubbery. She couldn't even pierce the potato with her fork. She never thought it was possible to ruin bacon, but this sure didn't taste like what Mrs. Philips made at home.

The poor quality didn't seem to hinder Zach's appetite. He ate steadily, though gnawing through the bacon slowed him down. She should've taken the time to make biscuits. She would bake up a batch before she left. She had already seen the honey. He probably had jam and butter around here too. But she just didn't have the time.

"Where did you say you were from?" she asked. She knew the answer, of course, but she wanted to see if the gash on his head had affected his memory.

"Louisiana," he mumbled around the bacon.

"Your voice reminds me of my cousin Harper," she said. "She's from Kentucky."

Zach nodded absently as he gnawed the bacon. Ellie didn't want to say too much about herself. She didn't want him to figure out who she was. But it seemed like a good idea to keep him talking. Not only to distract him from the pain, but also to make sure his brain hadn't suffered irreparable harm from the knock on the head.

"How did you learn of this place when you came from Louisiana? Or was it a series of happy coincidences that landed you in these mountains?"

He gave her a quick glance before turning back to his plate. She took a bite of hard potato while she waited. He looked as if he was measuring how much to tell her too.

"My father had a business acquaintance who came west," Zach said at length. 'He had written to Pa a few times about this area. Said the land could be had for a fair price and it was a good place for a man could start over."

"Start over from what?"

He looked up sharply. "From the War."

Ellie felt like a dolt. The War Between the States had ended the year before she was born. She had learned the travesties of the war in her history classes, but she had been comfortably insulated from the ravages of it all. Zach grew up in Louisiana. No insulation there.

"I imagine the work here keeps you too busy for going into town."

Zach stabbed at a piece of potato with his fork. The potato jumped off the plate. He barely caught it before it sailed over the edge of the bed. He popped it into his mouth.

"My family lost everything, the same as everyone we knew. Some remained and tried to rebuild. Like my family. It was too hard for most, and those who could, left. Pa stayed in touch with a few of them. He got letters occasionally. They tried to talk him into coming west. He wouldn't think about leaving. His parents were buried there. His and Ma's families had worked too hard, been through too much, to abandon the land they loved."

Ellie wanted to tell him she understood. Her life was in Willow Wood, despite the grief she'd endured and memories that tormented her. People still stopped to stare at her when she rode through town, morbid curiosity on their faces, though some tried to hide it. She could afford to go anywhere she wanted, but she never thought of leaving. It was her town, too, as much as theirs.

"What made you decide to come here?" She was sure it was a sensitive topic, but she wanted to know.

"Pa died. Then Ma took sick. She was never strong without him." His blue eyes darkened. "My whole life was spent rebuilding Cypress Springs. Over the last ten years, it had become a successful plantation again."

"Plantation?"

He pinned her with a challenging stare. "Before the war—before me—my family owned slaves. Four years before the Confederates fired on Fort Sumter, Pa freed every one and gave them a small stipend to start over. But he didn't believe in a government in Washington telling us how to run our lives or our businesses. He went to fight, leaving Ma, my two brothers, and sister Abigail there alone. My brothers were little. They both died from sickness the first year. That was the main reason Ma wouldn't leave after the war, even if Pa had wanted to.

"The plantation was far enough removed to miss the worst of the fighting and raids. It's the only way Ma and Abigail survived, along with a few of our former slaves. But there was no money to run the place. They barely grew enough food to stay alive. Mercifully, the war ended and Pa came home. There wasn't much to come home to, but he was determined to stay while so many of their friends and family had either been killed, burned out, or ruined."

His gaze had taken on a faraway look. Ellie couldn't look away. "You were born after the war?"

"March, 1866. Yesterday was my birthday."

She groaned aloud. "What a terrible way to spend your birthday"

Zach managed a smile. "It could've been worse." He gingerly touched the dressing on the top of his head. "I'm still here, thanks to you."

Ellie thought of how close she came to leaving him on the mountain to go for help, and her face burned with shame. A sore shoulder and the discomfort of sleeping on the floor for one night didn't compare to what Zach was going through. He could lose everything, and all she thought about was herself.

He tilted his head and regarded her thoughtfully. For the first time, the pain had eased from his features. "You're the first guest yo ever sit at my table. I don't reckon you're a guest, though, since you did all the cooking."

"I didn't do a very good job of it."

He swallowed the last bite on his plate. "It was fine with me."

"That's because you were nearly starving. I'm afraid there's nothing left."

"No matter." Weariness settled over him like a cloak. "The food should help me sleep. Your tea seems to be doing the trick." He lay back against the pillows.

Ellie hurried over to help him get situated. "I should check your head before you go to sleep. And your feet."

"My feet?" he mumbled as sleep dragged at him.

"Yes. The swelling in your knee may have cut off your circulation."

"I'm fine. When the snow lets up, I'll chop some firewood, Ma."

Ellie knew she had lost him. He was sound asleep. She pulled the blankets up around his chin. She stared down at him. It was the first time she'd seen his face when it wasn't drawn in pain. She imagined leaning forward and kissing his lips.

She jerked back as if she'd been burned. Where did that come from? She didn't know this man. She certainly had no right thinking about kissing him. After losing Matthew she vowed never to love another man. She had only loved two. Matthew and Papa. And they both disappointed and abandoned her.

She turned back to the stove. She had a lot to do before she could leave. She needed to prepare more food, fill the firewood box, and haul more water. She'd prepare the rest of the willow bark so Zach could make his own tea. If he could get to the stove, that is.

She thought again how dangerous it was to leave him here. He was nearly out of his head while he was awake, and now he was practically comatose. What if the fire went out while he slept? He could freeze to death without ever waking up.

She pushed the thoughts aside. She needed to get out of here while she had the chance. Someone who knew what they were doing could take care of him. She would start work again on her painting and get those soft lips out of her head.

She pulled back the muslin cloth over the window. She gasped aloud. Outside, she saw absolutely nothing but snow slashing horizontally across the pane.

Chapter Nine

Zach dreamed of an angel. A beautiful angel with long dark hair cascading around bare shoulders. He wanted to touch her, to see if her skin was as soft as it looked. To touch her lips. To kiss her. But his arms wouldn't move. His head felt strange. As if every beat of his heart pulsed blood out the top of it. He tried to put his hand over the opening in his skull to keep the blood from gushing out. He tried to tell the angel to help him. He couldn't form the words. His head hurt so bad. He wanted to throw up. He tasted burnt food in his mouth. Maybe the cabin was on fire. Maybe he was dead, and the pain was a memory of whatever had killed him. He thought he smelled lilacs, but maybe that was a memory, too.

A bright light flooded his eyes, obliterating every other sight and sensation. He twisted as much as his aching body would allow to get away from it.

The light lessened. Dots swam in front of his eyes. He blinked furiously. After a moment the angel's face came into focus. Only it wasn't an angel.

Ellie.

"What's happening?" he demanded around a parched throat. "What are you doing?"

"I was worried about you. You've been asleep for six hours."

"I thought I was supposed to sleep."

She swung the lantern away and stepped back. Blessed darkness fell over the alcove.

"I needed to see if your eyes reacted to the light," she said at his confused look. "Good news. They did. That means you don't have brain fever."

"Brain what?"

"Brain fever. It's very bad. It can kill you. Or turn your brain to mush."

"Maybe you're the one who has it."

She set the kerosene lamp on the table next to the bed and folded her arms across her tiny waist. "Very funny."

Zach tried not to notice the outline of her body in her soiled dress. He wished she wouldn't stand next to his bed like that. It made him think of how lonely he'd been the last few years. How empty his life was. He wished she'd just leave him alone so he could go back to his dreams of a beautiful angel with bare shoulders.

"You're the one who hit your head on the rocks," she said. "That's how you get it. From a severe blow to the head."

"What are you talking about?"

"Brain fever." Her brows slid together. "Can you understand me. Are you sure you're all right?"

She leaned in close again. The scent of lilacs swept over him, though not as strong as before.

"Tell me where you're from, Zach. What's your sister's name?"

He tried to turn away. "You already know that. I don't have brain fever. I don't even think it's a real thing."

"It most certainly is. It happens when your brain swells inside your skull and stops working properly. You wake up and can't remember how to pull your boots on. I read about an old king who got it from falling off his horse. He had to be led around by the hand the rest of his life."

"That was because his parents were brother and sister."

She sniffed. "How crude."

A smile played at the corners of her mouth. Zach forced himself not to smile back. He wouldn't say anything to make her smile again. He enjoyed teasing her and he had no right. He liked the flush in her cheeks and knowing he had caused it. After only a few hours he believed he had already gotten used to having her here, stumbling and clanging around the cabin and disturbing his sleep.

She moved down the length of the bed. "I'm going to unwrap your knee, but first I want to look at your feet."

"Why?"

"I told you already. I want to compare the left one to the right to make sure your circulation hasn't been impeded."

"Don't see what we can do about it either way," he said gruffly. He needed to get his mind off the scent of lilacs and the way her soft fingers kissed his skin.

"Neither do I," she admitted. "But first, let's look at the situation."

Before he could stop her, she slipped off his socks. Zach felt strangely exposed. No woman had seen his bare feet since his mother.

She knelt closer and looked all around each foot without touching them. "Ah. Hmm." Finally, she straightened. "Looks good. So, the problem looks to be limited to your knee and your head. And maybe your ribs."

"As long as I don't develop brain fever?"

She wrinkled her nose. "I think we can rule that out. You seem coherent enough, though I don't have any experience for reference."

He nearly smiled again.

"I changed the dressing on your head a few hours ago while you were asleep."

"You did?" Worry nagged. How had he slept through it? No wonder he was having odd dreams.

"A little bleeding, but the stitches are still intact. I suppose that's the most important thing. So, for now we'll focus on your knee. How is the pain since you had your tea?"

"Terrible."

"I'll make you some more when I finish. I didn't want to give you too much too soon in case it has adverse side effects."

She began unwinding the strips of cloth around the splints. Zach was alarmed at the way his knee had swollen around the wood. He braced himself for a fresh wave of pain when she took the braces away. He turned his gaze toward the window. He was surprised to see it was nearly dark.

"How long did you say I was asleep?"

"Six hours."

"Are you sure? If that's right, it can't be much past three o'clock. I'm surprised it's so dark already."

Her hands stilled at his leg. "The storm came."

"Storm?" He blinked away the fuzziness. Hadn't he expected snow yesterday? The pain had made the hours run together and overlap. He remembered the avalanche but couldn't quite grasp the particulars of how he got off the mountain and into this bed.

"There's at least a foot of snow out there." Her hands trembled. He thought he heard tears in her voice.

"Twelve inches of snow in six hours," he said in near disbelief. "We don't often get that much of a blizzard this late in the season."

"It's been a strange year."

He got the feeling she was referring to more than the weather.

She loosened the last strip of cloth and gently moved the pieces of wood from where they stuck to his leg. As expected, needles of pain shot up and down his leg. The sensation was almost pleasant as well as painful, like an itch relieved when scratched while hurting at the same time.

She gently positioned her hands at the back of his knee and squeezed. She moved carefully and slowly as she massaged the swollen flesh at the bottom and sides of his knee.

She looked up at his face. "Did any of that hurt?"

"Um, no. It eased the pain for a minute."

In more ways than one, he thought.

She straightened. "Good. If you'd had any broken bones or snapped tendons or anything else, you would've let me know. It looks like it might actually heal, and you'll walk on that leg again."

He felt like she'd punched him in the gut. "I never thought I wouldn't."

"It's a severe injury, and I have no idea what I'm doing. I wager it'll bother you the rest of your life."

"I don't care about that. It'll remind me of what my carelessness did to Clementine."

She stared at him a long moment. He could see she agreed. He wanted to defend himself. He didn't want her to think he was reckless and imprudent. But he didn't deserve understanding. He was solely responsible for the horse's death and his actions could cost him his livelihood. and his own injuries. His bad choices had followed him all the way across the country.

A mournful bellow sounded from the barn.

He straightened in the bed. "That's Bossie. I wonder what's wrong. There could be an animal in the barn."

Ellie shook her head as she placed the two straight splints on either side of his leg. They didn't chafe and dig like the ones she'd just removed. "That old cow has been fussing all afternoon. I left the paddock door open this morning so the animals could come and go, but I closed it after I saw how the snow was piling up. Trust me, there's nothing moving around in this storm except what belongs here."

The cow lowed again, louder than before. Ellie gave him a reassuring smile as she finished tying the splint into place. "She probably just misses you. She didn't give much milk this morning."

His eyes narrowed. "That's impossible. After missing last night's milking, she should've given more than you could carry."

Ellie bristled. "Well, she didn't. She only gave a few inches in the pail."

He sank into the pillows. He hadn't meant to snap. He didn't want to take his frustration at the situation out on the person who held his very survival in her hands.

"The problem can be easily fixed," he said. "She's engorged and in pain. If she doesn't get a good milking, she could develop mastitis. It can kill her, not to mention how she'll suffer."

Ellie's brown eyes glistened. "I'm sorry. I just thought she was—difficult. I've never milked a cow before."

"You've never milked a cow?" He couldn't keep the surprise out of his voice. "Not ever?"

Ellie tilted her proud chin. "We live in town. A milkman delivers our milk and butter."

"Okay, I'll give you a quick lesson. You have to save my cow. Grab a teat in each hand and pull down and squeeze at the same time."

"I did that. Nothing came out."

"Then you didn't pull hard enough. Don't worry, you can't hurt her. It causes her more pain when you don't do it." He formed his hands into fists and mimicked the motion in the air. "Pull hard and squeeze as you bring your hands down. Stick with it and the milk'll flow. Bossie's a good milker."

Ellie studied his hands as if committing the movement to memory. "You can do it, Ellie," he said gently. "It's easy once you get the hang of it."

She didn't look convinced. "So I've heard. Easy enough a child can do it.

Chapter Ten

Wind whistled around the corners of the cabin and under every eave, making Ellie worry the roof would lift off at any minute, exposing them to the elements. At home, safely tucked inside the Lundy mansion, she barely heard wind or rain. She often didn't even know a storm had passed through during the night until the maids arrived with mud splashed on their cloaks.

She sniffed hard to hold back tears that threatened. Fear of the storm outside was nothing compared to the pain that wracked her body from the top of her head to the soles of her feet, her shoulder worst of all. Her back ached from laying on the floor. Swollen sinuses from the unshed tears had given her a headache.

After she turned down the lamp and got down on the thin pallet on the floor, she had lifted her skirt to examine her legs in the glow of light around the stove door. Her knees and shins were covered with bruises and scabs from her fall from the horse. A knot on her right thigh must've been the result of a flying rock during the avalanche. Her hands and wrists ached from milking the cow; she could barely make a fist. Who would've guessed milking required so many muscles a person never knew she had?

She thought of the salve Mrs. Philips rubbed on her the time she was thrown from a horse and when she twisted her ankle on the stairs. This time, when absolutely every muscle in her body begged for mercy, there was no salve to ease her suffering.

She couldn't even complain. What was the point of pain if you couldn't use it to garner sympathy from every person within earshot? She certainly couldn't complain to Zach. He wouldn't have sympathy to spare with twenty stitches on top of his head and his knee the size of an elephant's.

Despite her best efforts, tears leaked down her cheeks. She shouldn't feel sorry for herself. It could've been much worse. But she couldn't help it. She wanted to go home. She wanted to change her clothes. She wanted to brush her hair and brush her teeth. She wanted a hot meal that didn't taste like sawdust in her mouth.

The worst thing about the whole situation was no one at home even knew where she was. She had packed provisions when she left the inn to protect herself in case she ran into trouble. But she hadn't done the most important thing of all. She hadn't told the Meeks where she was going or when to expect her back. It hadn't occurred to her to do so. She arrogantly came and went as she wished with no regard to the worry of others. What a foolish way to live. She put her own safety at risk, and now she was trapped by a blizzard in a tiny cabin with a strange man who could be any manner of criminal. While he might not be able to get out of bed, he had proven he could still shoot a gun. Even in his weakened state, she didn't think she could get away if he wrapped his powerful arms around her.

She shivered at the thought. It wasn't as frightening as she expected. It was—exhilarating.

Once she did get out of here, she would never see Zach again. She wasn't sure why it mattered. She had things to do in Willow Wood. After she milked the cow—successfully this time—she had checked her painting supplies in her saddlebags. The paints had been spared. But the legs of her easel were smashed to bits, and the corner of the canvas she had started for the Denver businessman had been crumpled in her fall. She couldn't sell it now. She would have to start over again.

Then there was the company, about which she seldom thought. Hershel List and Rodney Hammersmith were running *Lundy List Railroad & Mining* during her mourning period. However, she couldn't expect their goodwill to last forever. Half of the company belonged to her. While she trusted the men implicitly with financial and managerial decisions regarding the company, it was time she became involved. She wasn't stupid or incompetent. She had watched and learned from Papa all her life. She had her own ideas. She knew what was required to take the company into the next century.

The last few years she had become complacent. She had allowed her grief for Matthew to consume every aspect of her life. She was tired of living under an umbrella of self-pity and grief. She wanted to get back to living. Not relying on Harper and Logan to take care of her at home. And especially not allowing Mr. List and Rodney Hammersmith to manage her business affairs.

That meant going back to Willow Wood. Leaving this tiny, cramped cabin as soon as the wind died down. Forgetting all about the busted-up cowboy in the alcove who made her cold heart suddenly burst with life.

•••

Zach lay in bed, battling the bubble of laughter that threatened to spill into the dark night. Part of the humor came from the near delirium of pain in his knee. The willow bark tea had eased the pain enough to leave him feeling suspended halfway between wakefulness and the constant ache that pulsated through him with every heartbeat. Maybe he did have brain fever. Maybe he'd have to be led around by the hand the rest of his life. Unlike the king in Ellie's story, though, he had no one to lead him.

But much of the humor came from Ellie herself. Zach suppressed a chuckle every time he thought of how her face had glowed when she burst into the cabin lugging a full pail of milk with both hands.

"Look. There's milk. I did it. Bossie did it. We did it."

He had laughed, forgetting his pain for a wonderful moment. "I was beginning to think a wolf had eaten you."

She shook her head as she rummaged for the milk strainer. "It took some time to get the hang of milking like you said. But you were right. Pull and squeeze. Pull and squeeze. That's all there is to it. Thank goodness your cow is patient."

As if she had a choice, he thought.

"While Bossie and I were getting acquainted, I got to thinking."

Zach braced himself for whatever idea was about to come out of her mouth.

"All that snow may be a godsend for you. I can soak a cloth in the snow to make an icepack for your knee. And maybe one for the top of your head. I heard somewhere ice takes down swelling. At least I think I did. It should help more than just the tea alone."

She spent the rest of the evening tromping inside and out, applying compresses to his knee and his head for as long as he could stand it, and then returning the rags to the snow to freeze again. Just when Zach warmed up enough to fall back to sleep, she'd slap another icy compress in place, jerking him back to wakefulness.

Despite the icy water dripping onto the bedcovers, the swelling had gone down. The flesh of his knee no longer overlapped the splints she'd put in place, and his headache had lessened to a dull thrum instead of a marching band.

Now he listened to her gentle, oddly comforting breathing across the room. Ellie. He was still amazed at how God had put her on the mountain at the exact moment Zach needed her.

He hadn't realized how empty his cabin had been until there was someone else moving around in it. He never thought about being lonely. As far as he was concerned, he had no choice in the matter. It was his penance. The farm, the animals, the river, the dirt between his fingers, kept him too busy to think about why he was here. But sometimes in the midst of busy-ness, he made himself remember.

Forgetting was the coward's way. Zach Walsh was no coward. Sin came with a cost, a cost he accepted and willingly paid. But in the last thirty-six hours since this beautiful, nearly inept, effervescent woman stumbled into his life, Zach was reminded of the weight of his burden of debt.

He grew up playing with his friends around the abandoned plantation mansions left in the wake of the War Between the States. He didn't mourn the loss of wealth and prosperity earned on the backs of others' blood and sweat. He had never known that life.

All he had ever known was poverty and lack and hard work. He knew if a person wanted to build a life from the ashes, he had only his own ingenuity, two hands, and the Lord's grace to rely on.

He was born late in his parents' lives. Pa had run a successful law firm before the War and served on the state legislature while running a gentleman's plantation. During the War, he lost half his left foot to infection from a minor wound. He also lost his two sons to disease and malnutrition.

Abigail was twelve when Zach was born. She was a born leader and nearly became his mother as Ma's health deteriorated. By the time Zach was a youngster, Pa had restored much of his law practice, and he was earning enough to put back into the plantation.

Zach and his father rebuilt sheds and outbuildings. They improved the farm's irrigation systems and expanded some of the fields. They tore down a long-ignored section of the house and restored the remainder to much of its former glory. In Pa's shadow, Zach learned to make the most of little, and that you had nothing in this world but what God chose to lend you.

Pa died when Zach was eighteen. Ma slipped back into the debilitating depression that had plagued her since the outbreak of the War. Zach loved the plantation, but there was much he didn't understand.

Abigail's husband Carter Colegrove stepped in and offered to help maintain the business end of things. Zach was in over his head and jumped at the offer. He was young and naïve and didn't see the self-serving Carter was only interested in preserving the plantation for himself and Abigail.

Zach continued to work and barter and make do with little as Pa had taught him. He was too busy and too consumed with his own grief to realize Carter and Abigail were pushing him further and further aside until it was too late.

He worked every job he could find to make money. The plantation still carried debt. His dream was for Ma to see it free from creditors before she died.

But he was young. He needed to let loose and have a little fun now and then. It was why he gravitated toward Rusty Higginbotham and his crowd. Alcohol helped dull his sense of inadequacy and hopelessness following Pa's death. Zach didn't approve of everything Rusty and his friends did—barely skirting the edge of the law and sometimes outright breaking it—but staying home and facing Ma and the crushing responsibilities of the plantation were too heavy for his young shoulders. Especially after he learned the financial problems were mounting, no matter how much money he threw at them.

When he got in the fight that ended Rusty's life, Carter and Abigail sided against Zach. It didn't matter that the sheriff found no fault with him. They called him a killer.

He could see their point. He had allowed the liquor to dull his good sense to walk away before Rusty could draw him into a fight. Zach knew as well as anyone that Rusty Higginbotham was a stick of dynamite just looking for a spark. Zach had been that spark and Rusty died for it.

While Abigail and Carter accused him of bringing shame on the family, Zach knew what he needed to do. He went to the bank and paid off the liens Pa had taken out after the War. He presented the unencumbered deed to Ma where she sat in her bedchamber with Abigail and Carter.

"This is what your pa always wanted," Ma told him as her tears of gratitude splashed onto the heavy vellum paper. "We wouldn't have any of this if you and he hadn't worked so hard."

"He didn't build any of this," Carter had railed. "He used your fine husband's name to try to make the people in this parish forget he killed a man."

"He's taking advantage of you, Ma," Abigail said with tears in her own eyes. "He and Pa never respected Carter. Now he's trying to push us out."

Pa hadn't wanted Carter to have an equal share of the plantation and the law firm, so he willed Zach two thirds ownership to the estate. Abigail and Carter never forgave Pa and still resented him years after his death.

Though he wanted to pound Carter through the floor, Zach kept his eyes on Ma. He wouldn't give in to anger again. "I don't want anything from anyone. I'm doing it for you and Pa. I just wanted you to have it before I leave."

Ma placed her hands on either side of his face. "I understand, son."

Abigail stepped forward. "You can't believe him, Ma. He's up to something."

"He's trying to turn you against us," Carter added. "What can you expect from a killer?"

Zach stood and turned to face his sister and her husband. "You can have it all. I'm leaving the same way I got here. With nothing. Just do right by Ma."

The only things he took west were two horses and his saddle. After paying the creditors, he had just enough money to buy his small spread. Everything else, he acquired by bartering, trading, trapping, and labor for other farmers. As Pa taught him, he planned to build an empire from scratch. Though she was now gone, Zach wanted to make Ma proud as he had the day he handed her the free deed.

Part of what Abigail and Carter had said was true. Zach had been favored because of Pa's name. Out here where his name didn't matter, he would start on his own. He didn't deserve clemency or grace. He had been given it, nonetheless, and he would make sure God didn't regret His gift.

"Zach?"

His breath caught at the sound of Ellie's voice. He had nearly forgotten he wasn't alone in the cabin. He smiled into the darkness.

"Yes?"

"Is everything all right? Do you need anything?"

His insides warmed at the compassion in her voice. He hadn't been on the receiving end of caring or gentleness from anyone in a long time. Least of all, a beautiful woman.

"How did you know I was awake?" There was no point in telling her how much his body hurt. She had done all she could to help that.

"Your breathing wasn't regular enough for sleep. Would you like a cup of tea or another cold compress?"

He chuckled. "The wind would take you off the porch if you stepped outside. You need to get some rest yourself. Morning comes early."

She snorted. "I noticed."

Zach waited for her to say more. He knew she hadn't gone back to sleep. He imagined her there on the hard floor, staring into the darkness and listening to the wind. He wondered if it scared her. He should say something to comfort her. He wanted the conversation to continue, but morning did come early, and she'd been working nonstop since she walked through his door.

A gust of wind pulled at the shingles over their heads.

"Does the wind always blow off the mountains with such force?" she asked.

The wind didn't bother Zach. He barely noticed it. He had built the cabin as tight as a tick on a dog. "Yes. It's a lonely sound. But comforting too."

"Comforting how?"

"I know it's doing its job. It dries out the fields so I can plant, which means the stock and I will eat another year. It carries away pests and disease, keeping us healthy."

"I never thought of it like that."

"Everything God created has a job. A reason for being."

"The wind can also be destructive," she pointed out. "From the sound of it, it's trying to tear the roof off your cabin. Like the rockslide. It cleared the overgrowth from the side of the mountain, but we were caught in the middle of it. Your farm will suffer because of what it did to you. What it did to your horse."

"And you've suffered because you're stuck here with me."

She didn't answer. He wondered what she was thinking. He wished he had the nerve to ask. As far as he was concerned, her presence here was a blessing. But it was a curse as well. Her voice, her smile, the cold compresses, her bumbling attempts at the stove—every moment of Ellie Dixon in his life was a reminder of what he could never have.

Chapter Eleven

Zach awoke to the sound of singing. It took a minute for his pain-riddled brain to realize from where the sound was coming. He hadn't heard a woman singing in—well, since back home in Louisiana on Sunday mornings in church. He sure didn't expect to hear it in his cabin.

He relaxed into the straw mattress and let the gentle sound wash over him for a moment. The tune wasn't a hymn. It was a light romantic song he'd never heard before. Ellie must've heard him stirring. The singing stopped abruptly. Zach opened his eyes. Ellie was watching him from across the room.

"I'm sorry," she said. "I didn't mean to wake you. Sometimes I forget I'm not alone."

Last night when she thought he was asleep, Zach had watched her comb out her hair with her fingers and braid it again. This morning, wispy strands had once again escaped and floated around her face. Her eyes were relaxed from sleep, and the glow of the lantern cast her features in a pleasing light. Zach could barely catch his breath.

She must've mistaken his silence. She grabbed her duster and threw it around her shoulders. "I'll fix another ice compress and then check your stitches."

Before he could tell her he hadn't even noticed the pain, she was out the door. She came back in less than a minute with two frozen rags. She smacked them against the table to make them pliable and folded them into rectangles as she crossed the floor. Zach tried not to stare at her dark hair and the way her slim figure moved in her dress.

"You didn't wake me," he assured her as she positioned the first rag over the top of his head. The ice was not pleasant in the early morning chill, though the stove glowed with heat, but the compresses were doing their work.

She pulled the blanket aside to expose his knee. She examined it for a moment. "The swelling is down this morning. Your head looks better too. How did you sleep?"

"Like a log. I've never slept so much in all my life."

"That's a good thing. Your body needs it."

Zach maneuvered into a sitting position and leaned against the rough headboard. He ran his hand across his jaw. At this moment a shave would do him more good than anything. Though she had cut much of the hair around his stitches, blood had stiffened the ends and they scratched his neck. He was dirty, and he ached all over. He wanted to change out of the blood-stained clothes he'd worn on the mountain. He wanted to get out of this bed. Every move made him queasy. His head spun if he moved his eyes too quickly. He worried if he was safe with a razor in his hands or if he'd cut his throat.

He sure didn't trust Ellie with one.

He closed his eyes and tried to relax his head and shoulders into the headboard. "How's the weather this morning? Did we get more snow?"

"I don't think so. The drifts make it hard to measure. Some of the drifts are halfway up the side of the chicken house. Do you think the livestock in the canyon are all right?"

"They'll have to be for a few more days, at least."

"Maybe I could check on them for you. Saturn is a strong saddle horse. He and I can get through the snow."

Zach would've jerked upright if his head had allowed it. "No! I can't risk you getting hurt or lost. I have no idea what the conditions are. There are natural shelters out there the cattle'll find along the cliff walls. I don't know what you could do if they needed anything anyway, except report back to me."

He glared down at his busted knee. If she brought back a report that every head he owned was about to succumb to the conditions, there wasn't a blessed thing he could do to save them. For now, he preferred not knowing.

He thought he detected relief on her face that he didn't take her up on the offer.

"How are your ribs? Are you breathing any easier?"

He pressed his elbow against his side and inhaled as deeply as he dared. The catch was noticeable but not as worrisome as yesterday.

"I think I'll survive. I'll try to move around a little today."

"That's good to hear. You have work to do and so do I," she said with a smile that warmed his belly.

As if in response, a loud bellow sounded from the barn. "There's Bossie calling my name."

Ellie hurried to the other side of the room and sat down on the floor with her back to him. With a few deft twists, she tidied her braid and coiled it into a knot and secured it at the nape of her neck. She reached for her duster but changed her mind and took his coat instead. "Do you mind? This is the coldest morning we've had in weeks."

He could barely formulate an answer at the sight of her shrugging into his coat. It enveloped her, hanging nearly to her knees. She rolled the sleeves back a few times until her hands appeared and then took a length of twine she must've found in the barn and cinched the huge coat around her waist. She looked like a child playing dress up in her pa's clothes. She also looked like a vision he wanted to see in his doorway the rest of his life.

"I'll be gone for about an hour."

He knew she was telling him he had plenty of time to take care of his morning absolutions. Before he could respond, the door opened and closed with the familiar bang he had already gotten used to.

Zach stared at the door. Though every nerve ending in his body reverberated with pain, he barely noticed. He appreciated Ellie Dixon because she had saved his life. He tried to tell himself that was the extent of his growing attraction to her. It was only natural. It didn't hurt that she was an incredibly beautiful woman any man would be drawn to, especially a man like him who hadn't seen or spoken to many women in the last few years.

If he considered it, though, he knew it was more than that. That worried him more than his cattle stranded in the fields.

•••

Ellie hurried across the yard to the barn. The wind was quite manageable compared to yesterday when it buffeted her without mercy every time she stepped outside.

She hunched her shoulders inside the large coat. Zach's scent wafted up around her through the open collar. She snuggled deeper inside it and imagined his strong arms around her instead of the coat. She grabbed hold of the barn door and dragged it along the metal track, pushing thoughts of Zach away as she went. She had never been one of those silly women who gushed over a man simply because he was handsome and unattached.

She never gushed over men at all. Especially now. She had no interest in romance. Her one foray down that road had ended in humiliation and heartbreak, both of which she still dealt with on nearly a daily basis.

The acrid smell of three large animals confined to a small space assailed her senses, making even her eyes burn. A pitchfork leaned against the barn wall alongside a small pile of dry hay. She knew the purpose. While not looking forward to the chore that awaited her, she didn't mind it much. No living thing had ever depended on Ellie Lundy, unless she considered the household staff she paid every week. But they were Papa's employees. The man at the bank still signed Papa's name on their paychecks. Now, everything on this farm depended on her, from the cats to Zach. Though overwhelming, it wasn't the worst feeling in the world.

The animals stirred and watched expectantly as she moved to the tack box where the feed was stored. Breakfast for them first. Then milking. And finally, cleaning the stalls. Enough time for Zach to see to his needs inside the cabin. And hopefully enough time for her to forget those eyes that reminded her of a morning sky and calloused hands that raised the hair on the back of her neck every time his hand brushed hers.

She had once believed Matthew Dunleavy was the only man she would ever love. His easy, contagious smile had been the first thing about him that caught her attention. He didn't take himself too seriously. Matthew knew how to laugh and have fun. He was the polar opposite of every young man Papa wanted for her.

It was her determination not to fall in love with one of Papa's picks that thrust her into Matthew's arms. With three years of contemplation behind her, she realized she had fallen in love with him to spite Papa.

She shook her head at the childish, conceited girl she had been. She didn't know anything about marriage until her cousin Harper married Logan Kinski last summer. Their love seemed to mature and strengthen every day. Now she knew she wanted what Harper had. Not a husband she would grow to resent for his lack of ambition, but a man she could trust to always put her needs first. A knight in shining armor. A hero willing to climb a mountain to save her.

After the animals were fed, Ellie positioned the stool next to cow. She smiled at the first ping of milk hitting the bottom of the pail. "See," she told the cats waiting a few feet away. "I told you I just needed a little time to get the hang of it."

She wished Harper could see her. Or Mrs. Philips. They wouldn't believe their eyes. She could scarcely believe it herself. What was even more shocking was the sense of satisfaction that came with completing a simple task. No one had ever expected her to do anything she didn't want to do. Schoolwork came easy for her, and when it didn't, her teachers still gave her perfect marks. Mrs. Philips badgered her about learning the skills all ladies should know. But if Ellie pouted long enough or put her arms around the housekeeper and nuzzled her neck, the lessons were usually cut short.

Here, no amount of pouting or complaining got her out of what needed done. Zach hadn't asked her to do anything for him, but if she didn't, they would both suffer. The swelling in his knee had gone down and the poultice on his head she made from his instructions had prevented infection. For the first time in her life, she was needed. She was sore and hungry and tired, but she was also needed.

After she finished the milking and feeding and cleaning, she threw her saddlebag over her left shoulder since her right one still hurt like a toothache and headed inside. If Zach slept most of the day like he did yesterday, she hoped to work on her painting. The broken corner of the canvas meant she could never sell the painting, but no point in sitting in the cabin with nothing to do but snoop around like she had done yesterday.

Even with Zach's coat cinched around her, she was numb from the cold by the time she entered the cabin. She set the milk pail on the sideboard and went to the stove to warm up before removing the coat. Her stomach clenched with hunger. She wondered what Mrs. Philips had fixed for breakfast this morning. She could nearly smell fresh cinnamon rolls and crackling bacon. Thinly sliced that broke apart between her teeth the way God intended. She sighed aloud.

"Did you say something?"

Zach hadn't moved when she came in, and she thought he was asleep again. "I was just thinking about breakfast—"

The words froze on her tongue at the sight of him. He pulled himself up against the headboard. His face was freshly washed and shaved. She smelled the tang of soap from across the cabin. Her stomach filled with butterflies.

"I—see you were able to clean up a little."

He rubbed his hand across his cleanshaven jaw. "Amazing how much better a simple shave makes a man feel."

She nearly said it was amazing how much better it made a man look but stopped herself in time.

She crossed the room to examine the fresh bandage on his head. "I could've changed that for you after I finished breakfast."

He looked up at her, a strange look in his eyes as if he wanted to touch her hand on the bandage.

"I can't expect you to do everything."

"I don't mind," she said before she could stop the words. She did mind. She was selfish. She was used to people waiting on her, not the other way around. But with Zach…

She wasn't sure what it was about him that affected her so. She barely knew anything about the man except that he cared more about his horse than his own welfare.

"Bossie didn't give much milk this morning. And, before you ask, it had nothing to do with my milking technique. The chickens aren't producing either. I expect it was the storm."

"It always happens during storms like this. Shouldn't last but a day or two."

"I hope not." She put her hands in the pockets of his coat and drew an egg out of each one. "This is all we got this morning."

Carrying the eggs as gently as she would the crown jewels, she set them on the table and went to the larder. If there was cornmeal, she would mix up a batch of mush to go with the potatoes and bacon. All she needed was meal, salt, and butter. And water, of course, which was in ample supply thanks to the snow. She would save the eggs for cornbread to go with the beans she put on to soak last night before bed.

She set the food supplies on the table and recounted the measure of ingredients for mush. The sun hadn't crested the mountain yet, and she was already exhausted. She still had hours of work ahead of her before she could sit down and paint.

"How long do you think it will take me to get you to Scottstown in that flatbed wagon behind the barn?" she asked.

She had nearly jumped for joy at the sight of it when she went outside to dump the manure from the horses and the cow.

"Do you mean with Caesar and that horse of yours pulling it through the snow?"

"Well, yes."

Zach twisted his mouth in concentration. "About a month."

"A month? It's the end of March. The snow can't last but a few more days."

He tried to look serious, but she noted a teasing gleam in his eyes. "The snow has nothing to do with it. The buckboard only has two wheels."

"Two wheels!" The snow had drifted against one side and she hadn't seen anything below the wagon bed.

He looked to be enjoying the dismay on her face. "Last fall I was on my way back from town with a load of lumber when I drove off the road and into a ditch, breaking a couple spokes in two of the wheels. I couldn't get unstuck under the weight of the lumber. It took me nearly a week to tote the lumber the rest of the way home with a handcart. I put a sled runner on one side of the wagon so the horses could get it out of the ditch. I had planned to repair it before spring planting. The axel won't last all the way to town if we tried to pull it over the mountain with wheels on one side and a sled runner on the other. I doubt the horses would appreciate it either."

He cocked an eyebrow at her. "Don't suppose you're a skilled wheelwright?"

"You would suppose correctly."

She spoke lightly, but inside she wanted to cry. Her forearms and hands ached so badly from milking the cow she could barely stir the mush. Her back and neck were stiff from sleeping on the floor. She had always been proud of her thick, voluminous hair. Now it was a tangled, greasy mess. She didn't have a brush or a comb, so she had been picking out the worst of the tangles with the skinny end of a paintbrush. She could barely lift her right arm. She was miserable from the top of her knotted head all the way down to her blistered toes.

Zach was still watching her, probably wondering what she was thinking and if she was about to completely fall apart.

It took all her strength and resolve not to. She managed a smile. "It looks like you'll have to put up with my nursing and my cooking for a few more days."

He took the news surprisingly well.

Chapter Twelve

The mush didn't fry up nearly as well as Mrs. Philips's. Ellie still had no idea how to regulate the heat under the skillet, so some parts were burnt while others were gritty and undercooked. It didn't help that she used too much salt. Still, she ate every bite on her plate. Zach must've been just as hungry. After they finished, there wasn't a crumb left to throw out to the chickens.

After breakfast, she brewed another cup of willow bark tea, adjusted the splints around Zach's knee, and applied more ice compresses. He didn't complain about anything, but Ellie worried. His leg was swollen from the top of his thigh all the way to his ankle. She imagined it was black and bruised under his trousers. It was probably a good thing neither of them could see it.

So far, the poultice had prevented infection around his stitches, but she had no idea what was going on inside his head. Sometimes his eyes seemed to lose focus. Last night, when he threw up a cup of willow bark tea, she feared she had indeed poisoned him.

Her chief worry came from the way he winced every time he sat up or took a deep breath. His color wasn't as pallid as it had been the first day, so she knew he wasn't bleeding internally. But something was obviously wrong under his ribcage. She hoped he was only bruised on the inside like he was on the outside, and no major damage had been done that wouldn't eventually heal.

If only she could get him to a doctor, or at least to Scottstown and into one of the beds at the inn. There he would get enough to eat and his wounds cleaned with properly sterilized equipment. At the same time, the selfish Ellie liked having Zach to herself, though putting another's needs before her own was exhausting.

After she removed his ice compresses, she heaped two more blankets on top of him and banked the stove. With a full belly, two cups of tea inside him, and a toasty cabin, Zach fell fast asleep.

Two hours later, beans bubbled on the stove. No chores demanded Ellie's attention for the next few hours. She sank into the only armed chair in the cabin and took a deep breath—what felt like her first one in the last two days. She removed the pins from her hair and let the heavy mass of loose curls fall around her shoulders. She combed her fingers over her itchy scalp. What she wouldn't give to sink into a tub of hot, soapy bubbles all the way past her sore shoulder. She might not get out until Bossie called for her again.

Under the Bible on the table at her elbow was a thin tablet. Ellie carefully slid it out from under the Bible and flipped it open. Row after row of figures and abbreviations marched across the page. Dates. Notations she didn't readily understand. She turned to the next page. More figures and notations that looked too complex for a simple record of crop rotations and calf births. Zach Walsh was apparently planning to build a major operation out here.

The tablet reminded her of the ledgers that were a mainstay on Papa's desk for as long as she could remember. When she was little, she would sit on the floor under his desk, mimicking his moves and scribbling in her own tablets.

Tears tickled her nose. She hadn't entertained memories of Papa since she learned what he had done to Matthew. She still loved him and even missed him, but she didn't know if she would ever forgive him for what he did. He had brutally murdered the man she loved and dumped his body down a mine shaft as if he were a piece of garbage. To add insult to injury, he had let Ellie mourn for Matthew for two years and practically go out of her mind, all the while knowing he was never coming back.

The straw mattress rustled as Zach shifted in his sleep. Ellie quickly closed the tablet and slid it back under the Bible. She watched him for a moment, but he didn't awaken.

She wound her hair into a loose knot and went to the saddlebag she had left by the door. She set her art supplies on the kitchen table. Her busted easel went into the kindling box next to the stove. She propped the broken canvas against the butter crock on the table.

For the next few hours, she worked to fill in the colors of the sun rising over a mountain lake. This was one of a few commissioned pieces she needed to finish in the next few weeks. Capturing nature's beauty was where her heart lay. Over the last few months, she had seen she was hiding behind her canvases from her true responsibilities. Nearly every family in Willow Wood depended on the Lundy/List corporation in one way or another. She couldn't keep pushing those responsibilities into the laps of Hershel List and Rodney Hammersmith because she wasn't ready to do the job Papa left her.

The morning passed, and the sun cast its glare through the window directly onto her canvas. She moved it to the other side of the table and situated her stool in front of it.

She critically studied the painting for a few finishing touches. She mixed russet brown to just the right shade and dabbed the shape of a horse at the edge of the water, its head lowered as it drank from the stream. She darkened the paint and drew the silhouette of a man facing the rising sun. She set his shoulders as though he were welcoming the day and thanking the Lord for it.

Satisfied, she put down her brush. She wished the figure she had drawn could tell her why Zach lived alone so far from civilization. So far, he hadn't explained why there wasn't a woman here, except to tell her it was none of her business. Such a brusque reply meant there was more to the story than losing his family in Louisiana. Ellie couldn't help speculating on what it was.

Her stomach growled at the smell of the beans on the stove. It was well past noon. She was sure Zach would waken soon. She nearly laughed out loud at the notion. She had never set her schedule around anyone. Especially a man. The thought wasn't distasteful at all. She couldn't decide if her attitude had changed over the last year under her cousin's loving influence or because of the man gently snoring across the room.

She recapped her paint tubes and wiped her fingertips on the rag she kept close by. She leaned the canvas against the wall so Zach wouldn't see. She didn't want him to think she favored him more highly than she did if he noticed the figure that resembled him at the bottom of the painting.

"It smells good in here."

Ellie straightened and nearly banged her head on the stovepipe. Her cheeks flushed at his praise. "I'm sorry. Did I wake you?"

"No, my stomach did." He began the laborious task of pulling into a sitting position. His face was tight with pain.

She crossed the floor to the alcove. "Let me help. Are you sick?"

One corner of his mouth tilted upward, creating a tiny dimple in his cleanshaven cheek she hadn't noticed before. "Just hungry."

Relief washed over her. "Oh, I—"

The smile widened. "I know. You're worried about me developing brain fever. Before you ask, I'm from Louisiana and my sister's name is Abigail."

She pursed her lips in mock disapproval. "Well, excuse me for trying to keep you from dying in this bed. It will serve you right if you do have brain fever. Then you'll know I'm not overreacting."

"Are you wishing me ill will, Miss Dixon?"

The blood drained from Ellie's face at the fictitious name on his lips. "No, I didn't mean…" The words trailed away. She went back to the table.

"Since you're awake after sleeping away the better part of the day, I'll start a batch of mush to go with the beans. I don't want to use all the eggs for cornbread in case the chickens don't do their part tomorrow."

Ellie glanced at Zach out of the corner of her eye. He looked slightly befuddled at her rapid change in mood. Well, she couldn't help that. It was too late to correct him about her last name. Explaining why she hadn't been honest in the first place would force her to tell him she didn't trust him. If he knew who she was, he would treat her differently based on it, and she didn't want that.

"First I'll get you another cold compress and give you some privacy," she said as she slid her arms into his coat and ducked outside.

She stood on the narrow porch and let the cold air chill the flush in her cheeks. Once she told Zach her real name everything between them would change. No more teasing banter. No more easy conversation. No more gentle looks. It had happened her whole life. Until her cousin Harper, she'd never had a friend who liked her completely for her. They always associated her with the name on the railroad. They expected her to do certain things, wear certain clothes, go to the proper school. To act the part of a tycoon's daughter.

Most of the time she wasn't even sure who she was on the inside. Here in this cabin, she was slowing finding out.

Papa told her Matthew only loved her for her money. Ellie hadn't believed it. Matthew didn't care about money. Yes, he enjoyed gambling, but it was a game to him. He didn't care so much about winning great pots as he enjoyed the risk. After he disappeared, Ellie discovered the extent of his addiction. It wasn't harmless fun or the thrill of chance. He may have laughed off his habit as harmless, but he had made enemies who weren't. Enemies who wouldn't think twice about exacting revenge if he couldn't pay what he owed.

Ellie had believed Matthew loved her for her, not her last name. But there was no denying a wife with unlimited funds would make his life more agreeable should he land in a situation he couldn't sweet talk his way out of.

But it would make his life a lot easier to have a wife with unlimited funds should he land in a situation he couldn't sweet talk his way out of.

The longer Matthew was gone, the louder Papa's accusations rang in her head. Her money and position mattered even to Matthew. The realization had broken her heart.

She wasn't romantically interested in Zach Walsh. He was a handsome small-time farmer in a bad way who needed her help for the next few days. He was funny and smart, and she liked talking to him.

He would also be in a bad way if he couldn't get into the fields in the next few weeks to plant his crops or if the blizzard cost him any of his cattle. A man in his delicate situation would benefit immensely by cozying up to a woman with Ellie's access to money, no matter how strong his moral fiber.

She hated lying to him. But she couldn't risk seeing the light of opportunity in his eyes when he heard the name *Lundy*.

Chapter Thirteen

If he lived to be a hundred Zach Walsh would never understand women. Or at least not the one who had just skedaddled out of his cabin like a rabbit with a hound dog on her trail.

Sometimes he thought he and Ellie were developing a nice rapport. She was pleasant to talk to and even more pleasant to look at. He could tease her without her getting all het up and irritated. Then, like a splash of cold water, she'd shut down, leaving him wondering if he had insulted or offended her. True, he didn't have much experience with women. His sister had been nearly grown by the time he realized she was different from him.

He and his friends had been rough and noisy and rowdy. Girls tended to ignore them. By the time he developed a curiosity about girls and they began paying attention to him, he was too shy and uncomfortable around them to do anything but blush furiously if one spoke to him. He couldn't make his tongue put together two words when a pretty girl looked his way.

He was too busy working with Pa to miss female companionship. After what happened to Rusty, he knew no decent girl would have anything to do with him.

But this girl—this woman—was different than any he'd ever seen. Half the time she acted scared to death of him. The other half, she was either babying him or chiding him for sleeping away the day or trying to starve him to death with her terrible cooking.

Zach grasped his left leg and lowered it to the floor. He managed to keep it from thudding this time, but excruciating pain still shot up his leg at the increased blood flow.

Over the last two days of slipping in and out of consciousness, he hadn't dwelled much on what would become of his ranch without two good legs to serve him. His head would heal in a week or so, regardless of Ellie's worries over brain fever. The stitch in his side caused discomfort, but if he had punctured something important, he would've been dead by now.

His leg, well now, that was another matter.

Out here, a man was only as successful as his brains and his back and his legs allowed. The Lord had already seen him through plenty of adversity and shown him mercy and grace beyond what he deserved. But each day the sun came up over the mountains took him one day closer to calving time. One day closer to planting. Breaking ground with one horse brought enough problems without the hassle of only one good leg to follow the plow.

If calving went well, Zach could sell a few heads to buy the feed and provision for next fall. That plan left a lot to chance. The blizzard could've already cost him a cow or two in the canyon. Another one or two could deliver a dead calf. There was always the chance disease or pestilence could destroy the grasses in the canyon and the cows would look to him for sustenance. Selling calves early to buy feed for himself and the rest of the herd would put him farther behind in building his operation.

As he took care of his body's immediate needs, he prayed for acceptance of whatever the future brought. Worry only stole his peace and never accomplished anything. The Lord would see him through. Zach might have his own goals and timelines about building his operation, but it was ultimately in God's hands. Like the Apostle Paul had written in the book of Philippians; Paul had known want and he had known plenty, yet he learned to be content with whatever the Lord provided.

With the crude crutch under his arm, Zach shuffled to the sink and washed his hands and face. It felt good to move around, even if the simple act of taking two steps made his knee scream in pain.

He couldn't bear the thought of getting back in that bed, even though he knew he should. He'd sit up and read a while if his headache allowed it.

Banging on the other side of the door alerted him to Ellie's entrance before she burst through the door. He smiled to himself. He was still getting used to the sounds of another human breaking the silence of his day. And he liked it.

She dropped the compresses on the table and hurried around it to help him. "What are you doing over here? Let me help you back to bed."

Irritation at her fussing flared. "I don't want to go back to bed. I'm not a feeble old man."

She stopped and squared her shoulders. "Then what do you intend to do?"

"I'm going to go over there and sit in that chair and read the Bible. Is that all right, warden?"

Her jaw dropped, but he saw the smile behind her eyes. "You do whatever you want, Mr. Walsh, but I must ask, once you get down into that chair, how do you propose to get out?"

He glared at the chair. She was right. It sat several inches lower than the stools at the table. With his stiff back and hips and right leg weakened from supporting his weight, he doubted he could hoist himself out of the chair without injuring his left leg. In frustration, he shoved the crutch to the floor where it landed with a clatter. He and Ellie stared at it. The last of his strength evaporated. He leaned heavily against the table. He didn't know if he should apologize to Ellie or the crutch or to God for his outburst.

"I guess I'll go back to bed where feeble old men belong."

Unruffled, Ellie picked up the crutch and leaned it against the wall. "I found some pieces of lumber outside that look about the right length for a pair of crutches. There are some small pieces laying around the workshop in the barn that would work for the crossbars to rest under your arms."

Zach nodded, remembering. "I had forgotten about those."

"Proper crutches will make getting around much easier on you and I won't have to help as much."

She positioned her thin frame under his left side and helped him onto the stool at the table. She dumped the potatoes and onions from the wooden crate onto a pile on the floor and brought the crate to him. She grasped his left leg around the splint and set his foot onto the upturned crate. She put one of the icy compresses over his knee and then moved behind him.

"I must say it's easier to examine you at the table than on the bed."

Zach wanted to apologize. His pain and frustration at the situation had nothing to do with her. He wanted to put his hand over hers where she carefully removed the foul-smelling poultice from the top of his head. But he was afraid if he did, she would misunderstand. He didn't want her to think he was taking liberties. He didn't want her to think he was falling in...

The weight of the poultice fell away as Ellie carried it to the dry sink. Without a word, she prepared a pan of water and began washing the top of his head. The warm water felt heavenly but not nearly as wonderful as her fingers working along his scalp. After the wound was cleaned, she worked the rag through his hair, around his ears, and down his neck to remove the caked blood.

Zach tried to ignore her soft fingers on his head and neck. She was only doing what needed done. He had no right to imagine turning on the stool and pulling her into his arms.

"You need a haircut," she said suddenly.

Zach frowned. She sounded nearly as breathless as he was.

"But that's for another day," she continued. "I need to get the mush started. You can sit here and read while I finish our meal."

She took the Bible from the makeshift table on the other side of the room. It opened in her hand. "Zachariah Benjamin Walsh?" she read the inscription aloud. "Is that you? What a cumbersome name to put on a tiny baby."

"That's why I insist folks call me Zach. Ma liked Old Testament names. The more syllables the better. My sister is Abigail Keturah Elizabeth."

"That's a mouthful."

He chuckled. "Fortunately, Abigail grew into it. Is Ellie short for anything?"

"Eleanor. I was named for a grandmother I never met."

Her dark brown eyes bored into his as if she wanted to say more. He didn't know much about her beyond her name and that no one had taken the time to teach her basic domestic skills like milking a cow or frying bacon.

Her upbringing wasn't completely lacking, though, considering how gentle and attentive she'd been with him. When she found him on the mountainside, she could've climbed the hill, gotten on her horse, and ridden to Scottstown, leaving him to his fate. The fact that she didn't said more about her character than her lack of skill in the kitchen.

"I thought I'd read aloud," he said. "Is there a particular book or chapter you'd like to hear?"

She kept her back to him. "Whatever you want is fine."

A small scrap of twine marked a page in Jeremiah. The Old Testament prophets sometimes made for heavy reading. Zach decided to find a more inspiring passage for both of them. He flipped to the Book of Matthew and the account of the Sermon on the Mount.

Ellie poured the mush into a hot skillet as he began to read. After he finished two chapters, he closed the leather-bound book. "Do you go to church in Willow Wood?"

She scrubbed at a spot on the stove he figured was already clean. "Not as often as I should."

She didn't speak for a few moments. Finally, she stopped scrubbing and faced him. "I'm sorry. That's not true. I don't usually go at all. Papa and I seldom attended when he was alive. Not since I was a little girl. Even then, we only went when he wanted to impress an investor or business partner."

Zach thought of his brother-in-law Carter, the most inauthentic person he ever met. He believed Carter would say or do anything to build himself up in another's eyes.

"Business partner?"

Red spots appeared on her cheeks. Had he hit a nerve, or did she regret gossiping about her own pa?

"Papa was an important man in Willow Wood," she said at length. "He stayed too busy for things like church. I guess he didn't think it was important. After I got old enough to make my own decisions, I didn't see much reason to go either."

The casual statement made Zach sad. Christian fellowship was the biggest thing he missed about his self-imposed exile. He believed a fellow could worship the Lord anywhere at any time, but it wasn't the same as being part of a body of brothers and sisters to encourage and support one another.

"I've gone a few times with my cousin the last few months," she said. "I don't care for it."

She averted her eyes. "People stare at me. Harper says it's their problem, not mine." She managed a small smile. "But she's not the one they're staring at."

Zach's heart ached. She looked so small and vulnerable, he wanted to take her hand. He clasped his hands on top of the Bible. He didn't want her to get the wrong impression, but more so, he figured if he ever took hold of her, he wouldn't want to let go.

"Why do they stare at you?"

"Because of Papa." She snagged her bottom lip. "And me."

She added a pinch of salt to the cornmeal mush. Zach hoped she took it easy since she'd oversalted the last batch.

"I never used to care what people thought of me," she continued. "I was a stubborn young lady who believed she was always right."

She smiled at him over her shoulder, but Zach saw the pain in her eyes. "Everyone always said I was just like Papa. I was flattered by the comparison."

"Not anymore?" he prodded.

"I don't know. Most of the time I hate Papa for what he did. But sometimes—sometimes I understand it. I want others to understand too. I want them to see he did what he did to protect me."

Zach swallowed the urge to ask for details. He wanted to know just what evil her pa had done that made her hate him, but he could see she needed to tell the story in her own way.

After several moments, she went on. "Papa was killed last summer. He was thrown from his horse during a rainstorm. The hardest part of losing him is that I can't tell him how badly he hurt me. I suffered for two years because of him, and now…"

She shook her head as if to break the train of thought. "I'm sorry. I'm not the only one who suffered by Papa's actions. I always do that. I make everything about me. I don't know why I'm even talking about it now. It's over. I can't turn back the clock. I can't bring Papa back. I can't tell him how much he hurt me. How what he did still hurts. I can't bring—" Her gaze darkened as she turned back to the stove.

She removed the lid over the kettle of beans and stirred. "I shouldn't have said any of that. Even I know it's disrespectful to speak ill of the dead, especially your own papa. You asked me about going to church and I turned it into a diatribe about his faults."

Zach wished she would turn around so he could see her face. "I didn't think that's what you were doing."

He wanted to tell her she could tell him anything; that he would try to understand her pain and grief and doubts over whatever it was her pa had done. She wouldn't believe him. She didn't know him any better than he knew her. She probably feared he would react with the same condemnation and judgment she received from the people of Willow Wood. Maybe he would.

She replaced the lid on the pot. "My cousin says the only way to get past my fears about what people think is to give them to God. I'm not sure how to do that, especially since I'm not innocent myself. Why would God honor my prayers after what I've done?"

Zach rubbed his hand over a patch of stubble he'd missed with the razor. "Much of why I'm here is because I believed the same thing. I dishonored my pa's memory. I let my ma down, and everybody back home knew it. I was sure God would never forgive me. It took me a long time to accept that He forgave me the moment I went to Him with a contrite heart. That's how forgiveness works, Ellie. It isn't because we've earned it. God gives it because we can't earn it."

Chapter Fourteen

Ellie rolled onto her side, willing the floor to soften beneath her. Wedged between the table legs and stove didn't give her much room for sleeping, not that it mattered with tiny mice feet scuffling against the wall and her shoulder begging for liniment. Her mouth was swollen and tender from where she'd split her lip in her fall. She hadn't mustered the nerve yet to look at it in Zach's mirror. If she saw the damage, she figured it would only make it hurt more.

She had taken a few sips of the willow bark tea for the pain, but she hadn't wanted to drink too much in case it made her groggy and she couldn't hear Zach if needed her in the night.

Her physical discomfort wasn't what kept her awake, though. She had told Zach enough about herself and Papa that made her want to tell him the rest. She wanted to tell him she was tired of hiding. Tired of secrets. Until now, the only time she felt like herself was when she went into the mountains to paint. She could tell her stories through her art with no one judging the woman on the other end of the brush. They only saw the painting. Ellie Lundy became irrelevant. Something about being in this cabin— with Zach—bolstered her courage to step back into life.

From the sound of it, Zach was having no easier time falling asleep. She had extinguished the lamp an hour ago, but his breathing had not yet deepened into sleep.

She rolled onto her side away from her sore shoulder. "What did you mean when you said you let your mother down?"

He didn't speak right away. She began to wonder if he was asleep after all. Finally, he spoke. "I told you about my family's plantation. We still owned the land, but there was no money to operate the property. We were land rich and cash poor like most everybody in those days. I told you Pa had a law practice. I studied under him and did most of his clerical work. I planned to go into the practice while we rebuilt the house and the grounds."

Ellie thought of the tablet of figures under his Bible. She should have realized the meticulous detail in his notes had been done by a businessman who had studied law.

The straw mattress rustled as he resituated himself. "We had some good years in the fields. The law practice was growing again. Pa gave me a few pro bono cases, including one with a former slave who had been wrongfully accused of cheating a business in town. Ma looked healthier than I'd ever seen her. Then Pa died."

His voice trailed off. Ellie stared into he darkness and waited. She'd give him as much time as he needed.

"I didn't step in and take the reins the way Pa trained me to do. I was angry at God and angry at Pa for dying. I allowed my brother-in-law to take over many of my duties at the office. All I wanted to do was run with my friends. Instead of becoming the man of the family like Pa wanted, I turned to liquor.

"Ma's health declined rapidly. Not only was she worried about the plantation and the office, she had to worry about me, too. I stood aside as Carter took my place. Carter wasn't invested in the business the way I was. He loved the money and prestige of being a Congressman's son-in-law. Even though we had lost everything, we still had the name. It was one thing Carter didn't have. He wanted an easy way and he made one. By the time I came to my senses, most of what Pa had built was gone.

"Carter had been misappropriating funds from the law office for years, even before Pa died. I worked at any job I could find to pay back the clients Carter had cheated. Even after I made it right, everyone saw us as a crooked firm. No one wanted any part of us.

"Pa didn't believe in sitting back and bemoaning a situation. However it came to be, he strove to fix it. He wanted to repair our plantation. He wanted to repair the town. I think he would've liked to repair the whole South if he had the means. He hated what became of our part of the nation through corruption and greed. He wanted to make life better for everyone in Louisiana. For everyone in the South, regardless of skin color or the situation they'd been born into. I wanted the same thing."

"Didn't you say your pa died when you were eighteen?" Ellie asked. "I think you're putting a lot of blame on yourself. You were just a boy."

"Doesn't matter if I was eighteen or eighty. I was the man of the house. Ma depended on me. She was suffering, but I wouldn't look past my own pain. Instead of doing what my parents raised me to do, I watched the world go by through the bottom of a bottle."

Ellie forgot the hard floor and her aching shoulder. That must be the reason he didn't keep whiskey in the cabin. The bottle had made him shirk his responsibilities. "I'm so sorry, Zach," she said softly. "But I don't think it was your fault. Carter and Abigail took advantage of your youth and inexperience."

The silence lengthened again. Ellie meant to encourage him, but she feared her ignorance of the situation just made him mad.

"I was in charge, not them. I was supposed to finish what Pa started. I failed the plantation and I failed Ma. Believe me, I wanted to blame Carter, but he couldn't have taken from the company if I hadn't made it possible for him."

The mattress rustled again under his weight. "After I came west, I began to realize I could honor Ma and Pa's memories right here on this ranch. Pa taught me to build an empire out of nothing. It's what Ma wanted, too. Maybe empire is too grand a concept." He chuckled, and Ellie smiled in reply. "I don't want Pa's teaching to be in vain."

Ellie shifted on the thin pallet as guilt washed over her. Papa had sacrificed his entire life to build an empire for her. But she had not honored her inheritance. While she basked in self-pity and hid from her responsibilities behind an art canvas, she let someone else run Papa's company. She didn't believe Hershel List was pulling the shenanigans Carter had, but she hadn't done anything to ensure his integrity either.

As usual, she only thought of herself. "You're pathetic," she whispered.

"What?"

"Nothing. I was just thinking…"

Of how alike we are, she wanted to say. *Of how we let our past keep us from living and loving and accepting the gifts right in front of us.*

The wind buffeted the side of the cabin. She no longer worried that it might take the roof off. Though tired and headachy and uncomfortable, she felt safer and more secure than she had in a long time. Zach didn't speak again. She listened as his breathing lengthened.

She snuggled under the itchy blanket and the hard day's work claim her.

Chapter Fifteen

Ellie scratched a spot on the back of her head. She couldn't take it another day. Not one more day.

She was bruised and sore from jumping off the horse. Her back and neck ached from sleeping on the floor. Various burns dotted her hands and wrists from splashes of grease and hot water while she cooked. The tail of her dress was soiled with mud and grime and who-knew-what else she'd dragged in from the barn. If she didn't get a bath and wash her dress soon, she'd go out of her ever-loving mind.

When she got back in the cabin after her morning chores, Zach sat at the table with a steaming cup of coffee in front of him. He was freshly shaven. The scent of pine soap battled against the coffee. Though his clothes were as grimy as hers, his face and hair were clean. She'd be irritated at the injustice if she could keep her mind off his chiseled jaw and full lips long enough.

"The wind blew some limbs out of a tree last night," she told him. "They landed on the paddock fence and knocked some slats loose. Maybe in a day or two…"

She looked questioningly at his leg. The thought of being here another few days wasn't as distressing as it had been at the first of the week.

He continued sanding down the edges of a piece of wood for the crutch he was fashioning.

"I need to wash my dress," she blurted. "It's so stiff I can barely move." She wanted to tell him she needed a bath, but that was too personal to say out loud. Hopefully, he would deduce as much without her spelling it out. "Your clothes need a good scrubbing, too. Your pants are ripped, and there are blood stains on the shirt. If you had a tub big enough…"

"Big enough for what?"

Amusement shone in his blue eyes. Ellie surmised he knew exactly what she was trying to keep from saying. She had already searched for a tub in the barn and turned up nothing. Surely, he didn't bath in the creek all winter long.

"Do you have a tub for washing? The clothes as well as me."

He stopped sanding and looked square on at her. Ellie forced herself to look right back.

He jerked his thumb toward the other side of the room. "Right over there."

She looked, squinted, and looked again. All she saw was the small table where he kept his Bible and ledgers. Then she noticed the base of the table. It couldn't be. That couldn't be his tub. She crossed the room and took hold of the tabletop. Sure enough, the thin slab of wood lifted right off.

She stared in disbelief into the tub. "This is your— tub? How do you—"

Zach's laugh filled the cabin. "I suppose you're used to something bigger."

"Are you kidding? This one looks like my bathtub at home had a baby." She laughed at the ridiculousness of the situation. Tiny though it was, it would have to do.

She sobered and looked back at him. "There's only one other problem." She pursed her lips. How could she expect him to go outside and stay there long enough for her to soak in a tub? And how could she ask a perfect stranger—a man—to lend her something to wear while she washed her dress?

"I—um—"

"I don't have any dresses that'll fit you, if that's what you're asking." Zach didn't try to conceal his humor.

Ellie was so relieved she'd get a bath today he could tease her all he wanted. "I thought as much. I hoped, though, you might have an extra shirt and pair of trousers I can wear for the day."

"I'm sure we can figure something out."

•••

For the next hour Ellie toted bucket after bucket of snow into the house to melt down for bathwater. Zach didn't hear her talk to herself one time. He knew she was uncomfortable preparing for a bath in front of him, so he stayed out of her way as much as he could in the tiny cabin.

He found a length of rope in the chest at the foot of the bed and strung it up across the room alongside the stove. "So you can hang the wash to dry when you're finished," he said in answer to her questioning glance.

He threw a blanket over the rope to give her privacy for bathing, too, though he'd be outside all morning, and there was no chance of him walking in on her.

When she went out to fetch the last bucket of snow, Zach tucked the newly fashioned crutches under his arms and tested his weight on them. He took a few halting steps to get the hang of it. They were much more dependable than the tree branch he'd been using. The rags Ellie had wrapped around the top bars provided added cushion under his arms and made swinging his body between the crutches almost comfortable.

He went back to the table to wait for her so he could get the coat she'd been wearing since yesterday. His gaze landed on the sketchbook on the table he had seen Ellie sketching in every time she had a spare moment.

Zach itched to take a quick peek. He figured nothing would reveal more about her than the drawings between these covers. He glanced toward the window. He couldn't see her, but he was sure she hadn't gone far. His fingers moved toward the book's leather cover. Soft footsteps sounded on the porch. He jerked his hand back and shuffled to the door to open it. He wouldn't look in the sketchpad. Not without an invitation, no matter how curious.

He reached for the door handle. The door flew open and banged his wrist. Ellie nearly trod on his foot as she passed. "Sorry," she mumbled under the weight of the bucket, though her voice belied little sympathy, and even less patience for him being in her way.

Zach bit back a smile. He wished he could offer to help with the bucket, but he could barely maintain his balance between the crutches. Within a few days he'd be packing full buckets. For today, he'd just stay out of her way.

"I need to skin the animals I caught in my traps the other days," he said as he waited for her to take off the coat. "I'll be out there for a couple hours."

She handed over the coat and glanced at his knee. "You shouldn't be on your feet that long." She unwound the muslin curtain from around the string over the window. "I'll put the curtain back up when I'm finished so you'll know you can come inside. I won't be long."

He smiled, as much for her ingenuity as for the concern in her voice. It was nice having someone worry over him. "No need to rush. Skinning's a long job, and it has to be done.

His gaze slid toward the tub, partially concealed in the corner behind the blanket. The spring sun had already melted half the snow from the blizzard. Any day, Ellie'd wake up, saddle her horse, and head up over the ridge and he'd never see her again. For the most part, he had come to terms with his isolation. When Ellie left, it would almost feel like starting all over again.

Outside, he stepped carefully off the porch, mindful of the simple task for the first time in his life. His pride had taken a beating, along with his body, the last few days.

It wasn't easy hobbling across the sodden ground on his stiffened knee. Even with two cups of willow bark tea with his breakfast—burned potatoes, underdone turnips, and stringy bacon—and ice packs applied every hour, the pain was barely tolerable.

For the first time in nearly five years, he thought of how a swallow of hot liquor down his throat would take the edge off the pain. He wouldn't however, even if alcohol were available. He had hated the man he was when alcohol ruled his life. That man had been a disappointment and a failure. He didn't blame the alcohol, though. Every choice had been his own. Every foolish, reckless choice that led to the death of another man.

Zach had been too arrogant and self-centered to pay mind to the rumors scuttling around town about Rusty Higginbotham and his crowd. The group skirted the law from time to time, but their adventures were mostly for blowing off steam. They sometimes started fights over card games that didn't go their way. They "borrowed" horses and carriages to race through the fields, and nearly always turned the animals loose at the end of the night to find their way home. There were always girls around. Sometimes hired girls, but girls nonetheless. Their way of life was easier than Zach's and looked like a lot more fun.

Rusty was big and solid from working long hours on the railroad. There wasn't a man in the county willing to go up against him, and he knew it. Zach saw the wary looks in men's eyes when the gang strode into the saloon in Rusty's shadow. Rusty liked to stop, his muscular frame taking up the entire doorway, set his ham-sized fists on his hips and gaze around the room, challenging every man in the place.

Everyone, including the barkeep, withdrew into as small a target as possible and hoped they could end their evening without becoming the brunt of the big man's wrath.

Zach didn't know about the other fellows, but he had only joined the group to have a little fun; flirt with the girls, drink a little, dance a little and forget about losing Pa, if only for a night. He had no desire to punch in a man's face over a perceived slight.

He could always tell when Rusty was itching for a fight. When Rusty was in that sort of mood, Zach usually went home. He didn't want to be around when it happened, but he always came back the next night.

Zach had intended for that night to end the same. It started out well enough. It was harvesttime. He'd been working hard for every outfit that needed an extra man, and his pockets were bulging. He planned to keep it that way.

He kept the amount in his pocket to himself, though he knew the other fellows had their suspicions. He drank less than the others and didn't open his pockets for the girls who sidled up to him. When they realized he wasn't buying overpriced steaks or drinks, they moved on. The other men were too busy spending their own money to notice Zach was still nursing his third drink when John Henshaw and Teddy Galberth waltzed into the saloon.

John didn't go looking for trouble, but he didn't back down from it either. The animosity between him and Rusty was legendary. Rusty's knuckles whitened around his beer mug when he caught sight of John and Teddy. The girls stopped laughing and flirting.

The whiskey soured on Zach's stomach. He knew there'd be trouble. He sidled over to Rusty and kept his tone light. "That redhead in the corner isn't going to wait the rest of the night for you to make your move. If you don't stake a claim, I might see if she'll pay me some attention."

Rusty didn't take his eyes off John. "Go ahead. She's not near as good as she looks."

Zach's stomach sank like a stone. He'd do just about anything to avoid the coming storm. But he couldn't leave John and Teddy alone to walk into an ambush.

It wasn't long before John said something Rusty didn't like and fists began to fly. Zach tried to deescalate the situation, but John and Teddy were just as hungry for a fight. When the barkeep broke a pool stick over Teddy's back, the fervor went out of the fight. John and Teddy decided the night was over. Rusty, on the other hand, wanted to finish what he started. He and three of his lackeys started after John and Teddy.

"Rusty, no."

Rusty turned at the door and looked back, agape. No one told him what to do. Least of all, easy-going Zach Walsh.

"D'ya turn yella on me, Walsh?"

This was a road Zach didn't want to go down, but he'd seen enough fighting tonight.

"I ain't yellow," he shot back. "The fight's over, that's all. Let it go."

Rusty turned full on him and advanced away from the door. Zach's stomach dropped. Sweat rose on the back of his neck. It took effort to keep his arm from moving upward to mop the perspiration from his eyes.

"Only one decides when it's over is me, and I ain't decided," Rusty said in his deep, gravelling voice.

Zach exhaled slowly to control the rising adrenaline while maintaining a casual stance. "It's over." He indicated the upturned tables and busted chairs with a jerk of his chin. "Let's go back to the party. These girls here are waiting for somebody to dance."

Rusty advanced another step. "What party is that, Walsh? I ain't seen you spend a nickel all night. If you don't want to fight, I ain't gonna make you. But if you want to take what John's got coming, I'm happy to give it to you."

His hand snaked toward his thigh. Zach knew before that hand came up it would hold the long blade Rusty never left home without.

He put up his hands and swallowed around a dry mouth. "Now, listen, Rusty. I didn't come here tonight looking for trouble. Neither did those fellas you just run out of here. How about we let this blow over and go back to having a good time."

The whole time he talked, Zach vowed to never spend time with these men again. He didn't need friends that bad. He'd stay home with Ma and mind his own business.

"I knew you was yella. Ain't a Walsh in this town who ain't." Rusty lowered his shoulders and moved in, swaying from foot to foot.

Zach mimicked his moves, his eyes on the hand with the blade. He'd seen Rusty cut with that knife often enough to know only a fool took his eyes off it.

"I don't want to fight, Rusty, but I will if you force me into it."

Rusty barked out a laugh and lunged. A feminine voice shrieked as Zach dodged to the left. He grabbed the back of a chair and swung it between him and the charging man.

Rusty swatted the chair aside and kept coming. Zach moved in a tight circle, keeping his back away from the wall and the rest of Rusty's friends. He'd seen them grab a man's arms during a fight and pin them behind him to make it easier for Rusty to have his way with the blade or his fists.

Rusty lunged faster than a big man ought to be able to move and slashed downward. Zach deflected the blow with his right hand, though the brunt of it almost took him to his knees. Suddenly Rusty was all over him, pounding with his elbows, fists, and knees. Pushing, punching, slashing. A blow to Zach's forearm rendered his right arm nearly useless. He lowered his head and slammed into Rusty's barrel chest. His ears rang with the sound of bone cracking even as Rusty's arms tightened around him. Zach jerked to the side. The knife clattered to the floor.

Rusty slammed him to the floor. They rolled twice before Rusty came out on top. He grabbed Zach's ears with his huge hands and thumped his head on the floor. Zach saw stars and smelled and tasted blood. The top half of his body was useless, but he could still move his legs. He dug his heels into the floor and kicked and bucked to try to unseat the big man. It was no use. He was only draining his own strength. Rusty let go of his left ear and curled his fist. His face was so close Zach could smell his foul breath. The only thing in his field of vision was Rusty's yellow teeth. The first punch landed with extreme fury. Zach fought to remain conscious. Rusty's hand went back for another punch. Zach twisted hard. Using Rusty's momentum, he drove his shoulder into Rusty's sternum where he'd landed the head butt before he hit the floor.

The strength sagged out of Rusty like wind from a sail. He groaned and exhaled and landed on top of Zach like a bag of sand. Zach's hand closed around the handle of Rusty's knife. He rolled free of Rusty and clamored to his feet.

Rusty rolled over and looked up at him through puzzled and clouded eyes. His massive hands tore at his shirt as if trying to free it of a heavy weight. The others crowded in. Rusty wheezed as he searched the sea of faces. Someone ran out the door, presumably for the doc or the sheriff.

The barkeep came out from behind the bar. He eyed Zach warily as he took the knife out of his hand and circled back around the bar. Zach struggled to catch his breath. His ears were still ringing, and the sounds of Rusty dying came to him as if from the bottom of a well.

"Sheriff's coming," someone hollered.

A few of the gang ran off. Most of the women left as well. When Zach's vision cleared, the sheriff was standing beside him, along with two soiled doves and two men who'd been in the saloon.

"He's dead. He killed him," said the redhead with crooked teeth.

The barkeep came around the bar without the knife. "Didn't nobody kill him. I think he done had a heart attack."

The sheriff knelt beside Rusty's body and rested his hand on his chest. The doctor entered and the sheriff got out of the way. "Feels like his chest is crushed. What'd you do," he asked Zach.

None of it made sense to Zach. He couldn't form a word.

"Higginbotham was itching for a fight," the barkeep said. He motioned around the room to prove his point. "Look what they done to my place. He was on his way to finish what he started with John Henshaw when this one stopped him. It's a heart attack, I'm telling you, and none too soon. Higginbotham would 'a killed Walsh if he could 'a. I can't believe he didn't."

The doctor finished his examination. "His sternum's cracked. Near as I can tell, one of his ribs punctured his heart or maybe a lung. Don't make no difference now. He's just as dead."

The sheriff turned a long look at Zach. "Don't really matter how it happened. The man's dead and somebody's gotta be held accountable." He turned Zach around and put handcuffs around his wrists. "You're going to jail till we sort this out."

With the eyewitness accounts from the barkeep and the two other customers, Zach was released from jail two days later. The soiled doves were never asked to testify, nor were any of Rusty's friends. The town was divided. Half thought Zach was a hero, the other half believed him a drunken killer.

It didn't matter either way. Zach knew he couldn't stay in town. Not only had he shamed his family, he wouldn't be safe as long as Rusty's friends nursed a misguided thirst for justice. Zach would've felt the same in their shoes. Regardless of the exact cause of Rusty's death, he was just as dead, and Zach was the reason.

Chapter Sixteen

Ellie Lundy had never rushed through a bath in her life. When she was a girl, she played pretend games in the water, imagining she was a mermaid or a princess in a magical kingdom or stranded on a tropical island. In her teens, her baths often lasted so long she had to ring for a maid to add more hot water. Everything she did caused extra work and inconvenience for someone else. No wonder her friends so quickly abandoned her when she needed them.

Not today. She scrubbed furiously at her elbows and ankles in the rapidly cooling water, thinking of Zach outside on his busted leg just to give her privacy in his home. The ticking of the big clock on the mantle urged her to hurry as she stood and raked the course, faded towel across her body. She pushed her still damp legs into a pair of trousers, marveling at how easy it must be for a man to start each day. No slips, skirts, or petticoats to slow his progress. Now she understood why men were the ones to build bridges and fight wars and settle continents. Women were too busy getting dressed.

If she thought Zach could climb in and out of the tub with his splinted leg, she'd add more hot water for him. He'd probably appreciate a bath as much as she did. Since a bath in a tub was not in his immediate future, she dipped her soiled dress and underthings into the water. With a sliver of soap, she scrubbed at the grime on her dress and wrung out the full skirt.

She had never as much as rinsed out a slip in her life. The extent of labor that went into washing one dress, let alone an entire outfit and undergarments was staggering. As soon as she got home to Willow Wood, she was going to give every member of her household staff a hug, followed by a significant increase in salary.

She thought of the countless outfits she had splattered with mud or slush over the years. The torn hems, stained sleeves, and dingy bodices she handed over to someone else to clean and repair. She never gave the dresses another thought until the next time she opened her wardrobe and found them hanging as clean and crisp as the first time she put them on. Now she knew what went into making them so. She'd never cross a muddy street or mount a horse again without thinking about today.

After wringing out her things, she dunked Zach's shirt into the dingy water and left it to soak. She went to the window and wound the curtain around the rope to signal him back inside.

She finished scrubbing the shirt and slung it over the rope to drip dry. A fingernail snagged on the fabric and ripped below the quick. She gasped. "That was your last fingernail," she exclaimed. She turned her red, roughened hands back and forth in front of her. "No one will recognize you when you get home."

Her hands were chapped. The skin on her face was so dry, she thought it might crack open if she smiled too wide. Her shoulder hurt and sometimes popped when she moved her arm too quickly. Her top lip was still swollen, and she didn't think her mouth yet closed quite right. Every muscle in her body ached. If she wasn't afraid Zach would come in and catch her, she'd fall down on the floor and have a good cry. Even that would take too much energy, and the salt from her tears would burn the cut on her lip.

She heard Zach thump his way onto the porch. She folded her sore finger into her fist and went to open the door. She hitched up his trousers with her free hand. She had secured them around her waist with a length of rope, but they kept sliding down her hips.

Zach swung his way through the doorway between the crutches. Ellie grimaced at the mud splashed up his trousers nearly to his knees. She was not scrubbing those nasty things. Once he got his splint off, the pants would have to be burned.

She realized he had stopped just inside the door and was staring at her. His gaze dropped to her bare feet and slowly moved up her body, encased in the too-big pants, to her dark hair hanging loose around her shoulders. Heat rushed to her face. She had been in such a hurry to wash her dress before he came inside, she hadn't bothered to put her shoes on or pin up her hair. She hadn't even combed it yet.

She closed the door and stepped back from him. The only thing moving was his Adam's apple that slowly bobbed up and down as he stared.

"I—er—I'm sorry. I didn't want you to have to wait any longer to come inside." She wished she had somewhere private to finish putting herself together. Unfortunately, the tiny cabin didn't offer privacy. She had never fixed her hair in front of a man. Or finished getting dressed. She certainly couldn't send him back outside. Her cheeks heated in humiliation. What must he think of her! She couldn't do anything right.

Zach seemed to snap out of his shock at seeing a half-dressed woman in his cabin. "I'll empty the tub for you." He leaned one crutch against the wall and hobbled to the tub to grasp a handle.

"No, it's too—" Ellie realized what he was doing and cut off her protest. He was giving her time to fix her hair and jam her swollen feet back into her boots. She fought back the tears that she had been so stupid to put him in this position.

With no other choice, she sank to the floor between the table and the stove to partially conceal herself and put on her stockings. She was thankful she hadn't washed them, so she wouldn't have to walk around in wet stockings. She slipped on her boots and laced them up. She had found a comb in the bottom of her saddlebag and dragged it through her wet hair. At home, it often took an hour to comb, dry, and style her hair. She didn't have an hour today.

As soon as Zach dragged the tub to the porch and closed the door behind him, Ellie dropped her face into her hands and softly sobbed. What was wrong with her? She was twenty-six years old, for crying out loud. Practically an old lady. She should know what other women her age knew. How to milk a cow. Cook a simple breakfast. Not let a man see her bare feet.

She didn't have the luxury of sitting on the floor feeling sorry for herself. She swallowed back the tears and dried her face on the tail of the flannel shirt she wore over the trousers. It smelled like the inside of a cedar chest. And of Zach. The scent nearly brought fresh tears to her eyes.

Oh, Zach. Why did you have to be so kind and patient and handsome? Why couldn't you have been a crusty old trapper with a chew of tobacco in your jaw and a lecherous gleam in your eye? I would've ridden out of here that first night in the pitch black and let someone else figure out what to do with you.

Ellie went back to work on her hair. She couldn't have left even a crusty old trapper here to starve with a busted leg and possible concussion. But she wouldn't have to worry about falling in love with him as she nursed him back to health.

Was that what had happened?

She had fallen in love with Zach Walsh?

Impossible! She wasn't in love with anybody. Least of all, Zach. She didn't even know him. He certainly didn't know her.

She had loved Matthew Dunleavy. Passionately and completely. Her hands stilled in her hair. Had she? Or had the idea of shedding Papa's rigid standards mimicked love in her heart? Matthew embodied freedom and a carefree spirit, everything Ellie never thought she'd have as long as she carried the name *Lundy*. After he disappeared, the shine slowly wore off her image of him. Instead of love, she slowly realized it was pity she felt for him. Deep in her heart, she knew Matthew would never amount to more than what he was the last day she saw him.

Guilt plagued her after that realization. Guilt that she couldn't love such a sweet, guileless person, simply because he wasn't ambitious enough for her. She was a terrible, selfish person.

She twisted her wet hair into a knot and secured it at the back of her head. She blew her nose into a piece of paper and threw it into the fire. She blotted her eyes one last time with the tail of the shirt and went to the door to open it for Zach.

"I'm sorry. I wasn't—" She stopped talking. Apologies and explanations weren't necessary. Such things were bound to happen when two strangers were forced together in such a small space.

While he got settled at the table, she dried out the washtub and returned it to its position as a table base.

He motioned to the painting she had propped against the wall behind the stove. "Is that what you were doing when you came into the mountains?"

"I'm painting it for a businessman in Denver. He wanted a spring sunrise over the lake, so I needed to come out before the leaves opened up." She shrugged. "I guess it was all for nothing. The canvas broke in my fall, along with my easel. But finishing it gave me something to do while you were sleeping."

"May I see?"

Ellie didn't usually let anyone see her work until she was finished. But she wanted Zach to see. She wanted to know what he thought. She fetched the canvas and propped it against the canister on the table for him to see.

His eyes widened. "I know just where this is. At the bottom of the gorge where the creek empties into the lake."

Color rose in her cheeks, flattered that he so quickly recognized the scene. "I still have a lot of work to do.

There's no point in finishing it, though. You can see where the canvas buckled. It's worthless now."

"Worthless? Not by a long shot." He put his finger and thumb around the break and bent it back into place. "A little glue and it'll be good as new."

She smiled appreciatively. "Maybe so, but I can't sell a painting on a busted canvas."

He leaned forward and narrowed his eyes. "Is that me? And Clementine?"

Ellie laughed. "It's just a man and a horse. It could be anyone. It could be one of your neighbors."

"I don't have neighbors." He looked closer. "It is me. I'm flattered. No one has ever painted me before."

She started to deny it again. What was the point? He saw the truth on her face. She felt like a schoolgirl caught writing her beau's name on her tablet.

He sat back but didn't take his eyes off the painting. "It's beautiful. I want to buy it off you. How much? Oh, wait a minute. How famous are you? Can I afford it?"

She laughed again. She had forgotten how good praise felt. "I'm not that famous."

"Good, because I don't have much money."

"I'm not selling it to you. It isn't even finished. And it's broken."

"It doesn't matter. I want it anyway. I'd be honored to hang it on my wall. I'll make a frame for it to cover up that little busted spot."

Tears stung her nose. "Thank you, Zach. If you really want it, I'll give it to you. But don't take it just to make me feel better."

He dipped his chin and looked up at her. "I would never say I liked something when I didn't."

She blushed under the intensity of his gaze. "If you're sure then, I'll finish it before I leave."

He took the painting by the edges and held it up to the light. "This is the most beautiful thing I've ever seen." He gazed at her over the top of the canvas. "I'll think of you every time I look at it."

The look in his eyes made Ellie wonder if he was thinking of more than a painting.

Chapter Seventeen

If Zach's leg didn't hurt so bad, he'd go outside and find a chore to occupy the next few hours. He needed to get out of this cabin. He'd hitch Caesar to the plow and head out to the waterlogged field to begin breaking ground. He'd grab his ax and hack away at the tree that had fallen across the paddock fence. Anything to get the image of Ellie dressed in his trousers out of his head.

When he walked in and saw her standing there, a veil of thick burnished brown hair reaching nearly to her waist and those slender legs wrapped in his trousers, he couldn't catch his breath, and it had nothing to do with the stitch under his ribcage. Though the trousers hung on her like sails on a ship, the shape sent his imagination whirling. Though a wife wasn't in his future, it didn't stop him from thinking about one now and then, as the winter stretched long and lonesome, or when a new calf filled his heart with wonder and he wanted to share it with someone.

Now, in the middle of his cabin, stood the loveliest creature he'd ever seen, smelling warm and comfortable and intoxicating. It was all Zach could do not to reach out and take hold of her.

Shame colored his cheeks. Ellie wasn't here because she chose it. She'd been trapped by the avalanche the same as him. If she hadn't heard Clementine's death throes, she would've climbed up to the ridge and ridden back to Scottstown never knowing Zach was dying not twenty feet from the horse. His current carnal imaginings were unfair to Ellie and wrong in the sight of God.

He shifted on the stool, thankful for the first time for the grating pain in his knee to help dispel his impure thoughts.

Ellie circled the table as if to put a barrier between them. Zach didn't blame her.

"I'll make you a cup of tea. Your knee looks terrible. I never should've asked you to stay outside so long."

He looked down at the offending knee, swollen to nearly the size it had been the first day. It strained against the fabric of his pants and around the sides of the splint. But he wasn't in any position to pamper his body. He had work to do.

"I need to get used to moving around again," he said.

"You also need to give your body time to heal."

His insides warmed at the worry in her voice. "Walking helped the pain under my ribs." He stretched to prove his point. "Don't worry, I'll sleep this afternoon."

Without a word, she ducked outside and came back with a semi-frozen rag. She whacked it against the table to make it pliable and slapped it over his knee. Though Zach was used to her less-than-gentle ministrations, he flinched. He knew the cold compresses worked, but he dreaded seeing her coming at him with one in her hands.

"While we wait on the tea, do you think…" She snagged her bottom lip with her teeth and eyed him warily. "Would you mind—would it be all right if I cut your hair?"

Zach barked out a laugh. His hair? With all the pain and agony that wracked his body for the last four days, his hair was the last thing on his mind. Except for when she ran her hands through it yesterday.

"Why would I mind after everything else you've done?"

"Good. It's been driving me crazy. I just want to even it up a bit around the stitches. And maybe around your ears."

He threw up his hands. "Do your worst."

She grabbed the scissors off the windowsill where she obviously had them waiting. "I've never cut anyone's hair before, except for my dollies when I was little. They were never happy afterward."

"Why doesn't that surprise me?"

"I could shave your neck, too, if you want."

An image of a dismembered ear on the floor or a straight, bloody line across his throat nearly made Zach snatch the scissors from her hand.

"No, thanks. I'll take care of that sometime myself."

She took one of the towels off the line behind the stove and draped it around his shoulders. He clenched his teeth as the scissors went together and a hunk of his hair fell to the floor. He questioned his decision to sit here. He'd seen her skills at chopping vegetables. One slice of potato so thin it burned black as soon as she dropped it into the skillet. The next so thick it could choke a horse. He reminded himself a hat would cover a bad haircut, as long as he lived through the process.

The feminine scent wafting around him as she moved from one side to the next quickly took his mind off his own safety. The lilac scent he detected on her when they first met was gone. Now she just smelled clean and natural. Like a woman. A woman in his cabin.

"The paddock fence wasn't in as bad of shape as I feared," he said a little too loudly. "If the weather cooperates, in the morning maybe you can help me trim the tree and put the slats back in place."

"I'll do what I can. I tried to lift one myself. I couldn't even get it off the ground."

"They're water-logged from the snow and rain. They're much heavier now than they will be late summer."

The scissors paused against his neck. "It might be too soon for you to attempt such a job. Your stitches look better, but…"

"No sign of brain fever?"

She playfully nudged his shoulder. "It looks like you avoided that. Your knee bothers me most. It will probably cause you pain the rest of your life. After we fix the fence, I'll check on the condition of the trail to see if I can make it to Scottstown to send for the doctor? Maybe there's something she can do."

Zach knew better than anyone his knee needed medical attention. But he hated to think of Ellie leaving. "What will you do when you get back to Willow Wood?" he asked.

"I'll send the doctor straight out."

"No, not that. I mean you. What will *you* do?"

"Oh."

Zach couldn't contain his curiosity any longer. In the four days she'd been here, he still didn't know anything about her except that she painted, and her work was good enough for smart people to pay good money to get it. While in the barn, he had looked over her horse. It was well shod and in excellent condition. Her saddle was top quality. She had a housekeeper and was unfamiliar with household chores. She wasn't married and wasn't worried about getting home to children. The evidence said a lot, but only enough to raise more questions.

"I have to get back to my painting. The man in Denver isn't going to care about an avalanche slowing down my progress."

"How did a man all the way down in Denver hear about you? You must be more famous than you let on."

"Not really. Word gets around."

An evasive answer if Zach ever heard one. He wished he could turn around and look into her face. What wasn't she telling him? And why?

He had found the best way to get more information than he needed from a person was to ask about what seemed the most important to his or her heart.

"How did you get into painting?"

"From my mother." This time she answered without hesitation. "Everything I know, I learned from her."

Zach already knew that much, but at least it got her talking. "Was she professionally trained?"

"No. Like most artists, she was naturally gifted. Her parents probably didn't understand her any more than Papa understood me."

There she went again with a barely concealed slight against her pa. Ellie obviously had problems with the man. Whatever it was, was none of Zach's affair. Nor did he want to push her toward that subject when this was the first time they'd ever really talked.

"Did your mother understand you?"

"Oh, yes. We were kindred spirits. Or it seemed that way to me. She couldn't get out much because of her health, so I spent a lot of time in her room, reading and listening to her stories. And painting."

She stopped talking. The scissors continued to move around Zach's head. He waited; he knew she wasn't through.

"After Mama died, I realized I didn't know her at all. She had told me plenty of stories of growing up with two sisters. I could almost picture the little town in Michigan where she came from. But her—I didn't know enough about her at all. Why was she the way she was? She never complained about her physical limitations or the things she never got to do. Did she miss her parents? Why did she fall in love with Papa? Did she dream of doing something other than being my mother?

"You know how children are. We see our parents completely in that role. They are the ones who gave us life. We can't imagine there was ever more to them than that. No hopes, dreams, desires, or thoughts outside of us.

"It's only been eight months since I lost Papa. I had him my entire life, but I knew even less about him than I did Mama. Oh, I knew what everyone in Willow Wood knew. That he was strong. Stalwart. Arrogant. And good at what he did."

The scissors paused at Zach's neck. He hoped she wasn't finished, but he figured she'd stop talking once she finished cutting his hair and had to look him in the eye. It was easier baring your soul if you didn't have to look into the eyes of the one you were baring it to.

"Growing up, he was my hero. But I guess even heroes have flaws."

The sudden anger in her voice caught Zach off guard.

"He was a whitewashed wall hiding an evil heart. I want to grieve for him. I really do, but I don't know how." Her voice went soft, and Zach thought he heard tears. "He was my papa and I loved him. I guess I still do. But can you truly love someone when everything you thought you knew about them was a lie?"

Chapter Eighteen

Ellie wiped the stray snips of hair off the scissors with the towel from around Zach's neck and laid them on the table. She hoped he wouldn't notice the tremor in her hands.

Zach didn't own a proper teakettle. The pot of boiling water on the stove bobbled over the heat instead of whistling. She dropped a generous blob of honey into the tin cup, added the cheesecloth of willow bark and covered the cup with a saucer to steep. By the time she finished, she had regained enough composure to face him.

She wasn't sure what had gotten her started down this road of self-reflection, but it felt good to unburden herself with a man she barely knew and who didn't know her at all. Tomorrow after they finished the fence, she would climb on Saturn and ride out of this barnyard, never to return. Barring another avalanche or a completely impassable road, she'd ride to Scottstown to hire a wagon to come back for Zach. She would also hire someone to look after his animals for as long as it took for him to receive treatment in Willow Wood. He would resist the help, of course. He was too proud and stubborn to ask for it himself, and he surely wouldn't appreciate her taking matters into her own hands. Well, that was too bad. Sometimes a person needed to accept help whether it grated against their nature or not.

She looked across the table at Zach. He was staring at her. Her scissors had missed a few tufts of hair, and it was slightly longer on one side. Even with the flaws, he was even more handsome. She could only imagine how good he'd look without the dark circles around his eyes or the bald patch around his stitches. But the intense gaze he directed at her was what she noticed most. Every time he talked about his own pa, it was with reverence and respect. He couldn't understand a daughter who called her papa a whitewashed wall. She didn't owe him an explanation, but she wanted to give him one, nonetheless.

She settled onto the other stool. The upturned crate with his left foot resting on it was the only thing separating them.

"After Papa died, I turned all my attention to my art. It kept me from thinking about losing him. I didn't want to think about him or the night he died. He would've done the same thing if something happened to me. The day Mama died he went to work. He didn't grieve for her one day. At least not that I saw."

Ellie's stomach clenched at the memory. She seldom let her mind go back to when Mama died. In her mind, she was either the little girl who had a mother or the young woman who didn't have one. Never the eleven-year-old girl in between.

Sometimes she imagined that girl was trapped inside a snow globe like the one Papa brought her from Chicago when she was little. Frozen in time. Unscathed by the loss of that day. And if she did remember—if she lowered her guard and let the memories crowd in—it was like someone turned the snow globe upside down and shook it. As the tiny white bits of pretend snow whirled around her, she felt like she was holding her breath, afraid the glass would shatter, and all the little bits would come flying out.

So, she didn't think on it. But she wasn't safe inside the globe either. Anyone could come along and shake it and turn her world upside down all over again.

She wanted out, but she'd never be completely free as long as she stayed hidden inside the globe.

"I knew Mama was dying," she told Zach before she could talk herself out of it. "I think I had known my whole life. She tried to prepare me, especially as her time grew near. She didn't want me to think she had lied or sugarcoated the truth. She wanted me to know how much it broke her heart that she had to leave, but there was nothing she could do about it.

"I begged her not to go. I told her Jesus didn't need her. I did. She said it didn't work that way. People didn't get to choose. It was God's job to decide when people came into the world and when they left. We just had to accept it. After that, I sort of believed God was mean. Since He knew everything, He must've known how much I needed my mother. That meant he just didn't care."

Ellie exhaled a slow breath, determined not to cry. Now that she'd shaken the globe, she couldn't stop until all the bits had settled.

She didn't look at Zach either. It was hard enough saying the words out loud without knowing what he was thinking about her as she said them.

She kept her eyes on her hands and tore at a rising blister.

She looked down at her hands and tore at a rising blister. "That last day I stayed with her all morning, telling her I loved her and trying to be brave. I thought if she knew I wasn't going to act like a baby, she would be proud of me and find the strength to fight the disease that was stealing her from me. Then Papa came with the doctor and I had to leave.

"Papa yelled at me and said I was getting shoe marks on the bed. I wanted to cling to Mama, but I knew it would upset her if I didn't do what Papa said. She smiled that sweet smile of hers the way she always did and patted my hand and told me she loved me and she was proud of me. I didn't throw a fit, though I wanted to. I got off the bed and walked out of the room as straight and tall and ladylike as I could. I never saw Mama's smile again."

Ellie's vision blurred behind the tears. Her voice trembled. She didn't look at Zach. She didn't look anywhere but at the blister on her hand as she remembered Mama's bedroom door closing behind her.

"I sat in the hallway with my back against the wall for hours. Mrs. Philips tried to get me to go downstairs with her to the kitchen. She knew it would be a long process. I wouldn't even look at her. I wanted to be close in case Mama changed her mind and called for me. I thought if I was really quiet and really good, Papa wouldn't be mad at me for making marks on the bed and he'd let me come back in. I thought if I showed God how much I honored my parents the way the Bible told me to, He'd change his mind and not make Mama go. And if she did have to go, well, I wanted to be with her holding her hand, because if I was the one who had to go—I'd want *her* holding my hand."

She sniffed back a shuddering sob. Zach leaned over his busted leg and covered the hand with the blister. Ellie snagged the handkerchief out of her sleeve and covered her eyes so she wouldn't have to look at him. She wouldn't cry. Not now. Not fifteen years too late. If she cried for Mama, it would make her cry for Papa, too, and he didn't deserve her tears.

She turned her hand inside his and closed her fingers around his. The calloused warmth felt so good. She wished she could fold her whole body inside his hands and stay safe and warm and comforted forever. She pulled herself together and withdrew her hand.

After another deep breath, she continued. She couldn't stop now.

"I don't know how long I sat there. When the door finally opened, I couldn't get up. My legs and body were stuck in that position. I knew something was different. I wanted Papa to tell me I was wrong and Mama was fine. The doctor had given her some new medicine and it took care of whatever had been ailing her all those years. God had decided to let her stay with me instead of taking her away.

"I knew, though, as soon as I saw the look on his face there was no new medicine. God hadn't changed His mind. Papa was mad. Not sad like you'd think. He was mad. Furious. He always got that way when he didn't get what he wanted. He believed if you bargained strongly enough, got up early enough, worked hard enough, or paid enough, you could have anything you wanted. To lose the woman he loved more than anything else was like a slap in his face. It was like he made a bargain with God, and God didn't keep His end of the agreement.

"He walked right past me like I wasn't even sitting there. I didn't even have time to say his name. I wanted him to pick me up the way he did when I was little and hold me close and let me cry and assure me everything was going to be all right. I still had him, and he would make sure that was enough. He didn't. He didn't even look at me."

Ellie's voice cracked as the old hurt bubbled to the surface. "I finally got up and stood there frozen, watching him stride down the hall, his long legs eating up the distance to the stairway. I stared at him and willed him to stop and turn around and open his arms and let me rush into them.

"The doctor came out of the bedroom, looking almost disappointed that Mama had let him down. He glanced down at me but didn't speak. I guess he'd been through enough already without having to deal with a crying kid. He was still looking at me when the front door slammed downstairs. We both flinched. We knew it was Papa and we knew he was mad. I think we both felt responsible and a little scared about what would happen next.

"Papa was gone. Mama was gone, and I was alone with this man who never liked me. I wanted to cry and wail and kick my feet against the hardwood floors. I didn't care what anyone thought of me anymore. But I was too numb.

"Mrs. Philips appeared at the top of the stairs. She opened her arms and I ran into them. She had been baking bread that day and smelled like yeast. To this day when I smell fresh bread, I think of—"

She shook her head and blinked away the tears.

"She wrapped her arms around me, and for the first time I felt anchored to something. We cried and cried. I wanted to go into Mama's room, but the doctor had already shut the door and shook his head at Mrs. Philips. I knew I would never see my beautiful mama again. I'd never see her smile.

"Mrs. Philips took me downstairs. I slept with her that night. I kept asking where Papa was. I asked her all day. She said he was at the office. I don't know if he really was, but it made sense because he was always there. That's the day I learned he valued work over everything else. It shouldn't have come as a surprise. I knew he loved me and he loved Mama, but work was more important than either of us."

Ellie uncovered the tin cup and looked inside. "I'm afraid the tea's cold."

"Ellie."

She couldn't look up. She didn't want pity. Or judgment. Unburdening herself had been cathartic. She felt a hundred pounds lighter. She wanted to enjoy the moment before Zach told her she was wrong to hold onto resentment for fifteen years toward the man who had given her life. It was a sin in the eyes of God, and if she didn't change her attitude quick, fast, and in a hurry, she'd go straight to hell.

She carried the cup back to the stove. "I'll reheat your tea and remove that icepack too. There won't be much snow left by morning for cold compresses. Hopefully the worst of the swelling will be under control by then."

"Ellie."

She stared into the cup.

"I'm so sorry," he said when she finally looked at him.

She started to tell him it was all right. She had grown up fine without a mother. Papa had done his best to raise her on his own. He gave her everything she could want or need. He only wanted to protect her from her own foolish heart and stubborn will. He wanted her to have a good life with a successful man cut from the same cloth as himself. It wasn't his fault she fell in love with a gambler and a rogue who never would've made a good husband for her. He had just gone about it all wrong and made everything worse. He had killed a man, but he had done it to protect her.

"Everything he did, he did for me," she murmured. It was all she could manage.

Zach's bottomless blue eyes bored into hers. "I know."

"It was my fault. Everything's been my fault from the beginning."

His gaze softened further. He lifted his hand. She set down the cup and reached for it. His strong fingers closed around hers. Ellie closed her eyes and let his warmth and comfort wash over her.

"It wasn't your fault your mama died."

She opened her eyes. "No, not her. Papa. Papa died because of me. Matthew's dead because of me. Everyone—" She put her free hand on her stomach, thinking of her darling baby born too small to have a chance at life.

"I destroyed everyone I ever loved."

His fingers tightened around hers. "It's all right."

Keeping hold of his hand and her eyes locked on his, Ellie circled the table. She should warn him not to get close to her. Not to let her love him or he would suffer too. That's all she was good for. Hurting those she loved.

Her throat closed around the thought. She didn't love Zach. She couldn't. She barely knew him. He certainly didn't know her. Her love for Matthew had been self-centered and immature, inspired by rebellion toward Papa. Maybe this was the same. An immature infatuation she would recognize for what it was the instant she got back to Willow Wood. But this was nothing like what she felt for Matthew. Matthew had been a carefree, fun-loving boy. Zach was a man; a man who knew how to love a woman forever and always put her needs first.

For the first time in a long time, she didn't experience the familiar ache that accompanied thoughts of Matthew. Matthew had loved her, but he loved excitement more, the same way Papa had loved and revered business and success. Even back then when she looked into Matthew's dark eyes, she wondered if she would be exciting enough to hold onto him, or if he would soon grow bored and go chasing the next adventure.

She no longer wanted that kind of love; the kind that depended on excitement and fun and adventure. She wanted the kind her cousin Harper shared with her husband. Strong, mature, lasting love. Not fleeting and light-hearted.

Would she have that someday? Would she find it with a man like Zach?

When she got to his side of the table, he pulled her down onto the stool she had vacated. He leaned toward her and wrapped his arms around her. Her tears burst forth at the contact. Mindful of his sore ribs and busted leg, Ellie wrapped her arms around his neck.

"I didn't mean to hurt them," she said into his shoulder. "I was only thinking of myself. That's what I do."

He shook his head and wiped away a tear from her cheek. "No, Ellie. That's not what you do."

"Yes, it is. You don't know me."

"I know enough."

Zach looked like he wanted to say more. His face was only a few inches from hers. Ellie's throat constricted. She breathed in the fresh pine scent of him. Her gaze drifted to his lips, slightly parted, seeming to beckon to her. She had never wanted to kiss a man as much as she wanted to kiss him right this minute.

She should tell him the rest. It wasn't fair to come this far and then take the coward's way out. She should tell him about Matthew and what Papa had done.

If she truly wanted freedom from the sins of her past, she shouldn't let fear of reprisal keep her from confessing them all. But she didn't want the passion on Zach's face to be replaced with judgment. She had seen that look often enough when she walked down the streets of Willow Wood. She heard the whispers. She knew what good people thought of a woman who had a baby out of wedlock. She knew they called her *Crazy Ellie*.

No, it wasn't fair to give in to the pull of Zach's lips when he didn't even know her name. Kissing him wouldn't be fair to either of them.

She straightened and loosened her arms from around his neck. Ignoring the shock and dismay on his face, she pushed away from him.

"I'm sorry. I shouldn't have..." She dried her clammy hands on the trousers she wore and grabbed the softened compress from his knee. "I'll take this out and check on the animals."

She grabbed her duster from the peg and hurried outside without looking back.

Chapter Nineteen

Yesterday's sunshine had reduced most of the snow to slushy, soupy piles against the side of the cabin and outbuildings. Marshy puddles dotted the yard among green patches of spring grass. The sun shone through wispy clouds on a bright blue canvas, promising to dry out the rest of the yard by day's end. The end of the snow meant Ellie would be forced to make trips back and forth from the well for water. It also meant the roads would dry out, and she could make it to Scottstown for help. She should be bouncing up and down at the prospect of going home and getting back to her life. Instead, all she wanted to do was help Zach move the broken tree limbs off the paddock fence.

Zach leaned heavily against a fencepost to take the pressure off his left leg. "Shouldn't take more than an hour or two to repair this fence well enough to keep the animals inside."

Ellie studied at the tree laying across the fence. The branches of the tree had knocked several of the slats loose from the fencepost. Zach could nearly repair the damage without her, even with only one leg to stand on. What he couldn't do was move the tree limbs away from the fence. He pointed to the smaller of the tree limbs that had fallen across the fence. "If I chop those off, do you think you can drag them into a pile that I can burn later or haul away once I get the buckboard fixed?"

She looked doubtfully at his leg. "It'll be a bigger problem for you to hack away at that tree than for me to drag it off."

"We'll just take care of the worst of it for now. The way the tree fell across the fence creates a natural barrier to keep the animals in until I can fix it properly."

"Whatever you think."

Zach reached into his pocket and drew out a pair of leather gloves. "They're big, but they'll help protect those soft city hands."

"Soft city hands? Are you kidding?" She held her hands up and flipped them front to back. "They look like they belong on a field hand. They won't recover if I soak them in buttermilk for a week."

He snorted. "They're just not used to hard work."

Ellie wrinkled her nose and tried to look offended. She slipped her hands into the gloves and closed her fingers around the fabric to keep them in place. She put her fists on either side of the ax handle and held it out for Zach. "You get to chopping, Mr. Walsh, and I'll show you hard work."

He took the ax. "Just try not to get in my way and slow me down."

He shuffled toward the smaller limbs across the fence. Once his eyes were off her, Ellie blew out a slow breath to release the heat from her cheeks.

What was she doing? She had no business teasing and flirting with this man. They had nearly kissed last night. She still wanted to. She wanted to walk up behind him, take the ax from his hands, and lean into his arms. She wanted to tell him exactly who she was and let the chips fall where they may. She couldn't do any of that. She was on her way home as soon as they repaired the fence enough to open the barn door. Her family was probably worried sick about her. She needed to begin work on the painting for the businessman.

She would contact her friend in Chicago about displaying her work at an art gallery. She might even include some of Mama's paintings. She needed to find a business manager she trusted to oversee her half of *Lundy List*. Her responsibilities at the company were too great for her to do alone and still have time for her art.

The ring of the ax filled the air. Ellie forced her mind to the job at hand. Making sure to stay in Zach's line of vision so he wouldn't accidentally embed the ax in her skull, she grabbed hold of one of the branches and pulled. The branch remained in place. She yanked again. Pain shot through her shoulder.

Zach moved toward her through the branches. With two deft swings of the ax, he chopped the branch in two. This time, Ellie's half easily disengaged from the restricting branches.

Ellie watched his efforts and quickly figured out what he was doing. If she worked with him instead of grabbing branches willy nilly, she'd finish in half the time and with a lot less damage to her aching shoulder.

184

In less than an hour, they cleared away enough of the smaller branches to get close to the fence to repair the busted boards.

Zach leaned against the fencepost and mopped his sweating brow. "Good work, partner. I couldn't have done it without you."

"Isn't that what I said?"

She leaned over and scooped up a handful of sticks to get her eyes off Zach. She threw the sticks in the direction of the brush pile she'd created. As soon as they finished with the fence, she was going back to Willow Wood. Back to her big soft bed and wardrobe full of clean, lilac-scented dresses.

It would be easier to leave if Zach weren't so easy to talk to. Maybe it wasn't Zach but his ranch and the secluded setting that made it easy for Ellie to forget her past.

Be whoever she wanted to be.

Tell Zach only as much as she wanted him to know.

It wasn't fair to him. It wasn't even fair to her. But she didn't want to focus on that right now. Though she'd worked harder in the last five days than she had in her entire life, she couldn't remember ever having a better time.

She brushed her hands on the seat of the trousers and looked back at Zach. "What's next, boss?"

He was watching her strangely as if trying to read where her thoughts had been. "You've done so much already."

"We did the hard part. Let's finish."

He brushed his newly cut hair back from his forehead. "If you're sure you don't mind, there's a roll of barbed wire in the barn. Can you bring it out with a hammer and bucket of nails? We'll string wire between these posts until I can get to the sawmill for more boards."

With barely a nod and a glance in his direction, Ellie skirted the tree and hurried to the barn, amazed at the freedom of moving about in trousers. What would Mrs. Philips think if Ellie came downstairs in a pair the next time she went for a ride in the mountains? She banished the thought as quickly as it crossed her mind. Her long-suffering housekeeper had already dealt with enough from her. Ellie Lundy galivanting around Willow Wood in trousers would be the straw that broke the camel's back.

Careful to protect her hands and arms from the rusty roll of wire, she carried it back to Zach. After finding the hammer, nails, and a pair of wire cutters, they set to work.

Zach held onto the roll as if it weighed less than a paintbrush and unfurled it while Ellie carried the end to the opposite fencepost. "Do you want to nail it into place?" Zach asked.

"I would, but I don't want to show you up."

Zach grinned, and Ellie's heart melted a little. She quickly averted her eyes. The sun and the hard work and the pain in her shoulder were getting to her. Any feelings she thought she felt for this man were from isolation and his dependence on her. Nothing more. As soon as she got back to Willow Wood and back to work on what mattered, she'd put him out of her mind. He'd become a sweet memory of someone who helped her see beyond herself for a while. She wasn't the only person in the world with needs, and she was capable of meeting those needs.

She stepped out of the way to give Zach room to nail the wire into place. She watched his profile as he worked, committing the lines to memory. His straight jawline. The crinkles in the corners of his eyes. His concentration in doing a job right. She had no doubt he would build this ranch into an empire, even while missing a year to his injuries. He would eventually realize he needed a wife. He'd go to Scottstown and find a sweet young woman from among the strong families there, and the two of them would build a life on this very spot. He'd eventually tell her about the time he got caught in an avalanche and would've died if God hadn't sent a skinny, nearly inept woman out of the trees to help him off the mountain and nurse him back to health. He would claim he owed his very life to God's grace and Ellie Dixon—a woman who didn't exist.

Ellie pushed the thoughts aside. She wouldn't turn this day into an excuse to feel sorry for herself and bemoan the things she'd never have. She'd done enough of that already. It was time her eleven-year-old self broke out of the snow globe she had built around herself and learned to make a difference in the world, even if it was too late for her heart to know love.

The largest section of the fallen tree blocked Zach's access to the final fencepost and was too big for one man on one leg to cut away. Someday, when he was up to it, he'd tie the horse to it and drag it off. He leaned his hips against the largest branches as he explained it to Ellie.

"The tree will probably be enough of a barrier to keep the stock in without a line of wire."

Ellie looked past the tree to the fence. "For today. But once you get another horse, you'll need a secure paddock until she gets used to her new home."

She shimmied through the branches and climbed onto the tree trunk. "Hand me the wire and hammer, and I'll nail it into place."

"I know you don't want to show me up, but have you ever actually swung a hammer?"

"It can't be that hard. I've been watching you do it all morning."

He arched his eyebrows. "Just don't mash your thumb and don't fall outta there. We can't have both of us off our feet."

Ellie twisted the wire around the fencepost as she'd seen Zach do. She removed the gloves to grip the nail. She hit the nail with the hammer as hard as she dared in case she missed and hit her thumb. The nail barely stuck into the bark.

Zach laughed out loud. "You can't hurt it. Give it a good whack."

"I'm not worried about hurting the nail."

She smacked the nail a little harder. It slanted off center. She hit it again to straighten its path. The nail pinged and disappeared into the soft earth beneath where she stood. "Where'd it go?" she exclaimed.

"Gone forever. Try again, but you must hit it hard enough to drive it into the post."

"That's what I was doing." She set her mouth in a straight line. After only six whacks, the nail slid home and only a little bit crooked.

"Put in another one," Zach instructed, "to make sure it holds."

Ellie exhaled. Her shoulder throbbed. Another blister split open on her hand. When the second nail slid into place, straight and true after only four whacks, she let out a joyous whoop.

She pivoted on the log and held the hammer aloft. "I did it," she cried. She ducked between the branches, set her hands on Zach's shoulders, and jumped off the log. He grunted and stumbled under her weight. He wrapped his arms around her to catch her. His crutches dropped to either side of him as he sat down hard on the tree trunk, pulling her down on top of him.

Ellie gasped. "Oh, no. I'm so sorry. Your leg."

Zach didn't seem worried at all about his injuries. He tightened his arms around her. Ellie slid her arms around his shoulders and clasped her hands behind his neck. She hadn't been this close to a man in years. His hard-muscled arms enveloping her felt as strong as she had imagined. She wanted to stay here in his arms forever. Safe. Content. Loved.

She should pull away. He didn't love her, and she didn't love him. They were only together out of necessity. He had told her very little about why he lived in this remote cabin except that he wanted to be left alone. She hadn't told him why she had chosen a solitary life.

But she didn't pull away. She couldn't. His blue eyes held onto hers, drawing her closer. His lips parted. He tilted his head to avoid the sore spot on her mouth, and he pulled her against him.

Ellie tightened her arms around his neck as their lips met, gingerly at first, and then stronger as the kiss deepened.

After a long moment, she broke the kiss. "I'm sorry. I didn't mean to hurt you."

"You didn't hurt me." His voice was hoarse and dry. He traced the cut on her lip with his forefinger. "I hope I didn't hurt you."

"Never," she whispered.

Ellie knew she should pull away, but her arms refused to let go of his neck. He moved his mouth toward her, and she went willingly.

His lips explored hers. Ellie curled her fingers in the hair at the back of his neck and sank deeper into his kiss.

"You're so beautiful, Miss Dixon," Zach whispered, her breath warm on her face.

She stiffened and pulled completely out of his arms. How could she let him kiss her like that when he didn't even know her name? She stood and moved away from him. "I—um—I need to get my things together before..." She couldn't finish. She shoved the hammer into his hands and hurried to the house.

Chapter Twenty

He shouldn't have kissed her. He shouldn't have taken advantage of the situation. But when a beautiful woman fell in his lap, what was a man supposed to do?

Zach gave the pliers one last twist, a little harder than he intended. The wire snapped and zinged into the paddock.

He should be sorry for kissing Ellie, but he wasn't. He'd been wanting to do exactly that for a long time. He'd do it again if given half the chance. The only thing that bothered him was the look on Ellie's face when she pulled away. Obviously, she didn't share the same passion he felt for her.

Zach never claimed to know much about women, but he sure thought Ellie had begun to have feelings for him. Yesterday, after telling him about losing her ma, he thought she wanted him to kiss her. Then, just like today, she pulled out of his arms and ran out the door like a scalded dog. Had he misread the situation, or was something else going on?

Zach glanced toward the closed cabin door that has just slammed shut behind Ellie. Hope swelled in his chest. Maybe her fleeing had nothing to do with him and everything to do with her denying her attraction for him.

He grasped the coil of barbed wire in one hand and hobbled to the barn. The soggy ground sucked at his crutches with every step, making for slow progress.

Inside the barn, Ellie's attempts to keep order were evident everywhere he looked. She was a hard worker; he'd give her that, especially considering she'd never hefted a pitchfork before the moment she walked onto his property.

He stored the wire and tools, then opened the paddock door to allow the animals to go in and out. A spring breeze was as much of a cleaning the barn would get today. He was too tired for anything else. His head pounded. His armpits chafed against the crutches. The pain under his ribs made a deep breath uncomfortable. And his knee—his pitiful knee. He grimaced at the swelling around the splint. He needed to get off his feet, and quick.

Pain and weariness were a good thing. Once Ellie rode out of the barnyard, Zach would sleep until someone arrived to reset his knee. Then his body could begin to heal. He could get back to running his ranch and forget all about the angel who saved him on the mountain.

Or he could walk away.

Saddle Caesar and ride out of here. That seemed like the simplest solution to a whole lot of problems. Sell the property and what was left of the cattle and start over somewhere else. Someplace where he didn't have to worry about picturing Ellie Dixon every time a door slammed, or he bit into an underdone piece of meat.

He wasn't sure such a place existed.

Ellie glanced up as he walked through the door and then purposely turned her back to him. She had changed back into her own clothes. While disappointed he could no longer see the outline of her long legs, his fool heart skipped a beat at the sight of her in feminine attire with her copper-laced hair coiled neatly at the back of her head.

She removed the lid from the pot on the stove and stirred. "The beans are nearly hot and a cup of tea is steeping. You should eat and lie down to stretch out your leg. I'll be on my way soon."

Zach nearly said; "Or you can fetch the parson, so you don't have to go."

What was he thinking?

Instead, he took off his coat and hung it on the peg next to her duster. "I'm sure your family is worried about how you fared during the storm."

Ellie set a bowl and spoon on the table. "They probably think I'm still at the inn in Scottstown, hard at work on my painting."

Zach didn't have much appetite. He sank onto the stool and positioned his foot on the upturned crate. While the food heated, she gathered her painting supplies from the windowsill.

"Could I see some of your sketches?"

She turned and stared at him.

"If you don't mind, that is. I've seen you working in that tablet. I was just—curious."

A flush of color warmed Ellie's cheeks. "If you're sure you want to see them."

"You always do that."

Her dark brows slid together. "Do what?"

"Dismiss yourself. Everything you do, you act like it doesn't amount to anything. Especially your painting."

She glanced at the paintbrushes clenched in her fist. "I don't mean to. It's just…"

Zach suspected he already knew what she was thinking. Her pa had dismissed her art. Maybe everyone else in her family treated it like a silly hobby to occupy her time rather than a passion that defined her.

"I didn't ask to be polite," he assured her. "The painting you gave me is better than anything I've ever seen hanging in a museum. That fellow in Denver is going to be mighty pleased when you finish his. I'd like to see what else you're working on."

Her cheeks colored further, and her hands trembled as she took the sketchbook off the sill and handed it to him. He patted the stool next to him. "Could you sit beside me and explain what I'm looking at? I'm not very sophisticated."

A bubble of laughter erupted from her lips. She circled the table and sat on the stool. Her nearness made the blood stand still in Zach's veins. It took him a moment to remember what he was doing and focus on the sketchbook instead of the warmth of her body next to him

He opened the pad and blinked in amazement at the intensity of the first drawing. A windowpane filled the page. Feminine knuckles gripped the pane. Beyond the glass, a city street bustled with activity. Everyone on the street seemed oblivious to the house and the woman looking out. Though done in charcoal, the drawing was so vivid, Zach could nearly hear the crowd as they moved past the window.

He wanted to ask about the woman. It had to be Ellie herself. What had happened that made her feel like an observer to her life rather than a participant? She told him people stared at her, but she never explained why. Is that why she felt so invisible and alone? But it seemed too personal to ask. If his hunch were right, any questions would embarrass her. If she wanted him to know, she'd explain without him asking.

"This is amazing," he said without taking his eyes off the picture. "I can see the grain in the wood on the windowpane. And the little girl with the braids; I can almost hear her laugh."

He doubted it was what Ellie wanted to hear. She probably wanted the emotional response the painting had evoked in him. He didn't have the nerve to tell her that.

He flipped to the next sketch. He was relieved it wasn't of another morose young woman about to jump off a bridge. But it was equally gloomy. He saw a close-up rendering of a tree branch, stripped bare by winter. Beyond the branch, a thin cloud covered the lower half of a sliver of moon. Zach nearly turned the page but stopped and looked again. The detail made him almost imagine he could feel the cool bark of the tree under his fingers, slick from a recent rain, and smell the wet earth beneath his feet.

He held the sketchbook at arm's length and tilted his head to study the picture further. He lowered the book and turned to Ellie. Her eyes flitted from him to the picture.

"This is..." He nearly said *good.* But good didn't begin to describe the way the sketch made him feel.

A knot formed in his belly. He fixed his gaze on the drawing and rubbed his hand across his jaw. It was just a tree limb covering a moon. But somehow so much more.

"It's..." he started again. He exhaled in defeat. She wanted the truth. He'd have to give it to her even if it hurt her feelings. "Ellie, I've never seen anything like this.

It's..." He stopped again and searched for the best way to describe the experience, even if she didn't like what he said.

"I've seen many a tree in my time. I've climbed them, fell out of them, sat in their shade, burned them for heat, and even skinned the bark off one to make this table."

He looked her square in the eye. "But I've never looked up at the moon through a tree's branches and felt—sad. Is that how I'm supposed to feel?"

He could tell the critique wasn't what she expected, but he wanted to understand why she saw the world the way she did.

"You're supposed to feel how you feel," she said. "That's the thing about art. It's different for everyone."

He studied the picture again to make sure he hadn't made a snap judgment. "Well, that's how this makes me feel. Alone. Heavy. Despairing." He shook his head. "It's beautiful. Your talent is amazing..."

"But?" she asked as his silence lengthened.

"I don't like it," he burst out. "If I had to look at this thing every day I'd probably jump onto a pitchfork. I like pictures that make me smile. That lift my spirit. Like geese traveling across the sky. Or the effects from the wind sweeping down the canyon, cleansing away the vestiges of a hot summer day. Are all your drawings like this?"

"No. The ones I've sold are more commercially appealing. Like geese flying or a dog chasing a rabbit."

"But these, they're more like..." He looked into her smoldering brown eyes. He didn't want to insult her. He didn't want his words to hinder the way she looked at her art from now on. But the woman he'd lived with for the

last six days was not this person. She was beautiful.
Warm. Funny. Giving.

He wondered if she knew it as well.

"These are how you see the world?"

She glanced away. "Sometimes."

He wanted to ask why. What happened that made her
feel this way? He laid his hand over hers. "Don't
apologize for letting the world see who you are."

"I don't. Or, at least, I try not to." She pulled her hand
free. "I've never shown these to anyone before."

Zach's heart swelled. What did that mean? Did she
want him to see the real Ellie inside the beautiful
package? Or she knew she was leaving soon, so what
difference did it make what some random mountain man
thought about her and her work?

"Thank you."

She picked at a blister on the pad of her hand. "I don't
like disappointing people. They expect—things—you
know. My family loves me. They worry about me. I don't
want them to think I'm—beyond repair."

"Are you?"

"Ellie, how is that possible? You're..." He almost
told her she was the most amazing woman he'd ever met.
That if he stopped to think about it for two minutes, he'd
realize he didn't want to live without her.

"None of us are beyond repair," he said instead. "Just
like that canvas you wanted to throw out. God can make
something beautiful out of a busted canvas."

"I know."

He slammed his hand on the table. "Do you know,
because you don't seem to?"

Ellie jumped, startled.

Zach gritted his teeth to rein in his frustration. "Is that how you talk to everyone? You agree with whatever they say because you think it's what they want?"

Her brown eyes flashed. "That's not what I was doing. I believe God can make something beautiful out of anything. I just don't believe He always does."

Zach exhaled. "You're right. Not everything in life is beautiful. Sometimes it's ugly and scary and unfair. But it's real. We can't hide from it."

She set her lips in a hard line. "You think that's what *I'm* doing? You're kidding, right? You're the last person to accuse someone of hiding."

She swept her arm around the cabin. "You live here all alone. You have no neighbors. No wife. No evidence that you came from anywhere, beyond a few names scratched in a Bible. In the six days I've been here, you've told me nothing about your life before you got here except for what I dragged out of you."

"I wasn't accusing you of anything, except maybe telling people what they want to hear so they won't demand anything else from you. I don't want to know the Ellie who fixed my leg or who never milked a cow. I want to know the Ellie who draws these pictures." He tossed the sketchbook onto the table.

She jumped up and circled the table. She slid the pot of beans to the cool side of the stove and wiped her hands on the towel tucked in the sash of her dress. She turned to face him but kept the table between them.

"No, you don't, Zach. That Ellie is selfish and cowardly. But at least she knows it. Unlike you. There's more to you being here than grief over losing your family and your pa's law firm. You came to these mountains to hide, the same as me. At least I know what I'm hiding from. We're alike, you and me. We pretend we don't need anybody. We pretend what we have is exactly what we want because it's easier than getting hurt again. But we're only fooling ourselves. The only thing sadder than being a coward is being one and not knowing it."

Anger flared in Zach's gut. "You don't know anything about me."

She flung her hands down as if to cool them off. "Exactly! I've been trapped in this blasted cabin for six days and I don't know the first thing about you. Except no one in Louisiana seems to want you back."

Zach couldn't decide if he wanted to throw something, shout something, or storm out of the cabin. Storming out of anywhere was out of the question with his busted leg. Which only made him madder than knowing she wasn't wrong.

"I'm no coward," he bit out.

She sniffed. "Prove it."

He stared after her as she went to the door and grabbed her saddlebag. She plunked it down on the table and reached for the sketchbook. Zach dropped his left foot to the floor and nearly cursed at the jolt of pain that surged up his leg. He grabbed hold of her wrist. He lurched to his feet and yanked her against him.

Ellie's breath caught in her throat as his arms tightened around her. The soft, clean scent of her—her hair, her skin, her freshly laundered dress—wafted up around him. Zach let go of her wrist and buried his hand in her hair. A few pins came loose and fell to the floor. Her wide brown eyes scanned his face before finally settling on his mouth.

Zach held her head in his hand and stared down at her for a long moment. He lowered his mouth to hers. The kiss was deep, hungry, and long overdue.

"Hullo, the cabin." A man's voice called out.

Zach frowned and lifted his head.

A woman's voice sounded from the trail. "Ellie?"

Ellie wriggled out from between Zach and the table. She scooped one of the hairpins off the floor and jabbed it into place.

"Ellie Lundy?" the woman's voice called out again.

Zach leaned heavily against the table and blinked to clear his head. "Who is Ellie Lundy?"

Ellie straightened her bodice, patted her hair into place, and ran for the door.

Chapter Twenty-One

Ellie's heart pounded as she threw open the door. She didn't stop to throw her duster over her shoulders before running outside. She hoped her blazing cheeks would be attributed to the sight of the familiar pair of buckskins in the dooryard pulling the mud-spattered buggy and not Zach's kiss.

"Ellie!" Harper Kinski squealed. "Logan, we found her." The petite blond stood and awkwardly climbed down from the buggy before her husband had a chance go around to help her.

Guilt warmed Ellie's cheeks. Her cousin was expecting a baby in late summer. She shouldn't be riding all over the countryside looking for her.

The two women met in the middle of the yard. "Ellie, oh, thank God," Harper cried. "I was so worried. We've all been worried. Are you all right? We thought you were at the inn, so we looked there first. Then Mrs. Meeks said you went into the mountains Monday morning to paint and she hadn't seen you since…"

Harper shuddered and pulled Ellie closer. She hugged Ellie so tight, neither could draw a complete breath.

"I'm fine, I'm fine," Ellie said around Harper's gushing. "I was worried about you worrying about me. There was no way to get word to anyone that I was all right, but as you can see, I am."

She was glad she had changed into her dress after fixing the fence. It wouldn't do for Harper and Logan to see her wearing a strange man's clothes.

"How did you know I was here?"

"We saw your horse in the corral. We thought you might've met up with some kind of trouble on the road. An accident or your horse went lame. Then the blizzard came. When we found out you hadn't been at the inn for days…" Harper's eyes misted. "My imagination went wild."

After securing the horses, Logan came over to the women and put his hand on his wife's elbow. "Slow down, dear. Ellie looks none the worse for wear. I told you everything would be fine."

Harper took a deep breath and sniffed back tears. "I know. I'm sorry. Mrs. Meeks figured you headed home when you realized a blizzard was coming. We told her we hadn't seen or heard from you in nearly a week. We'll have to stop there on our way home and tell her we found you to put her mind to rest."

Harper stopped talking and stepped back to look her up and down. "You are all right, aren't you? Are you sick? You're so thin."

Ellie laughed for the first time. "Eating my own cooking is all. Another week and I may have starved to death."

Harper frowned. "Your own cooking? Whyever for?" Her hands tightened on Ellie's elbows as she gazed around the dooryard. "Doesn't a family live here? A woman?"

Ellie opened her mouth to answer, but Harper was no longer looking at her. Ellie turned to follow her gaze to the cabin. Zach stood framed in the doorway, leaning heavily on the crutches. Even with the crutches and his injured left leg dragging behind him and the dressing on his head, he managed to look rugged and masculine. Dangerous even, if a person didn't know better.

Logan put a protective hand on the small of Harper's back. "Ellie?" he asked, his eyes fixed on Zach.

Ellie wrapped her arms around herself, suddenly aware of the cold. She started toward the cabin. Harper and Logan fell into step after her.

"This is Zach Walsh," she said when they reached the porch step. "I don't know if you heard, but there was an avalanche Monday on the mountain. That's why I didn't make it back to the inn. It knocked me off my horse, and I wrenched my shoulder and split my lip. Zach was caught in the worst of it. His horse was killed. As you can see, he was badly injured, and he almost died himself."

Harper's mouth dropped open. "You saved him?"

Ellie and Zach exchanged glances. A flush crept up Ellie's cheeks. "Well, I—helped him back to the cabin."

Harper's eyes narrowed.

Logan was staring at Zach, too, suspicion all over his face. He snapped to his senses first. He climbed onto the porch to shake Zach's hand. "Logan Kinski. This here's my wife Harper. She's Ellie's cousin."

"Zach Walsh," Zach repeated for manners' sake. "Pleasure to meet you." He smiled at Harper. "I've heard a lot about you, ma'am."

Harper's eyes dashed from Zach to Ellie. "Yes, a pleasure…"

Ellie's stomach clenched. Harper was already figuring out the situation. She was thankful her cousin hadn't seen her wrapped in Zach's arms a moment ago.

"Let's go inside. I'm freezing, and I'm sure you two are tired from your ride from Scottstown." She glanced at Harper's rounded middle and thought again of the trouble her impetuous behavior had brought on those she loved.

A dozen unasked questions filled Harper's eyes as Ellie ushered them inside. Harper and Logan glanced around the cabin. Their eyes lingered a moment on the single bed in the alcove.

Zach seemed to notice it, too. He quickly filled the silence. "I thought I was going to die on that mountainside after the avalanche hit. I was buried under rubble. My horse was dying. I would've been dead up there myself if Ellie hadn't come along."

Ellie directed a smile of appreciation at him she hoped the others wouldn't notice.

Harper's eyes misted with fresh tears. "Mr. Walsh, it must've been divine providence that put you and Ellie on that mountain together. Ellie needed protection from the coming blizzard and you obviously needed help getting home."

Zach dipped his head. "Ma'am, I believe the same thing."

Logan helped Harper out of her wrap. Ellie circled the table to take it from him and hang it up. "I'm so sorry you had to come looking for me. You must be worn out." Harper's delicate condition was barely discernible, but Ellie figured travel over rough, muddy roads was challenging, nonetheless. "I'll make some coffee. The beans are hot. I was preparing to pour Zach a bowlful."

She stopped talking at the familiarity in her words. It sounded like she had already set up housekeeping with this stranger.

Zach moved forward to pull one of the stools out from under the table. He indicated the other one for Logan. Logan shook his head, deferring to Ellie.

Harper sat and Logan dropped his hand onto her shoulder. "We feel much better now that we found Ellie. We couldn't rest until we knew she was safe." He added the last part with a hard stare at Zach.

"I was preparing to head to Scottstown," Ellie said quickly, motioning to her half-packed saddlebag.

Harper rested her hand on the sketchpad in the center of the table as if in challenge. She knew Ellie would never leave it behind.

"I was going to send someone back for Zach. He needs medical attention. Better than I could provide. His knee was completely dislocated when he was thrown from his horse, and I had to stitch up his head. When the blizzard locked us in, I couldn't get out any sooner."

Harper and Logan stared at her. She forced her mouth to stop talking. The more excuses a person made usually indicated a bigger lie.

Zach turned to Logan. "I'm sure your horses could use a rest, too. I can help you unhitch the buggy and take them to the barn to warm up."

Logan nodded and followed Zach's lurching gait out the door. When the door closed behind the men, Ellie went to the stove to return the beans to the heat.

Harper put her hands to the small of her back and stretched. "You look mighty comfortable at that stove."

"What does that mean? I'm just doing what has to be done."

Harper pursed her lips thoughtfully and then lifted a shoulder as if to say it didn't mean anything.

Ellie wasn't fooled. Harper knew better than anyone that Ellie Lundy's way of doing what needed done was to ring for a servant to do it.

She moved the pan of water next to the beans to heat for coffee. "Now that I know how much trouble cooking and cleaning and toting are, I'm raising the whole household's pay."

Harper laughed. "They'll be glad to hear it. Now tell me a little about that busted up cowboy."

Warmth flooded Ellie's face despite her effort to keep her feelings hidden. She took her time rinsing out the tin cup Zach used for his coffee and the small bowl she used for a cup. She had promised everyone coffee, but now she remembered Zach didn't own enough dishes for company.

"Like I said, he was on the mountain the same time as me. Neither of us realized the other was there until after the avalanche. He had been collecting pelts from the river. I was on my way back to the hotel."

Harper shook her head in wonder. "I suppose it's nothing short of a miracle you were there. I don't want to think what would've became of Mr. Walsh if you hadn't been."

"He's told me the same thing many times."

Harper kept quiet while Ellie poured coffee into the tin cup and slid it toward her. She waited until Ellie filled the little bowl and sat down. Instead of taking a drink of the coffee, Harper covered Ellie's hands with her own.

"We didn't start to worry until the blizzard hit. We figured you were at the hotel, warm and cozy, working on your painting without a care. Then the snow began to melt and you still didn't come. By last night, I couldn't bear it another moment. I told Logan we were coming after you this morning no matter what condition the roads and trails."

Ellie smiled warmly at her cousin who she loved like a sister. "I'm glad you did. If you'd been another five minutes, I would've passed you on the road."

She blushed slightly at the lie. Another five minutes, and she would probably still be kissing Zach.

Harper lifted her cup and looked around the room over the rim. "You still haven't told me about this man."

"What do you want to know?"

"Everything. Where is he from? Is he—honorable?"

"Yes, he's honorable. He's been nothing but a gentleman from the moment we met. Of course, his injuries were too grave for him to be anything else. Not that I think he would've..." Her voice trailed off.

Harper cocked her head. "He's very handsome."

"I thought married women weren't supposed to notice those things about other men."

"You don't lose your eyesight when you marry."

"I suppose not."

Harper studied her for a moment. "So..."

"So, that's all. We were thrown together by the avalanche. Literally. I had to set Zach's knee on the mountain. I'm afraid I did a terrible job of it. The swelling was frightful. He lost a lot of blood, too, from where he landed on his head on the rocks. He needs to see Lisette Dutton as soon as possible. The first few days he was too weak and in too much pain to travel. Not that he can travel anywhere without a wagon. With the blizzard and threat of more avalanches, the roads were too dangerous for me to head to Scottstown on my own. I couldn't leave him alone that long anyway the first few days."

"He seems to have recovered well," Harper observed.

"Only because of necessity. As I'm sure you noticed outside, a tree fell on the paddock fence and we had to fix it this morning so we could let the animals out of the barn."

"We?"

Ellie exhaled in frustration. "Yes, we. He couldn't do it on his own."

"But you think he's handsome?"

Ellie sighed again. "Yes, Harper, he's handsome. I don't think there's any disputing that. But his looks have bearing on the situation. I've slept every night on the floor." She pointed to the spot between the stove and the table. "Just ask my aching back."

Harper stroked Ellie's arm. "I'm sorry. I don't mean to sound like I don't trust you. Or him. It's just an unconventional situation, to be sure."

"Unconventional or not, he needed me. Believe me, I actually considered leaving him on that mountain to go for help. I didn't think I could do anything for him on my own. If Saturn had taken off, we'd still be up there trying to figure out how to get home."

Harper wrapped her arms around Ellie. "I shouldn't have been so suspicious. It's just that when I saw him standing there, looking so tall and strong, and with you in the fragile state you've been lately."

Ellie pulled out of her cousin's arms. "I'm not fragile."

"You have to admit you've been through a lot the last couple of years. If you remember, that's why I came here from Kentucky."

"Because of my melancholy. Yes, I remember. That's why Papa sent for you and how you met and fell in love with Logan."

Harper's face softened. "Now, maybe you've found love yourself."

Ellie hoped to keep her emotions off her face. "Harper, I wouldn't fall in love with a man I barely know."

"What about him? Is he in love?"

Ellie gasped. Her cheeks filled with heat. She wished she had an excuse to get up and occupy herself with a chore. "Of course not. He doesn't even know who I am."

"How's that? You've been here for six days."

Ellie picked at a torn cuticle. "He doesn't know my last name. I told him I'm Ellie Dixon."

"Why?"

"He's the first person I ever met who doesn't know I'm rich. He didn't know a thing about me except I was a woman on the mountain who could help him, and I wanted to keep it that way. Even you had preconceived notions about me when you got off that train last summer."

Harper didn't try to deny it.

Ellie added a dollop of cream to her own cup and stared into the liquid as it softened and swirled. "It felt so nice to be myself for once. Not Hugh Lundy's daughter or heiress to a railroad. Oh, Harper, I told him things I've never been able to tell anyone. Not even you. It was so freeing. I just couldn't tell him the most important part."

"What will you tell him when we get to Willow Wood? He's bound to figure it out when he sees your house."

"He has no reason to see it. He'll stay at Dr. Dutton's office, and I'll never see him again."

Harper narrowed her eyes. "You don't mean that."

"Why don't I?"

"Oh, Ellie, that man loves you." Harper leaned forward and gazed into Ellie's eyes. "Do you love him?"

"No! I told you, I don't even know him." She thought of their words earlier. He would probably never forgive her for calling him a coward. Yes, he kissed her, but that only meant he was attracted to her. Not that he loved her. "He certainly doesn't know me."

Harper fluttered her hand in the air. "All right. My mistake. But no matter what happens between you, you owe him the truth. About everything. If you don't tell him who you are and how you feel, you'll never forgive yourself."

"And I'll never forgive myself if he hates me for lying to him."

"He won't hate you once you explain yourself. And if he hates you, well, you'll know what kind of man he really is."

That was the problem; Ellie already knew. And Harper was right, she did love him.

•••

Lundy.

The name kept running through Zach's head. Ellie Lundy. Why had her cousin called out *Lundy* when they rode into the yard if Ellie's last name was *Dixon*?

Had she lied about her name? If so, what else had she lied about?

Zach's conscience rebuked him. He hadn't exactly been forthcoming with his secrets either.

He pushed the misgivings aside as the name *Lundy* kept nagging at him. He was sure he'd her about his secrets either.

As host, it was his obligation to unhitch the pair of horses from the carriage, but Logan ended up doing most of the work. Once the horses were unhitched—with barely a word exchanged between the men— Zach led the way to the barn. Ellie's horse came to the paddock doorway and nickered in recognition. The newcomers shook their heads and whinnied in reply.

Logan looked around the barn. "Solid. You build it yourself?"

Pride swelled in Zach's belly. Ellie was the only other person who'd seen the inside of the barn. "This place was bare earth when I got here. Barn and corral were the first things to go up. That little tack room in the corner is where I slept the first six months."

Logan uncinched the harnesses and reins and hung them over the sides of the stall. Zach wished he could help, but it was all he could do to stand.

"What do you run out here? Cattle? Horses?"

"Cattle. I'm just starting out. I hope to build a herd of horses, too, someday."

Logan nodded. "I got a few hundred head myself in a canyon north of Willow Wood. It'll be a few years yet before the whole property's completely mine. Harper and I are building a house out there. We hope to be moved in by the summer. But with Ellie to consider, we can't make solid plans."

What did that mean? Zach wondered. Ellie had told him she lived with Harper and Logan, but he hadn't thought she was their ward.

Logan was watching him. "Don't know if Ellie mentioned her pa died last year."

"She told me."

If she couldn't support herself on her own that would explain why she lived with her cousin.

"She doesn't have any other male relatives," Logan continued. "Closest thing she's got is me. I've known her for years, and Harper considers her a sister. That would make her my sister-in-law."

Recognition registered on where Logan was going with the conversation.

"I guess what I want to know is if you behaved respectably toward my sister-in-law." Logan squared off in front of Zach. His hands curled into fists.

Zach sized the man up. He was nearly half a head shorter than Zach and not quite as broad. But he was hard-muscled and looked like he could handle himself in a fight. He also had righteous indignation on his side if he believed Ellie's honor had been besmirched.

Zach held up his hands, palms out. "Everything here's been above board since the day your sister-in-law led me into the yard on her horse. I'd testify that to a preacher. I was hurt, as you can see. Worse than I've been in my life. I told her, and I'll tell you, I wouldn't be standing here defending myself if she hadn't come along. I'd be on that mountain next to my dead horse, picked apart by the buzzards by now. Even if I didn't owe Ellie my life and my gratitude, I'm a Christian man. I would never behave dishonorably to a woman. I'm not that sort."

Logan studied his face the whole time he talked. Apparently satisfied, the stiffness slid out of his shoulders. "I appreciate that, Walsh. I didn't come here to kill a man, but I was ready to make a hard choice when I saw you step outta that cabin."

Zach chuckled. "With this gimp leg and dressing on my head?"

"A man can behave mighty deplorable, even with a gimp leg and a busted head."

Zach thought of Ellie in his arms only a moment before Logan and Harper rode into the yard. The man wasn't wrong.

"I'm glad I didn't force you into that position."

"Where you from?" Logan asked, trying to look like the answer didn't matter much.

"Catahoula Parish, Louisiana."

"I'm from Indiana myself. Moved here four years ago. Is this what you've always done? Ranching?"

"Pretty much. My family had a place. Lost it in the War. I figured I'd try to build something under a different sky."

Logan studied him another moment. "I reckon that's what drove most of us here."

Each man studied the other, contemplating the words left unsaid. Secrets. Escaping a hard past had sent many a man westward.

"We best get back to the house and get some grub in our bellies," Zach said. He didn't say as much, but his knee throbbed from spending so much time moving around on it today.

Logan let him take the lead toward the door. "I can stay here and tend the place while you and the women go to town and see to that leg."

Zach nearly told him that wasn't going to happen in a month of Sundays. No other man would tend his stock while he lounged on his backside in a soft bed in town.

He immediately recognized his sinful pride had reared its ugly head again where it had no right. God may just have allowed him to get stuck in that avalanche to knock some of the stubbornness out of him.

"I appreciate the offer. Best to see what damage has been done if I plan to ever get back to work."

Chapter Twenty-Two

E llie rode Saturn alongside Zach and Harper in the buggy as they headed toward Scottstown. The women had secured his splinted leg with the pillow from the bed and lashed it down with a rope. He felt like an infirm old man and half expected them to tuck a blanket under his chin against the chill in the air. But the most humiliated part of the trip was leaving Logan Kinski behind to tend *his* stock for however long it took him to recover.

Harper maneuvered the buggy around the worst of the ruts on the trail, but it was still a bone-jarring trip for Zach. Due to washouts and minor rock slides, they were forced to go around the mountain instead of over it, which would've cut the duration of the trip in half.

Harper asked him about landmarks they passed. Zach answered every question as best he could and asked his own about her family and life in Kentucky. She was only talking to distract him from the pain. He appreciated her efforts. What he needed distracted from, though, was Ellie. Now that they were on their way to a doctor and help for his knee, he'd probably never see her again.

Especially since she considered him a coward.

Finally, the buggy reached Scottstown. Harper stopped in front of a two-story lap-board structure, the most impressive building in the settlement, that housed the inn and a small café. As the women went inside to gather Ellie's things, Zach worked the kinks out of his back as best he could. He'd like nothing more than to climb down and walk around a few minutes, but that was out of the question in his current state. He would never take two strong legs for granted again.

Fifteen pain-filled minutes passed before Ellie and Harper came back out. Ellie stashed a brocade traveling bag in the boot of the buggy and climbed back onto her horse.

"I'm sorry we took so long. Mrs. Meeks was beside herself with worry. It took some doing to assure her I was well and in no need of medical attention."

They were the first words Ellie had spoken directly to him since he kissed her. He grimaced. He was sure Mrs. Meeks was curious about a lot more than Ellie's health after spending nearly a week in the cabin of recluse Zach Walsh. He didn't care what people said about him, but he hated to think of Ellie being subjected to more whispers and finger pointing.

They rode for what seemed like hours to Zach's leg before a small farmhouse appeared in the distance. As they drew near, several red-headed children ran to the fence and climbed onto the slats to wave and call a greeting.

Harper waved back and called to each of the children by name. "That's the Ransom farm," she told Zach. "We're not far from Willow Wood now."

Zach looked at Ellie, but she kept her eyes averted. Stubborn woman if he ever saw one. He hoped she realized he could be just as stubborn.

In the center of town Harper pulled the buggy to a stop and handed Zach the reins. "I need to run an errand. Can you handle the carriage the rest of the way to the doctor's office? It's just one street over. If I run into her, I'll tell her you're waiting for her at her office."

"You have an errand now?" Ellie was incredulous. "How will you get home?"

"I'll walk."

Ellie glanced at Harper's midsection. "Should you be walking?"

Harper chuckled. "Goodness, Ellie, it's only two blocks. Exercise is good for a person."

She climbed out of the buggy. "It was nice meeting you, Mr. Walsh. I'm sure we'll be seeing more of you."

Zach wondered if there was a hidden meaning in the comment. He tipped his hat. "The pleasure was mine, Mrs. Kinski."

After she set off across the street toward Endicott's General Store, Zach tapped the reins against the horses' flanks. He looked directly at Ellie, who was still going out of her way not to look at him.

"Your cousin is a thoughtful lady," he said.

"I don't know what I'd've done without her the last year. And Logan too."

"After you lost your pa?"

She pursed her lips and gazed down at him from atop the bay. Zach wanted to reach out and grab her hand. Pull her to a stop and make her talk to him. But not in the middle of the street with everyone watching. Suddenly, he found himself staring at her mouth, and he couldn't think of anything but their kiss in the cabin and how he hadn't wanted it to stop.

Color crept into Ellie's cheeks as if she knew what he was thinking. Or maybe she was thinking the same thing.

"The doctor lives on a ranch outside of town," she said crisply. "If she isn't in her office, I'll send someone after her."

"No need to do me any favors," Zach returned. "I reckon I can take care of myself."

Her full lips turned down as her eyebrows shot toward her sable-colored hairline. She gazed pointedly at his left leg stretched out in front of him.

Okay, so maybe she had a point, but Zach wasn't in the mood to back down. "Just point the way if I'm keeping you from something."

He immediately wished he could take the words back. She'd been worrying her right shoulder all week, and her mouth was still scabbed and bruised. The doctor should have a look at her too. He started to apologize, but she spoke first.

"Don't be stubborn, Zach Walsh. I'm not leaving you until the doctor's seen to your leg. And your head."

And then what? he wanted to ask. *Will you leave me then? Or can I get you to change your mind?*

Halfway down the next street Ellie pointed out a large white house with a doctor's shingle hanging over the door. There was no carriage in sight. "I'll see if she's here," Ellie said.

"Hello there," a woman called from across the street. Zach turned to look. A small, steely-haired woman was waving from the porch of an immaculately kept house. "Yoohoo, Ellie Lundy."

There was that name again. *Lundy.*

As he watched, the woman stepped off the porch and crossed the street. Ellie changed course to meet her. "Good morning, Mrs. Rusk."

"The doctor isn't in," the woman said. She looked up at Zach, her gaze taking in the dressing on his head and his splinted leg. "What'd you get yourself into, young man?"

"Mrs. Rusk, this is Zach Walsh. He was caught in an avalanche in the mountains last week."

"And you're just now getting him to town?"

"The blizzard struck the very next day."

She mulled over Ellie's answer while gazing suspiciously at Zach. "I suppose that would present a problem."

"Do you know if Dr. Dutton is at the ranch?" Ellie asked.

"I haven't seen her yet today. Alveda Pratt had surgery here last week. I figure Lisette went out to the house to check on her, though I wouldn't know for sure. She doesn't tell me much, even when I come right out and ask."

Zach glanced away so the woman wouldn't see his smile. Ellie's face fell. "Oh, dear. We must find her. She needs to look at Zach's head wound. His knee also needs properly set before the damage becomes irreparable if it hasn't already."

"You might as well wait here then. The doctor could be back any minute. Or she could stay gone all day. Like I said, nobody tells me anything." Mrs. Rusk lifted her bony shoulders and turned to head back across the road.

Ellie looked at Zach. "I'm sure the office door is unlocked. I can help you inside and then go look for the doctor."

"I don't think the two of us can get me out of this buggy without breaking my other leg."

Ellie set her hands on her hips. "Well, we have to do something." She cast her gaze around the street. "The blacksmith's shop is one street over. There are always men hanging around there. I'll enlist a few to come help me."

"I'd rather fall out on the street than have a group of men haul me inside like a sack of wheat."

"There's that stubborn pride of yours again, Mr. Walsh," she chastened. "When will you learn you're going to have to accept help?"

"I will as soon as you tell me something first." Before she could ask what, he snagged her hand and held on tight. "Tell me why everyone in this town calls you Lundy."

The blood drained from her face. She pulled her hand free. "What?"

"You told me your name is Dixon. Nobody else seems to know it, including your own cousin."

"I—uh—I didn't know you. I wasn't sure I should tell a strange man—"

"You thought you'd be safer with a stranger if he thought your last name was Dixon? I'm not buying it. Give me the real reason."

She pulled her hand free. "Zach, we don't have time for this. It's cold. I'm going to find help to get you inside."

"How long does it take to tell a person your true last name?"

"My name is Lundy. All right? I'm Ellie Lundy. My father is Hugh Lundy. I didn't tell you because I didn't want you to—to judge me."

"Judge you? Why would I do that? Lundy doesn't mean anything to me—"

Recognition suddenly clicked. "Hugh Lundy? The railroad Lundy? The mining company Lundy?"

A muscle in her jaw tightened. "Yes. I'm Hugh Lundy's daughter. I didn't tell you because I didn't want to see the look on your face when you found out."

"What look?"

"The look on your face right now. The one that says I'm a helpless rich girl who never milked a cow or reached under a chicken for an egg."

Zach barely kept from laughing out loud. "Woman, you are anything but helpless."

His words surprised her into silence for a moment. "You believe that because you didn't know who I was. Now that you do, you'll forever see me the same as everyone else. Crazy Ellie. Pitiful Ellie. Delusional Ellie who locked herself in her room for two years because her beau left her."

"Would you be quiet. I don't know what you're talking about."

"Not now, but you will."

She pinched the bridge of her nose. She looked like she wanted to cry but didn't want to give in to tears. "In those mountains with my art, I'm the woman I want to be. Strong. Confident. Talented. No one stares at me for falling in love with a man who was no good for me. For not seeing who he really was. They don't whisper when I walk into a store. Or pull their children against them as if I'm a monster."

Zach wanted to touch her. To smooth the hair back from her face. To make her see he wasn't like everyone else. He couldn't reach her from where he sat in the buggy, and he didn't think she wanted him to anyway.

"Ellie, I know what it's like to be stared at. To be defined by one careless, stupid mistake."

She didn't seem to hear. "In the mountains I don't get anything I don't earn for myself. My last name may have opened a few doors in the beginning for my art, but clients buy because of what they see—what they feel—not because of who I am. That's how it was when you first asked me my name. If you didn't know me, you couldn't judge me. The only things you knew were what you saw for yourself. If you looked at me sideways, it was because I earned it, not because you thought you might get something from me."

"I don't want anything from you."

As soon as the words were out of his mouth, Zach knew they were a lie. He did want something. He wanted it all. Her smile. Her off-key singing. The determined set of her jaw when she tried something new. Her childlike joy over hammering a nail into a fencepost. He wanted the dejected little girl she had been, and the strong, determined woman standing before him.

Most of all, he wanted her love. But what would a woman in her position want with a crippled cowboy who couldn't manage a struggling ranch of thirty head of cattle? He was beneath her station in every way. It was only a matter of time before she realized it too.

A man on a horse rounded the corner. Ellie's eyes lit up. "It's Grayson Dutton, Zach, the doctor's husband. He can help me get you inside." She raised her arm and waved. "Marshal Dutton, over here."

Her gaze slid back to Zach. "The doctor'll fix you up now. It's almost over."

She was more right than she knew.

Chapter Twenty-Three

Ellie slid the last pin into place in her clean hair. It had taken Mattie Sue two hours to get the tangles out before she could wash it. Her scalp still tingled from the tugging and pulling, but the discomfort had been worth it. The scraped places on her skin tingled, too. After a long, luxurious soak in a tub of steaming, lilac-scented water, Mattie Sue had coated her sore spots with ointment and rubbed her dry elbows and feet with lotion before helping Ellie into a clean chemise and dress.

Ellie felt like a new woman. On the outside, at least.

The filthy, torn dress she had worn for almost a week—not counting the day and a half she spent in Zach's clothes—lay in a heap on the floor. Mattie Sue had offered to take it downstairs to the laundry, but Ellie told her it could wait. The dress was beyond repair, but she wasn't ready to consign it to the rag bag. Now that her mountain adventure was over, the dress was the only reminder of her six days with Zach Walsh.

Six days. Such a short time, but in many ways, it seemed like more than a lifetime.

Would she see Zach again? Did he want to see her now that he knew who she was? A lying, conniving, crazy, inept rich girl who had lied to him from the moment they met.

He had said she was anything but helpless. Did he mean it? Ellie had never received a higher compliment. A compliment she *earned*. But what did it matter now?

By the time she and Grayson Dutton got Zach out of the carriage and into the doctor's office, Lisette had arrived and taken over his care. She complimented Ellie's stitching of the head wound and assured her she had field treated his knee the best way anyone could have.

The muscles and tendons had been damaged, but Dr. Dutton offered a hopeful prognosis for recovery. The injury would bother Zach the rest of his life, but after the first year, the worst would be behind him. The kneecap could pop out of joint now and then if he stepped down wrong, but he would live. As long as he exercised and followed the doctor's instructions, an occasional limp and bothersome ache during rainy seasons were the likeliest lasting effects.

Ellie hadn't missed the despondency on his face as the doctor talked. A year of recovery. How would his ranch survive a year if he couldn't run it?

While the doctor settled Zach into a bed, he insisted she examine Ellie's shoulder and any other complaints. Ellie hurried out of the office before the doctor could get near her. If Zach had to deal with a bothersome ache for the rest of his life, she could handle one a few more days.

Directly after the avalanche, all Ellie wanted was to get back to the comforts of her beautiful mansion on the hill overlooking Willow Wood. As Saturn carried her through the massive gate, for the first time in her life, the house didn't feel like a home.

Ellie had never lived anywhere but here. The house was a magnificent structure that, according to Papa, had taken three years to complete. The tan river rock had been carted in from all over the Northwest. A mill and foundry was built at the bottom of the hill for the sole purpose of providing workmen a place to cut slate shingles for the roof and eaves and saw and sand lumber to build a house worthy of Hugh Lundy.

The result was a masterpiece of architecture. The grounds had been shown as much attention to detail and completed the austere affect of the property.

Ellie had always regarded her home with pride. Pride for Papa's hard work and Mother's artistic design. Today she saw the imposing structure the same way as many of Willow Wood's residents. Cold. Impersonal. A waste of space and resources. All a person truly needed was a cozy cabin in the woods with someone they loved.

She left Saturn with Burt, the stable manager, to brush down and feed. As she left the stables, she glanced into the empty stall that had housed Papa's favorite horse Sundancer, the way she always did when she walked by.

She had Burt sell Sundancer the day after Papa died. Everyone tried to talk her out of it. They said she would regret it, knowing how much Papa had loved that horse. But Ellie couldn't bear seeing Sundancer or hearing him bang against the sides of his stall, as if determined to get out to go find Papa.

Ellie never knew where Papa was going that stormy night he saddled Sundancer for what would be the last time. A few days after he was laid to rest in the cemetery next to Mama, the sheriff brought Ellie the contents of the saddlebags he had slung across the horse. Before fleeing the house, Papa had taken a substantial sum of money from his safe, along with property deeds from all over the western half of the country. They included drilling rights to a mine in Arizona Ellie never knew he owned.

She hadn't known where he was going or what his plans were that night when he rode out into the storm. He was a hunted man and would be for the rest of his life. But she didn't doubt he would survive and survive well if he had made it out of Willow Wood. She imagined he planned to make his way to Mexico, selling properties along the way and stockpiling more money to see him to the end of his life.

Her papa would never settle into a simple existence as a peasant in the Mexican countryside. He couldn't help himself. Wherever he ended up, he would build an empire. He would call himself something else in his new life, but he would always be Hugh Lundy.

Just like Ellie would always be Ellie Lundy, no matter what she called herself to Zach.

He was right. She wasn't helpless. Not anymore.

Maybe she never had been.

A few years ago, she had realized people meant it as an insult when they compared her to Papa. Hugh Lundy was driven, determined, and willing to run over anyone or anything that stood between him and what he wanted.

But he also loved with all his heart. Ellie knew it now in the way he built this house for Mama. In the way he destroyed his own life in a twisted effort to protect Ellie.

Ellie *was* like Papa. Not in the way many people thought. But she was strong. And determined. And she loved with all her heart.

She stirred through the messy pile of belongings Maddie Sue had brought from her saddlebags. Her fingers closed around her beloved sketchbook. She flipped to the back and the sketches she had done while staying in Zach's cabin. The ones she hadn't gotten to show him.

Her heart ached at the sketch of the view outside his cabin door. She smiled at the likeness she captured of his horse Caesar. The long-suffering milk cow. The impatient cats crowding around her ankles for milk. Even the goose looked as irritable in print as she did in real life.

Matthew had barely looked at Ellie's artwork. When he did, he praised her for mountains that looked like mountains and pronghorn sheep that looked like the real thing. But he never saw the emotion behind each piece. He saw her art the same as Papa had. As a lark, a harmless hobby to fill her time, not a reflection of *her*. Maybe that's all it was at the time.

She wondered if Zach understood because he experienced the same self-imposed isolation. He said he knew what it was like to be stared at. Feared for one careless, stupid mistake. The words had barely registered when he said them just before Grayson Dutton rode into the yard.

Elle lowered the sketchbook and stared across the room. What mistake was he referring to? She should've stopped thinking about herself long enough to ask. Now she may never have the chance.

She loved him. She knew it now. She loved him with the maturity of a woman, not a rebellious daughter who only wanted to lash out at her controlling father.

Did Zach love her back? How could he? He wasn't ashamed of his last name. Everything he did was to honor his family name. He could never understand a daughter unwilling to admit where she came from.

A gentle knock sounded at the door. "Ellie?" Harper whispered before she stuck her head into the room. "I thought you might be sleeping."

Ellie arched her sore back and looked across the room to her large bed. "That sounds heavenly. It's too close to bedtime now, though. If I take a nap, I'll be up all night."

Harper s blond brows rose in question as she came the rest of the way into the room and sat on the Queen Anne's chair. "Isn't that what you usually do?"

Ellie wrinkled her nose. "There's only one reason to stay up all night, and that's brooding."

Harper cocked her head. "Are you all right?"

"Just thinking."

"About what?" Harper looked like she already knew the answer.

"How is the house coming along on the ranch?" Ellie asked instead. "It should be about ready for you and Logan to move in."

Harper drew back. "Ellie, are you kicking us out?"

"No. Well, maybe. You put your own plans on hold long enough for my sake. You're going to have a family soon. You need time to get settled in before the baby comes."

Harper laid her hands on the soft swell of her stomach. "Logan thinks that would be best, but we don't want to leave you before—"

"Before I'm ready?" Ellie finished. She opened the sketchbook to the drawing of the hands on the windowpane and handed it to Harper. "I've never shown you this before."

Harper studied the drawing while Ellie continued.

"Even before I met Matthew, I felt like I wasn't a real person. I had plenty of friends. We went to parties and laughed and had loads of fun. The only time I was alone was when I was cooking up another grand adventure. I almost thought if I sat still with my thoughts—with just me—I'd realize how empty my life was. How shallow. After I lost Matthew, I realized I had no true friends. That they could get along just fine without me. It was my own fault. I hadn't been a friend to them either. I couldn't be bothered with their problems. It shouldn't have come as a surprise when they abandoned me after Matthew disappeared. I would've done the same thing to them."

She glanced at the dirty dress on the floor. Her heart swelled at the memories it brought.

"I'm not feeling sorry for myself. On the contrary, I feel better than I have in ages. It's just—I know what love is now, Harper, and it's because of you. You left your entire world to come here to help me—a practical stranger. I didn't make it easy for you, but you demonstrated true grace. Logan has showed me how a mature man loves and respects his wife. Zach..."

She shook her head. She wasn't ready to talk about him.

She nodded at the drawing in front of Harper. "I no longer feel invisible, that the world is moving past without me. Now I feel—peace. I don't know if it's God. Or you and Logan. Or spending so much time in the mountains with my canvas and my paints."

Harper leaned forward, her eyes shining. "God can use people, or His creation, or whatever it takes to reach you and let you know He's here."

Ellie nodded. "I know that now. That's why I want you and Logan to focus on finishing your house so you can move to the ranch as soon as possible."

She turned back to the mirror and massaged a sore spot on her scalp. "I won't be around much to keep you company anyway. Monday morning I'm going to Papa's office to talk to Mr. List about the company. I already set up an appointment with Ned Yates at the law office to discuss my business holdings. I should send a team to Arizona to see what should be done with a mine down there. I own half of one of the most powerful corporations in the country. It was time I acted like it."

Harper gasped. She jumped out of the chair and spun the stool around so Ellie was facing her. She pulled her to her feet. "Do you mean it? Logan and I will help you however we can. Neither of us know anything about running a company like Lundy List, and I don't sure want you sending my husband to Arizona."

She laughed. "But I'll do anything else to help. Oh, my goodness, this is so exciting."

Ellie laughed along with her. "It is exciting. And terrifying. I never let Papa talk with me about the company. I always thought he'd be here to take care of things. Now it's all on me."

Harper squeezed her hands. "I have faith in you, Ellie. We all do. You're stronger than you think."

"I know that now."

Harper pulled a handkerchief from the sleeve of her dress and dabbed the end of Ellie's wet nose. "What about Zach? Are you…"

"I don't know. I really don't. Oh, Harper, I think I love him. No, I know I do. He'll probably never forgive me for lying about who I was. I can't blame him. But whether he does or not, my first responsibility is with Lundy List and this town. I want the company to continue to bless Willow Wood. I want it to play a role in building this nation the way Papa intended."

Harper pulled her into another brief embrace. "I'll pray for you. I'll also pray for Zach. The two of you should talk. You need to tell him exactly how you feel."

Ellie sighed and sank back onto the stool. "Believe it or not, I'm more intimidated about talking to him than I am Mr. List."

"Don't let fear cost you the man you love."

Ellie nodded at Harper's reflection in the mirror. "I won't. I'll probably always be a little afraid and unsure. I guess that's a good thing. But I won't spend another moment of my life as a coward."

Chapter Twenty-Four

After church on Sunday—having actually listened to the sermon for the first time in as long as she could remember—Ellie packed a luncheon basket and headed to Dr. Dutton's office. As expected, the doctor wasn't in, but the front door was unlocked. She called out to announce herself.

"Zach? Are you here?"

"Don't know where else I'd be," Zach called back from a large room at the back of the house where Lisette kept patients who needed to stay overnight.

Ellie's heart lurched at the sound of his voice. She never guessed she would miss a person so much after only one day. "Don't be a grouch," she scolded when she reached the doorway. "I brought lunch. Have you seen Dr. Dutton this morning?"

Zach tried to look irritable, but she saw warmth in his eyes. Had he missed her as well? "She stopped in this morning, poking and prodding with those ice-cold hands of hers. Reminds me of someone else I know."

"I don't know who that would be. Now, sit up so you can eat."

Zach scooted up on the bed, and Ellie positioned another pillow behind his shoulders.

"She and the marshal brought me a visitor," he said as he settled into the pillow. "Cute red-headed baby girl. Looked just like her mama. Not the least bit shy. Even let me hold her a minute, though holding onto her was like wrestling a catfish."

Ellie chuckled. She found a stool and pulled it alongside the bed. "That baby's a social butterfly. Everyone in town treats her like their own, holding her and passing her around every chance they get. She was named for Grayson's mother, Josie Dutton. His parents were some of the earliest settlers in Willow Wood."

She opened the basket and set a crock and two bowls on a small table as close to Zach as she could get it. "I hope I'm not disturbing you."

He shook his head. "I was about to go out of my mind from boredom."

"I figured as much." Her hands trembled as she prepared the lunch. All she could think about was being in his arms yesterday. She had called him a coward. Then he yanked her against him to prove he was anything but. Heat coursed through her limbs at the memory.

She cleared her throat. "I...um...thought I'd join you for lunch if you don't mind."

"The doc left a pot of soup for me in the kitchen. She said she'd stop by after church to serve it and see if I needed anything."

"Oh."

"I told her not to bother. I convinced her I'd probably be asleep and she'd only disturb me. I figure she'd appreciate a day with her family as much as I'd appreciate a day without her. I expect either she or her husband will stop by tonight to make sure I'm still breathing."

"I'll prepare you a bowl of the soup if you prefer, but I brought some of Mrs. Philips' chicken and dumplings. No one in their right mind passes up her chicken and dumplings."

Zach pulled back in mock horror. "Isn't she the one who taught you how to cook?"

Ellie laughed. "She tried, but I was a terrible pupil."

"I'll say," he mumbled under his breath.

She slid the fullest bowl toward him, along with a roll the size of his fist. Zach bowed his head and blessed the food, and they began to eat. After a few minutes of eating and complimenting the absent cook, Ellie dabbed her mouth with a napkin she had packed in the basket.

"I didn't come just to make sure you had lunch. I wanted to talk to you."

"I'm glad you did. I think I got used to you banging and clanging my pots together and slapping ice cold rags on my head. Now I can barely fall asleep in a quiet, comfortable house."

Ellie appreciated the teasing. She had been unsure what to expect when she walked through the door. He didn't seem angry with her, or even annoyed. But he didn't know the whole story yet.

"Until yesterday you didn't know my last name," she began. "Now that you're in town, it's only a matter of time before you know it all. I want you to hear it from me."

Zach pushed aside his empty bowl. "You don't owe me an explanation, Ellie. I've been thinking about what you said about the way people treated you because of your last name. My family was plantation owners. A lot of folks hated us for that reason alone. They wanted Pa to fall on his face. Get his comeuppance. Others saw we were rebuilding and believed it meant we had money hidden somewhere. Or they were jealous because they had nothing left. One thing I've learned, we can't help the way people react to us. I'm sorry anyone ever made you think you needed to hide who you are."

Ellie put her bowl back in the basket and then his. "The first time you saw me you thought I was an angel. Remember? You didn't know a thing about me except that you needed me to get you off the mountain. I've been judged my whole life because of Papa's wealth. People assume I'm spoiled and demanding and used to getting my way. Maybe I am. But with you, I was completely anonymous. No history, no expectations, no judgment. It was freedom."

She wrapped the spoons in a napkin as she gathered her thoughts. "That isn't what I came to tell you, though. I want to tell you about the night Papa died. I told you I was in love once. Or I thought I was. To be honest, I don't know anymore. Matthew Dunleavy was a lot of fun. He was different from Papa in every way. Everything with him was light and easy and uncomplicated. He didn't take life so seriously the way Papa did. He just wanted to have a good time.

"Papa hated him. He believed Matthew was beneath me. He said Matthew was only interested in my money. He said I was a fool for falling for his charms."

Her voice cracked. Even after three years, the words cut as if they'd been spoken yesterday.

"Matthew wasn't like that. He didn't have a nefarious bone in his body. He didn't look far enough down the road to be conniving. He lived his whole life for the moment he was in without a care about what might be coming around the bend. That's all right when you're young and silly and in love. Eventually though, you realize you have to grow up."

She closed the basket lid and sat back on the stool. "I realized it anyway. I don't think Matthew ever did. I wanted more. I still want more. I knew I would never have it with him the day I told him I was going to have a baby."

The color drained from Zach's face. "You were going to what?"

Ellie didn't look away. She didn't come here to apologize for her past. Only to make sure he knew.

"One night Papa and I had a terrible fight. He said Matthew was a worthless gambler and he was using me. I told Papa he loved his money more than he loved me. I told him I wished he wasn't my papa. I wished he was dead."

She squeezed her eyes shut. Her cheeks burned with shame. She remembered how Papa's face had turned red. So red she thought he would explode, that he would strike her. Then his steely gray eyes went flat. He looked at her the way he would a horse that went lame. It was a shame, but he wouldn't lose any sleep over its loss.

"I wanted to take the words back as soon as I said them. I didn't wish Papa were dead. He was the best papa I could've asked for. But I was so proud. Just like him. I wanted to hurt him for hurting me. I never said I was sorry. Not that night. Not ever. I'm not good at admitting fault. I never told him I loved him again either. That would be the same as an apology. I wouldn't apologize because I was right. At least, I thought I was.

"That night, I went to Matthew. I wanted to punish Papa. I knew it was stupid and reckless and a sin, but—I can't undo it. I thought Matthew loved me enough to…"

She took a deep breath. Now that she started, she couldn't stop. Zach needed to hear everything, even if it meant he could never look her in the face again. And she needed to say the words out loud. Words she'd never spoken. Thoughts she never fully processed.

"I thought he loved me enough to change who he was. That was maybe the stupidest part of all. You can't change a tiger to a lion, no matter how much you want to.

"I didn't want to tell you about the baby, Zach. I didn't want to tell anyone. I even convinced myself it wasn't true for a time. When I told Matthew, I thought he would make it right. I thought he would explain to Papa how much we loved each other, and he was going to give up gambling and marry me and go to work for the company and everything would work out. Instead, all I saw on his face was panic and fear, and even disappointment. I believe he almost hated me at that moment. I knew then he would never give up anything for me. He loved me but not enough to take care of me and our child."

"Where is the baby?" Zach's voice was barely audible.

"She didn't survive. She came too early. I don't even know if the baby was a girl, but that's how I think of her. I named her Rebecca after Mama. I love her, and I miss her every day. She'll always be a part of me, and even though I sinned, I don't regret her."

She looked at Zach, wishing he would say something. He didn't.

"I didn't tell Papa about the baby, but somehow he knew. He never forgave Matthew. I'm not sure if he forgave me. He wanted to protect me. In his twisted logic, he thought he was doing what was best. He didn't want me to ruin my life with a man like Matthew. He did what he always did. He took care of things. That's who Papa was—a fixer. He saw a bad situation and took matters into his own hands."

She clenched her eyes shut to build up her nerve.

"My papa killed Matthew. He murdered him and let me and everyone in town believe Matthew left town to escape gambling debts. Harper and Logan uncovered the truth. The night Papa died he tried to kill Harper. When he realized he couldn't get away with it, he ran away. It was storming and the drive was wet. He fell off his horse."

The image of Papa's body on the drive, slick with rain, filled her mind. She swallowed the bile that threatened to empty her stomach.

"Papa's gone and I'll never have the chance to tell him I loved him. Despite everything he did, I love him still. I'm sorry I was an ungrateful, willful daughter. Maybe if I'd been better, obedient, he wouldn't have needed to…"

She pushed the thoughts away. She couldn't go back and change who she was just like she couldn't change Papa or Matthew.

"For the last eight months I focused my attention and energy on my art so I wouldn't have to think about Papa and Matthew and my baby. But they'll always be part of my life. Part of who I am. Zach, you made me realize I'm not beyond hope. God can still use me if I let Him."

Zach didn't say a word, which was probably just as well. Ellie stood and took her cloak off the back of the chair. She took her time buttoning it and looping the basket over her arm, giving him time to speak. To say something.

After a moment she turned toward the door. His voice stopped her.

"I'm glad you told me, Ellie."

When she turned back to look at him, his expression was unreadable. "Nothing you did changes the fact I wouldn't be here if not for you. You saved my life."

Was that how he would always think of her? The woman who set his knee and kept him warm and dry for a few days? It may be enough for him, but she needed more.

Chapter Twenty-Five

"Hello, anyone here?"

Zach pulled himself upright in bed as far as he was able. His head thrummed with pain at the movement. Even with Dr. Dutton's medicine coursing through his system, he hadn't slept much last night. He rubbed his hand across his bristled jaw. He hadn't shaved since Friday. He had spent his Monday watching the progression of the sun across the polished floor and wondering how long Dr. Dutton planned to keep him here. Not long if Zach had anything to say about it. Crippled or not, he had a ranch to run.

"The doctor stepped out," he called to the man at the front door.

Heavy boot treads moved in his direction. Zach straightened the blanket over his legs and adjusted the dressing on his head. If he'd known he was in charge of receiving the doctor's patients when she was out of the office, he would've asked for a desk.

Logan Kinski stepped into the doorway, looking the picture of health and vigor. Zach liked the man a little less because of it.

"I'm not here to see the doc. I came to give you a report on the ranch."

Zach irritation evaporated into the warm sunshine spilling through the large windows. He motioned to the stool where Ellie had sat yesterday while she bared her soul to him.

Logan sat and ran his hands around the brim of his hat. "Burt and I rode across your property this morning. He's the stable manager at the Lundy mansion," he said to Zach's questioning look. "Used to be my job, but Burt's got it now. Anyway, no need to worry about your fencing. It survived the storm, so I turned the cow and horse out. We drove the other cattle closer to the barn. It'll be easier to manage them there."

Zach nodded as Logan talked. Logan didn't need to explain the details. Both men knew what the cattle needed, but he appreciated the update.

"Three of your cows have calved. You have two pretty little heifers that appear in good shape. Unfortunately, we found a bull calf in the gulley near the creek. His mama obviously went down there during the blizzard. He didn't make it, but the cow looks fine. The other seven are about to drop their calves any day from the look of things."

Zach listened to the account but couldn't muster much enthusiasm about the ranch or his cattle. He wanted to ask about Ellie. He could tell she needed something from him when she left yesterday. He hadn't been able to give it. He didn't know if he ever could.

"I appreciate your help the last couple days. I plan to be outta this bed tomorrow. Then I can relieve you. I'll find a way to pay you back for the work you've done. Ellie said you're raising a house on your property. As soon as my leg's healed enough to move around, I'll come out and do whatever I can to work off the debt."

"You don't owe a debt for getting caught in an avalanche. It's what neighbors do out here. You would've done the same for me."

"Where I come from, a man doesn't ask others to pay for his own hardship."

Logan's lips flattened. "That's not what I thought you were doing."

Zach nodded begrudgingly. He glared at his left leg, encased in a splint much less cumbersome than the one Ellie had fashioned. "I know. I'm sorry. It's just this whole situation. It really grates on me."

Logan watched him for a moment before speaking. "You one of those fellas can't admit when he needs a little help?"

"Don't know. I've never been in the position before. But I believe the Good Book. Pride goeth before a fall, it says."

"And a haughty spirit before destruction," Logan finished. "Everybody always leaves out that part."

"You saying I got a prideful spirit?"

"Only you can answer that."

The two men studied each other. After a few moments, Logan drew in his legs to stand. "I best be getting on. I haven't been to the mansion yet. I want to spend some time with my wife before I head back to your place."

"I appreciate all your help, Kinski," Zach said. "You were under no obligation when you rode into my barnyard the other day."

Logan stood and brushed the lint off his hat. "I reckon I've not spent a night away from my bride since the day we married. It gave me some anxious sleep, considering her condition."

Zach looked up at him. He didn't like another man hovering over him. Maybe he did have a prideful spirit. He needed to spend some time in prayer about it, among other things.

"I appreciate you forsaking your own concerns for mine. Many a man wouldn't have offered to do what you did for a stranger."

"That's where you're wrong. Like I said, the men around here are ready to pitch in when there's a need. If you plan to stay, you might be called upon to help someone else someday."

If he planned to stay.

Zach didn't tell him he'd been thinking about little else since arriving at the doctor's office.

"How's—er, how are the women faring without you?"

He gave himself an inward kick as Logan's eyes filled with mirth. He had just said he hadn't been home yet to see Harper.

"I reckon they're fine. When I get there, I'll be sure to tell them you asked."

"No need for that," Zach said. "I don't want them thinking—"

"You don't want Ellie to know you asked about her?"

There was no point in denying it, so Zach didn't answer at all.

"I won't tell her," Logan said. "But I am a little curious. Guess you can blame it on me living with two women for the last year."

"Curious about what?" Zach snapped.

"About what you plan to do about Ellie. Living with her and Harper has also made me aware of things men don't generally notice. I wouldn't have been paying as close attention if I wasn't worried about Ellie spending six days in a cabin with a man none of us knew. Maybe that's why I picked up on the spark between you."

"Spark? What spark—"

Logan went on as if he hadn't spoken. "Ellie cares for you. You care about her, too, or your face wouldn't be turning that shade of purple right now. You probably love her. As her closest male relative as it were, it's my duty to know your intentions. You gonna marry her or what?'

"Marry? I told you nothing untoward happened between us. If I could get outta this bed quick enough, I'd punch your face for suggesting such a thing."

Logan raised his hands and backed up a step, chuckling. "Easy there. I didn't say something unlawful happened. I'm just saying it's within my rights to get a shotgun and drag you both in front of a preacher."

"We were out there alone because of this," he gestured at his leg, "in case you forgot."

"Doesn't matter. Any judge in this state would see my side of things. Not a one of them would fault me if I shot you right now."

Zach stared at him a moment, then laughed. "Ellie doesn't seem like she needs a man to preserve her honor. If she hasn't shot me yet, I'm not much worried you will."

Logan looked almost disappointed. "I reckon not. But I believe I know her well enough to know what she does need. A man who'll love her in spite of her last name. In spite of her past. A man who knows what it's like to need grace."

Zach looked up sharply. Did Logan know something? Had he somehow learned what happened between him and Rusty Higginbotham in Louisiana? Impossible! No one west of the Mississippi knew about that night.

"No one needs to tell me about grace," he bit out. "If God's forgiven a person for their past, it sure isn't my place to hold it over their head."

"That's good to hear," Logan said evenly as if he didn't hear the venom in Zach's voice. "So, I suppose it doesn't bother you at all that she's one of the richest women west of the Rocky Mountains. Maybe the richest."

Zach's stomach sank. "I reckon that would bother most men."

"Would you love her more if her situation was poverty instead of wealth?"

"I never said I loved her at all."

Logan raised a hand again in a gesture that said he wasn't here to argue the point. "I just asked if it'd be easier to love a poor girl than a rich one. Or a plain girl instead of a pretty one."

Zach snorted. "Don't tell me it hasn't bothered you living in another man's house with Ellie and her cousin and a staff catering to your every need."

Logan pulled up. "No one caters to me."

Zach laughed out loud. "That's what I thought. It's easy to expect me to accept Ellie's wealth, but your pride has you defending yourself against taking something you haven't work for."

Logan crossed his arms over his chest and rocked back on his heels. "I admit it took a little getting used to.

I worked for Ellie's father for three years before I met Harper. Now I've gone from stable manager to man of the house. The point is, I love Harper and Harper loves Ellie. Both of us will do anything to protect her. Including shooting a man who tries to take advantage of her position."

His face hardened and he stared unblinking down at Zach. Zach wished again he could stand and look at the man eye to eye. Whatever Logan had to say, Zach hated that he was forced to sit down for it.

Logan exhaled, long and loud. "I reckon it's better that you didn't know who Ellie was the whole time she was in your cabin. You'll never have to ask yourself if you love the woman or if you love her money. She won't have to wonder either."

Zach nearly reminded him he'd still not said anything about loving her. Logan wasn't stupid, though. It was pointless to defend himself against something so obvious.

"She's the heiress to an empire. My family lost everything in the War. I have nothing to offer her."

Logan nodded thoughtfully. "I reckon that's for Ellie to decide. You love her. If you didn't, you wouldn't agonize over this so much. You'd just marry her and move into that big mansion and accept a gentleman's life of ease. I wouldn't count on that happening, though. Ellie Lundy's not the kind who'll give a man something for nothing. Her pappy was a strong man. It'll take an even stronger one to fill those shoes. Maybe you're not the one."

"That sounds like a challenge."

"Nope. Just an observation."

When the front door slammed shut behind Logan, Zach began the long process of getting out of bed and crossing the room to reach his pants and shirt. He was nearly dressed when he heard someone come in the back door. Leaning awkwardly on the crutches, he hurriedly finishing buttoning his shirt.

When Lisette Dutton saw him standing nearly dressed, she hurried across the room to him. "Mr. Walsh, where are you going?"

"I appreciate all you've done, Doc. My leg feels better already without twenty pounds of lumber strapped to it. But I have to go. I need to talk to Ellie."

"That's fine. I'll send for her. You can talk to her right here. You need to stay off your feet for at least another week so the swelling on your knee..." She stopped talking when she realized Zach wasn't paying attention.

He glanced around the room for his belt. "That'll have to wait, at least another few hours. I'm going to Ellie. Now"

The auburn-haired doctor tilted her head. "How do you propose to get there?"

Realization nearly made Zach throw down the crutches in frustration. "I don't suppose you could lend me a horse for a spell."

"You won't be getting on and off a horse unassisted until summer."

Zach's first inclination was to curse the avalanche and the continued inconveniences it presented. He supposed God intended it to teach him humility, a lesson sure to be hard learned. He situated the crutches under his armpits. "Reckon I better get to walking."

The doctor's eyes gleamed at his determination. "My buggy's still hitched outside. You're welcome to it. I can't have you collapsing on the road. Folk'll blame it on my doctoring."

Chapter Twenty-Six

Ellie sat on the wide veranda facing the street. The ten-foot-tall metal gates stood open to the town, not that she often had visitors. While Papa was alive, the front gates were closed unless he was expecting a business associate. Even then, most visitors were encouraged to use the back gate. He claimed he didn't want his day frittered away with frivolous interruptions. Nor did he want curious neighbors poking their noses into his business. Ellie suspected it was more than that. The gates were always open when Mama was alive. Though Papa never admitted it, Ellie knew he closed himself off from the world after Mama died.

She had told Zach Papa hadn't grieved one day for Mama. He had gone back to work the way he always did. Now she realized she was wrong. He had grieved every day. The huge gate and the stone walls that locked him inside with his grief were his proof.

She should've asked him about Mama more. Everyone knew he didn't want to talk about his late wife, so the entire household tiptoed around the subject. Ellie wished now she had forced him to talk. Even if he didn't want to divulge his loss, she should've made him listen to hers. Now it was too late. He was gone, and she didn't understand him any better than one of his employees.

So many things may have been different if she had worked to know Papa. For all his evil deeds, she still believed there had been good in him. Mama loved him. That meant something. Her gentle mother wouldn't have fallen in love with a monster.

Papa had also loved Ellie. As soon as she intimated a want or desire, he made sure she got it. He urged her to go away to university, but when she resisted, he didn't force the issue.

Two stubborn people, she and Papa. Cut from the same cloth; unable or unwilling to bend, to apologize, to say the words that weren't said often enough. She would never know the depths of his love or how losing Mama had shaped the man he became.

Ellie opened the sketchbook on the table beside her. She had come out to sketch the open gate and the view of the street. Through the gate, she had a clear view of the Trego mansion. In a few months there wouldn't be any Tregos left in Willow Wood.

At the first of the year Felicity Trego had married Ned Yates, the lawyer Ellie was scheduled to meet with tomorrow. In June, Belinda Trego was marrying Carl Rayburn, the man she reportedly loved for twenty years. Who knew! Belinda had never shown an interest in men or anything outside her family's factory, Trego Leatherworks, which she ran nearly single-handedly since her father's death. Then Felicity fell in love with Ned, Belinda reunited with Carl, and Willow Wood was still trying to catch up.

Ellie doubted she would ever do anything to surprise anyone.

She looked down at the sketchbook. So far, the page was blank. Her pencil hadn't made the first mark. She couldn't stop thinking of the papa she would never fully know. She didn't want to live with regrets. Papa would be disappointed in her if she did. He would tell her regrets were a luxury only for the weak.

She took up a pencil and began to draw. With determined strokes, she sketched the strong lines of her papa's jaw, his firm mouth, his thick eyebrows.

Since August, she had kept all memories of him out of her head. Now she wanted to remember. Tears blurred her vision as her hand moved across the paper. She didn't need to see. She knew the face, the lines, the man.

She turned up the corners of his mouth and added light and shadow to his eyes. Papa always assumed a serious countenance for a picture. Not today. Her own face softened as she drew the man she had grown up with; the man who only wanted the best for her, the man who held Mama's hand as her health deteriorated, who pushed her wheeled chair through the garden, who adjusted the shawl around her shoulders when they moved into the shade of the willows.

Ellie would remember that man today.

A carriage slowed on the street and turned into the long drive. She recognized Lisette Dutton's horse, followed by the carriage as it came into view. But the man driving wasn't Grayson Dutton. This man was—Zach.

She nearly dropped the pencil and sketchbook in her haste to stand up. She set the sketchbook facedown on the table and strode to the end of the veranda. She hugged her arms around her middle though the early April day was warm.

"What are you doing here?" she called to him. "Does Dr. Dutton know you're out of bed? Does she know you stole her carriage?"

Zach laughed, the deep rumble causing a flutter in her middle. "She sent me here with her blessing. Well, not a blessing. Exactly. She just knew she couldn't stop me."

He pulled the carriage into the shade at the bottom of the veranda steps and began the arduous descent to the ground. Ellie considered going down to help, but she knew his pride wouldn't appreciate it. So she waited.

He swung down using only his strong arms and landed on his right foot. He took the crutches from the seat and lurched to the bottom of the veranda. Ellie opened the front door and stuck her head inside. She heard Debra moving around in the dining room where she'd been cleaning earlier. She called for the maid to bring two glasses of lemonade and a plate of cookies.

By the time she finished with her instructions, Zach had reached the top step.

She motioned to a wide wooden chair. "You're getting better at moving around on those things."

"Necessity." He dropped into the chair.

Instinctively, she grasped his left ankle and lifted it onto the footstool. She wanted to chastise his foolishness for coming when he should be at the doctor's office resting. She was alarmed by the red in his face and the way his left leg trembled against the footstool. She was also secretly flattered he'd gone to the trouble.

"Logan came by the doctor's office a while ago to give me a report on my cattle."

She sat down on the chair beside his. "I know. He's inside with Harper now. Mrs. Philips is preparing dinner. Should I tell her you'll be joining us?"

He ignored the invitation. "Three of my cows calved during the storm. Only lost one. Good considering the weather and them being in the canyon without me."

"Why are you telling me this?"

"Because none of it mattered. Naturally, I hate to think of losing a calf or how the cow may have suffered with it. But I wasn't interested in cattle or anything else on the ranch."

He stared at her as if she should understand. "I'm afraid I still don't follow."

"I didn't care because of you," he exclaimed. "None of it mattered because you weren't there." He gestured with one hand around the veranda. "This is you. This is where you belong. Not my cramped little cabin with no indoor water. This—" he gestured again. "I can't compete with this. I can't offer you anything, Ellie Lundy. I can't even offer you a whole man."

She followed his gaze to his splinted leg. What was he talking about? Was he—

The front door opened, and Debra stepped out with a tray. The maid couldn't have come at a better time. It gave Ellie a chance to think. She jumped up and took the two glasses and set them on the table. Her hands shook, and the shaved ice clinked inside the glasses. "Thank you, Debra." She took the plate of cookies, leaving the maid with the empty tray. "You don't need to come back to collect anything. I'll bring the dishes inside when we're finished."

Ellie took her time returning to her seat. She took a sip from the glass, letting the cool liquid soothe her throat. It was hard to believe a blizzard had dumped a foot of snow in the mountains last week, and today she was perspiring inside her dress. She recognized the perspiration had little to do with the sunshine.

Zach glanced at the door to make sure the maid wasn't coming back. He ignored the glass and plate of cookies. "I thought I was prepared when I came up this hill. But the closer I got and the more of your house that came into view—" He released a low whistle.

"It crossed my mind to keep driving and circle back to the doctor's office. I've known people with money, but you must have more than every person I've ever met combined."

She gripped the glass, irritation bubbling. "I don't know what you want me to say. I told you why I didn't tell you my last name. I should've explained in the beginning, but the topic doesn't organically lend itself to conversation. Pass the salt, and by the way, I own a railroad."

"You're right. You didn't owe me anything. Not then and not now."

So why was he here?

"I won't apologize for my situation, Zach. Tomorrow I'm going to Papa's office to see to my holdings at the company. I'm not sure how it'll happen, but it's time I faced my responsibilities there. I've closed myself up in this house long enough. I appreciate everything Harper and Logan have done for me, but I'm not a child. I don't need protection."

He sat back in the chair. "I didn't come expecting an apology. I came to give one. When I first realized who you were, I thought I was angry because you hadn't told me your name. It took me about five minutes to realize it wasn't anger I was feeling. It was pride. If your name had been anything but Lundy, I guess it wouldn't have stung so bad. You told me you've been judged your whole life because of who you are. I went and done the same thing. I'm sorry."

Zach rubbed his hand over his roughened jaw. "I hope you'll forgive me for that, but it's not the only reason I'm here." He took a deep breath and looked toward the street.

Tears stung Ellie's nose. Had he come to tell her goodbye? Would she see him after today? Whatever happened, she prayed she was ready. The idea of walking through the company door tomorrow sat like a cannonball in her stomach. She was eager to step into her role at Lundy List. She was also afraid she was in over her head. Everyone in town would be watching. Watching to see if she had Hugh Lundy's brains and leadership skills. Or if she would fall on her face. Ellie wasn't even sure herself. She had been so comfortable at the cabin. At peace. Every day was a struggle but simple. But it wasn't her life. Her life was Willow Wood and running Papa's company.

She blinked away the tears while Zach seemed to gather his thoughts. *I don't want to lose him, Lord. I love him,* she prayed. *But I'll do whatever You need from me for this town. If I must put my duties first at the sake of what my heart wants, give me strength to accept it.*

"Ellie, I am the biggest hypocrite you'll ever meet."

Ellie jerked her eyes open at the sound of Zach's voice. Had she missed something? "I—"

"You were right," he continued. "There's more to me coming west than my pa's death. Back home, I wanted to hide from my responsibilities, and I started running with some rough characters. The leader of the group was dangerous. He liked to drink and fight and break things and make noise. One night it went too far. He was determined to start something. He and I got into a brawl. He was a big guy. Sometimes big guys have weak hearts. I guess I hit him the right way at the right time." His voice broke. "He died at my feet."

The blood drained from Ellie's face.

"I took a man's life, Ellie. The witnesses said it wasn't my fault. They told the sheriff Rusty was looking for a fight that night. But none of it changed anything. The man was still dead because I was somewhere I shouldn't have been, doing things I knew better than to do. That's why I came west. I couldn't stand the looks in folks' faces. Especially my Ma's. I let her down, and I wasn't man enough to face it."

Ellie couldn't speak. She didn't know if she was angry or shocked or sad for the man who died. Or for Zach.

He sat forward and rested his elbows on his knees. He clasped his hands and stared at them. "I never thought a woman would want me after what I'd done. I didn't think I deserved that kind of happiness. When I came west, I thought this would be my life. I'd build a little cabin on a ranch and raise cattle and horses and live as many days as the Lord gave me. And I'd live them alone paying penance to my parents and to the man I killed.

"Then I met you. When Logan came to see me today, I realized I didn't care anything about that cabin or the ranch. A week ago, it was my whole world. Now…"

He lifted his head and looked into her eyes. "Well, now, it means nothing if I have to go back out there without you."

His hand reached for hers, and Ellie took it. "The Lord forgave me for what happened to Rusty. But my pride made me think my sin was too great for me to forgive myself. It nearly convinced me I couldn't love you. That I could never have you. But I do love you, Ellie Lundy. Your name can't change that, though I pray you might think about changing it someday."

Ellie's stomach tightened. "Zach—"

He dug his right boot into the veranda floor and pulled his chair closer to hers. He grabbed her other hand. He looked around, his gaze taking in the front of the house and the manicured approach from the street. "I can never offer you anything you don't already have."

Ellie's chest felt like it would explode. "I would never ask you to."

He shook his head. "But I'd want to. I want to give you the world, but it looks like you already own it."

She laughed around a throat tight with tears.

Zach leaned forward, but he couldn't reach her over the splint on his knee.

Ellie shifted her chair, so her knees faced his outstretched leg. They leaned together and their lips met. Warmth and sweetness washed over her as she melted into him. After a few moments, the horse at the bottom of the steps snorted and stamped its foot. They laughed at its impatience and pulled apart.

"I love you, too, Zach," she whispered.

He glanced away. When he looked back, his eyes were hopeful. "Are you sure it'll be enough? I'll be enough?"

Ellie opened her mouth to tell him she would never want anything but his love and this moment. She remembered her prayer from a few moments ago, and a thought occurred to her.

She straightened. "There is one other thing I need from you. I need someone to help me manage my share of Lundy List. I want it to be you."

He dropped her hands, and distance fell between them. "I don't know anything about railroads or mining."

"Neither do I, except that they're a lot of work. You know how to build a business from scratch. You told me so yourself. You've practiced law. This should be a piece of cake for a man with your experience."

What experience? I was a kid when I did all that."

"You're not a kid now, and you're still doing it. I saw your books."

"My what?"

"Your ledgers. I looked through them the first day at your cabin while you were sleeping. I wasn't snooping. Well, maybe I was. I was bored and looking around, and I saw the ledgers you keep for the cattle. I knew then you were a businessman at heart. I need someone like that at Lundy List. Someone I can trust. Someone with as much to lose as I have."

"I won't take a charity position."

"Good, because I'm not offering one."

Ellie swiped her hand across her damp eyes as excitement swelled in her bosom. "We've got work to do, Zach Walsh. Papa put his entire life into this company. Into Willow Wood. I want to do the same thing. The way I look at it, both of us—together—can honor our parents by making Lundy List more successful than it is today. We're almost to a new century. The nation is changing, and it will keep changing. I want our railroad to be at the forefront."

Zach looked down at his knee, the horse at the bottom of the veranda, the impressive stone gate, before bringing his gaze back to her. "I don't want to disappoint you."

"Then don't. Help me."

He reached forward and brushed his thumb across the fading bruise on her lip. "I hope you know what you're doing."

She smiled. "We'll learn together."

They leaned into each other. The kiss began softly but quickly intensified. Zach was the first to pull away.

"I think you better agree to marry me before Logan comes out here with a shotgun and chases me off your fancy porch."

"What?"

He kissed her again. "Will you? Will you marry me?"

"You know I will."

Ellie's heart seemed to stand still as their lips met. This was what grace felt like. God had answered her prayers. She no longer needed to hide from her past. She could fulfill her duties to the people of Willow Wood and still have the desires of her heart. She was forgiven, and it felt wonderful.

The End

Coming Soon

If you have enjoyed Ellie's story, or any of the books in the Willow Wood series, please take a moment to leave a review on Amazon, Goodreads, or any other marketplace or blog that allows reviews. Honest reviews are the best way for new readers to discover my books.

Then, download a copy of the next book in the series, the much anticipated:

A Cowboy for Meggan: Willow Wood Brides Book 6

Chapter One

"Where'd you say you were from, young man?"

Shane Casey tore his gaze away from the young woman sitting across from him on the stagecoach. He'd been trying not to stare since the moment he saw her before they boarded the stage in Smithfield. It wasn't easy. Her hair was as black and shiny as a raven's wing and looked as soft. She was tall and slim as a willow branch, only a couple inches less than Shane's nearly six feet of height. She had smooth porcelain skin and lush red lips that kept drawing his gaze. But what really grabbed his attention were those mesmerizing emerald green eyes. He figured they were even prettier when she smiled. From the firm set of her jaw and proud tilt of her head, he doubted he'd ever know for sure.

Her traveling companion was another matter altogether. The old lady had introduced herself as Gloria Hennessey before they climbed aboard the stage. She was short and round with thinning gray hair combed into a tidy bun. Laughing, faded blue eyes shone out from a face amass with wrinkles. Probably because she smiled so much and never stopped talking.

Back at the station, as Shane took her hand to help her into the stage, she had introduced the younger woman as her granddaughter Meggan Jones. Meggan rewarded him with a ghost of a distracted smile that didn't come close to reaching those green eyes as she rejected his offer of assistance.

Shane had briefly hoped the old lady would doze off once the stage got moving and he could pass the trip home to Willow Wood getting to know Miss Jones. It didn't take two minutes to realize that wasn't going to happen. Mrs. Hennessey showed no signs of drowsiness, and Meggan showed even less interest in getting to know him.

He hoped Mrs. Hennessey hadn't noticed him staring at her granddaughter. Not likely since she hadn't paid Meggan any more mind than Meggan paid Shane.

"I'm from Willow Wood, ma'am," Shane told her.

"Has it been long since you've been home?"

Shane felt like he'd been on the road for a month of Sundays. His boots and britches were caked with dust. His face bore the signs of travel, too, he was sure. He hadn't shaved since he left St. Louis, and his dark hair was mashed flat against his head under his Stetson. As soon as he got home, after hugging his ma and tasting some of her fine cooking, his first order of business was a hot bath and a warm shave.

He wouldn't mind coaxing a smile out of the brunette across from him first.

"Yes, ma'am. Besides a few visits home to see my ma, I've been gone for four years."

"Four years? My, my. What kept you away so long?"

Out of the corner of his eye, Shane saw the brunette stiffen in her seat. She pursed her lips and glanced at her grandmother.

Shane waited half a breath to see if she was about to say something. She hadn't uttered as much as a peep, and he was curious to know what her voice sounded like—or if she even had one. When it became apparent she wasn't going to say anything now either, he turned his attention back to her grandmother.

"I left Willow Wood to study animal husbandry. After I finished school, I worked with a few animal doctors for the experience. The last one was in a little town in Missouri. Too far for coming home for visits."

"Missouri. Did you hear that, Meggan? My, my, that's where we're from. Kansas City."

Shane heard an intake of air as Meggan's green eyes widened. Her jaw clenched tight. Shane was sure she'd speak this time since something had obviously gotten under her skin. But after a visible effort to bring her emotions under control, she turned toward the window, dismissing them both.

Mrs. Hennessey didn't seem to notice Meggan's irritation. "Are you home for good?" she asked Shane without a glance in her granddaughter's direction.

A bubble of enthusiasm spiked in Shane's gut, despite Meggan's lack of interest. He'd worked a long time to see his plans come to fruition, he couldn't believe they were finally within reach.

"Yes, ma'am. I'm going to raise me a strong line of working horses and open my own veterinary clinic."

"My, my, that's quite ambitious for a young man. I expect your parents are very proud of you. And anxious to have you home too."

"Yes, ma'am. It's just my ma, though. Pa passed away when I was little.

Mrs. Hennessey reached across the expanse of seats and patted his hand. "Well, I wish you all the success in your new venture. You sound like a very industrious young man. Doesn't he, Meggan?"

Shane didn't bother looking to see if Meggan had an opinion, one way or the other, since he already knew she wouldn't. He suspected Mrs. Hennessey knew, too, and only included her granddaughter in the conversation out of habit, not because she expected a response.

"I hope so, ma'am," he said.

The old woman tilted her head and gave him a playful smile. "Is there a young woman waiting for you in Willow Wood, Mr. Casey?"

Meggan stiffened, though she didn't look away from the window. Was she curious, too, or simply annoyed her grandmother would ask a question only an old lady could get away with asking?

Heat rose under Shane's skin. "Uh, no, ma'am. My work...keeps me pretty busy."

"I suppose it would. Well, you just never know. Love generally comes when we're not looking for it. Isn't that right, Meggan?"

Mrs. Hennessey finally succeeded illiciting a reaction from her granddaughter. Meggan gave her a withering look, which the old woman chose to ignore.

"Where are you ladies headed?" Shane asked to steer the conversation in any other direction.

"Seattle. Have you ever been?"

"Granny!" Meggan hissed between clenched white teeth. Her eyes went round in warning. Mrs. Hennessey stared expectantly at Shane—unaware of, or in spite of—Meggan's agitation.

Shane looked back and forth between the women, wondering what he'd missed. Though he'd been too busy the past year or two to pursue a romantic engagement, he would've liked seeing Meggan Jones again and possibly making a better impression on her. That wouldn't happen with her in Seattle.

"No, ma'am, I've never been," he answered Mrs. Hennessey.

"Neither have we. I'm looking forward to it. I love traveling; seeing as much of this magnificent nation as time allows. So does Meggan."

Meggan stared at her grandmother's profile, her full lips pressed together in a hard line. After a few moments of waiting for a reaction that never came, she exhaled and turned back to the window.

Why did she care if Shane knew where they were going? He hadn't kept his own plans a secret. Maybe she feared he was a highwayman bent on following them into the wilderness to rob them—or worse. Or she was tired of her grandmother telling their business to everyone they met on the road.

Whatever the reason, Meggan's ire was lost on the old lady. Mrs. Hennessey smiled at Shane and opened the bulging, well-worn scrapbook on her lap she had shown him nearly the instant the stage got rolling.

When she first removed the scrapbook from her satchel, Shane had groaned inwardly and prepared for a deluge of pictures of children, grandchildren, and newspaper clippings of their accomplishments and deeds. Instead, she had turned the scrapbook around to show him a Wanted poster and gleefully recounted how the man in the rendering had murdered two guards during the robbery of a federal payroll in the Texas Hill Country.

Shane listened with morbid curiosity to more stories of criminals and their villainous acts as she flipped through the pages. It seemed an odd hobby for an old lady who looked more suited to rocking babies than collecting Wanted posters. He had to hand it to her; she sure knew how to spin a good yarn. He imagined she could make a fair living writing dime novels should she take a notion.

She looked up to make sure she still had his attention.

"Here's a good one. This is Harold Watkins. You'd think he was a bank clerk or watchmaker from the looks of him. I suppose that's why he was so good at what he did. Harold lived with his mother in a small apartment in Lawrence, Kansas. Everyone in the neighborhood thought he was a mild-mannered man who sacrificed his future to care for his dear mother."

Mrs. Hennessey's eyes brightened with every word of the story. "Not our Harold. He was a confidence man of the highest caliber. Because of his mild demeanor and ability to lower the defenses of everyone he met, he was able to talk trusting old ladies out of every dime they had. Took advantage of so many. He was so charming and agreeable that even after his crimes were exposed, many of his victims refused to believe he meant them any harm and defended him in court. Isn't that right, Meggan?"

The old woman snickered without giving Meggan a chance to answer. "He's not cheating old ladies anymore, no sirree. Justice finally caught up with him. My, my, thieves and swindlers don't know when to quit. They get away with something once, or even a hundred times, and they think they'll keep getting away with it." She shook her head as she stared at the picture of Harold's bespectacled face.

She was right; he did look like a bank clerk.

"Arrogance. It's the downfall of many an otherwise shrewd individual."

Meggan muttered something under her breath Shane couldn't hear over the creaking of the stage. If he hadn't seen her lips move, he wouldn't have known she had spoken at all.

Mrs. Hennessey turned a few more pages. "Ooh, you'll like this one." Her pale blue eyes shone with excitement.

"This here is Earl McCaffrey. My, my, he was an evil man if there ever was one. He was a lawman, don't you know, who murdered the girl he was courting along with her mother. Earl had a bad reputation—much deserved, by the way—and the girl's parents forbade her from seeing him. Rumor had it that Earl had already gotten away with murdering three people in cold blood.

"He once shot a boy in the back who he said was stealing a pig. For goodness sakes, the boy had already dropped the pig and took off toward home. Earl fired anyway, killing the poor thing right in his tracks. Even the man who owned the pig said the boy's family was hard up, and he wished he had done something sooner to help them before it came to such a desperate act."

Mrs. Hennessey shook her head and managed to look disapproving, but her eyes gleamed in the dusty interior of the coach.

"Anyway, the girl's parents caught her sneaking out with Earl a time or two. Her pa threatened to kill Earl if he ever came back. Nobody knows if the girl came to her senses or if she was completely bewitched by Earl's charms, but one day he went out to the house when it was just the girl and her mother there. Maybe he tried to get the girl to run off with him. Maybe he argued with her ma."

She shrugged as if it didn't matter. "Either way, he killed them both. Her pa came home and found them laid out right there in the dooryard, slaughtered like hogs. Earl went on the run for nearly a year. Justice finally caught up with him on a little farm in Missouri near a place called Wilcox. Got his neck stretched, he did. Thank the Lord," she added as an afterthought.

Shane sat back against the wall of the coach. He wasn't sure if he was more distressed by the grisly story or the cavalier way in which the genteel old lady told it.

She sighed and smoothed her hand over the ruthless murderer's face. "If I was a little younger, why I'd think mighty serious about hunting down these animals myself and hauling them in for the reward," she said, pronouncing it re-ward.

She closed the book on her lap and regarded Shane with wide eyes. "Wouldn't that be a hoot? Why they'd never see me coming."

Shane nearly laughed out loud until he realized she was serious.

"Granny, for goodness sake!" Meggan exclaimed. "Why must you say things like that?"

Shane's eyes widened, more surprised by the sound of Meggan's voice—as lovely as he had imagined—than by Mrs. Hennessey's admission.

Indignation stiffened the old lady's spine. "Why not? Sounds a lot more interesting than sitting around embroidering samplers. Don't you think so?" she directed at Shane.

Shane figured just about anything was more interesting than embroidering samplers, especially since he wasn't sure what they were. But he didn't think hunting down outlaws like Earl McCaffrey was a practical occupation for a woman of any age.

Both women stared at him, waiting. He'd been trying to get Meggan's attention for the last two hours. Now that he had it, he wasn't sure what to do with it.

"Well, I...uh...I'm afraid you won't find many bandits hiding from the law in Willow Wood. The biggest crimes you usually hear about are young boys snitching apples off of trees."

Mrs. Hennessey looked disappointed. Meggan turned back to the window.

"Are you staying in town for the evening?" Shane asked, though he already knew the answer. Willow Wood was the end of the line for the stage, and the trains had already pulled out for the day. The ladies wouldn't be continuing to Seattle tonight.

Mrs. Hennessey brightened. "We're staying at the Grand Hotel."

Shane's spirit lifted. Tomorrow morning, he was meeting Lester Cheney at the hotel to inquire about his first acquisition of horses. Maybe he'd arrive a little early and see Meggan—and her grandmother—in the dining room. Outside the window, he recognized the familiar rise and swell of the landscape. Home. Anticipation stirred in his belly. Though he didn't regret a day of the last four years studying or working with some of the top equine doctors west of the Mississippi, it sure felt good to be back in Willow Wood.

The coach slowed and the driver called out to a man on the ground. Before the dust settled, Shane threw open the door, unfolded his long legs, and climbed out.

He turned quickly before the driver could take the privilege from him and offered his hand to Mrs. Hennessey. "Ladies, may I be the first to welcome you to Willow Wood, Idaho."

The old woman smiled warmly at his gallantry. "Thank you, Mr. Casey. You have made our journey a most pleasant one. Hasn't he, Meggan?"

As soon as the older woman's feet touched the ground, Shane reached back into the coach to help Meggan. Gazing down at him with those penetrating green eyes, she hesitated a moment before taking it.

She looked like she was about to say something. Something more than thanks. More than an apology for her grandmother's odd conversation.

After she stepped down, she clung to his hand a heartbeat longer than necessary before slipping free. Shane felt like the wind had been knocked out of him. Was it his imagination or wishful thinking? He'd give anything to know what was behind that guarded expression.

"Oh, Meggan, what a lovely town," Mrs. Hennessey crooned, breaking the spell. She groaned in a refreshingly unladylike manner. "Oh my, my tired bones are so happy to be out of that coach. I believe we might rest here a few days."

"Granny," Meggan said, her voice once more fraught with warning.

Or exasperation. Shane couldn't tell which.

He turned to the older woman. "The Grand Hotel is just across the way, ma'am. Do you need an escort? I'd be happy to help you with your bags."

She giggled. Her eyes flitted past him to Meggan, assuming—correctly, he had to admit—the reason behind his eagerness to assist them. "The driver will help with our bags and send someone for our trunk, I'm sure. But thank you for pointing the way, Mr. Casey. As long as the hotel has a dining room, we'll have dinner there tonight. Should you have no other plans, feel free to join us."

Meggan's jaw tightened. Shane considered accepting just to see that light flash in her green eyes.

"I'm afraid I can't, ma'am," he said instead. "My ma is expecting me."

"Yes, of course. I do hope we run into you again, Mr. Casey."

"You just might," Shane said with a glance at Meggan. He tipped his hat and watched them head across the street in a swish of skirts and chattering banter from Mrs. Hennessey to the driver, now turned porter.

Shane picked up his bag from the ground and turned in the direction of the Trego house on the high hill that overlooked Willow Wood. The older sister, Belinda had written in her last letter that he wouldn't need to rent a horse when he got to town. The sisters would supply as many as he needed until he could secure his own and properly begin his practice.

Over his shoulder, he watched the short, rounded figure of Mrs. Hennessey and the tall, willowy Meggan step off the street and into the shade of the hotel awning. Before the driver could set down the bags to open the door, a cowboy jumped forward to do it for him. The cowboy smiled broadly and tipped his hat at Mrs. Hennessey before directing his full attention to Meggan. Across the distance, Mrs. Hennessey's singsong voice called out her thanks and appreciation for all the helpful cowboys in Willow Wood. Meggan glided through the door without sparing the man a glance.

Shane continued on, pleased the cowboy holding the door had made no greater impression on the beautiful, enigmatic Meggan than he had.

Chapter Two

Meggan removed the last pin from her hat and set it on the bureau. She walked through the doorway of the adjoining room and looked at Gloria Hennessey, the woman everyone believed was her grandmother.

Sometimes, even she believed it.

"Must you tell everything about us to every stranger you meet?"

Why did she bother to ask? She already knew the answer.

Gloria looked at her through the reflection of the dressing table mirror. "Whatever do you mean, dear?"

"The cowboy on the stage. You didn't know anything about him. He could've been an undercover agent. Or a thief. You told him our real names, where we're from, and where we're going. You even told him where we're having dinner."

Gloria spun around on the stool in front of the mirror to face her. "Wasn't he the handsomest thing? And such an interesting young man. Has his whole future mapped out. I admire a man who can make a plan and see it through. Not like the worthless bag of bones that turned my young, foolish head. Did I ever tell you about him? Martin Coss, the laziest excuse of a man on God's green earth. Now, that Shane Casey, he'll amount to something, you mark my words. I bet every young woman in this town is excited to have him back." She arched her thinning eyebrows at Meggan.

Meggan stalked across the room to the bureau and began straightening the toiletries Gloria had dumped out of her carpetbag. She didn't want the older woman to see how the comment had stung. She wished Gloria didn't insist on pointing out every handsome, eligible man they met only to remind her another woman would wind up with him.

Meggan focused on what she was doing and not Shane Casey. Yes, he was handsome with his thick dark hair and deep brown eyes. And interesting too. She would've loved to have gotten to know him better. She never got a chance to talk to anyone her own age about anything of substance. Especially a man. But there was no point in getting to know Shane or bemoaning the way things were. After Gloria rested for a day or two, they would continue to Seattle where she'd meet a whole new group of people she'd never see again after Gloria decided it was time to move on.

Shane's intelligence and enthusiasm were evident in the way he talked about raising horses and building an animal husbandry practice. But as usual, Gloria spent the whole time talking about herself and her blasted fascination with killers and thieves. She refused to see how every word out of her mouth could bring justice down on their heads.

Meggan was sick of it all. Sick of Gloria's games, the lies, the Wanted posters, the feigned interest in others to serve her own end.

Meggan glanced at the trunk the bellman had put at the foot of Gloria's bed. All their earthly possessions—their entire life and being—shoved into one battered trunk.

She wasn't a materialistic person, but it didn't seem right. A person should have more to call their own than what could fit into a trunk. She longed to sit in a chair that hadn't hosted a thousand backsides before her. Sleep in a bed molded to her body and not someone else's. She was tired of living like a guest everywhere she went. She wanted to belong. To see a caring face when she looked across the table. Hear an old friend call her name. Most of all, she wanted to stop looking over her shoulder, afraid an enemy from her past had caught up with her.

Her irritation at the situation bubbled over.

"I just don't understand why you need to tell everyone your life story the moment you meet them. You know how dangerous it is. I don't see why you can't be quiet and listen to their stories for once. It's common courtesy. Not to mention, you learn a lot more by listening than talking. Isn't that what you always say? And you wouldn't attract so much attention."

Gloria cocked her head and grinned. "I don't think I'm the one who attracts attention, dearest."

Meggan exhaled in frustration. What was the point in talking to Gloria about anything? She would always do everything exactly the way she wanted, and Meggan couldn't do a thing about it. It had been that way since the day she moved in with the Hennessey sisters when she was ten. After Grandma Elsie died, she didn't have anywhere else to go. Alice and Gloria lived across the hall and had helped take care of Grandma as her health deteriorated. If they hadn't taken her in, she would've been sent to an orphanage.

Sometimes, she wondered if an orphanage would've been better. There, she may have been adopted. She could've had a normal life. Brothers and sisters. Friends. School. Handsome suitors and dances. Parents to hold her when she cried and teach her more than how to spot an easy mark in a crowd.

"You talk too much," she insisted. "You shouldn't have told Mr. Casey we were from Kansas City. You heard him say he spent time in Missouri. What if he read the papers? What if he knows about the robbery? It's a wonder you didn't tell him what's hidden in your trunk."

Gloria's jaw tightened. Meggan had finally struck a nerve.

"Don't be ridiculous. He was an interesting young man. All I was doing was making conversation to pass the time. You should try it sometime. Our lives would be a lot easier if you tried charming men with the gifts the good Lord gave you instead of acting so stuck up all the time. But no, you leave all the real work to me."

"I have no intention of batting my eyelashes and acting like a simpleton to distract some poor lout while you count the money in his money belt."

Gloria rolled her eyes. She shook the wrinkles out of a pale blue frock and laid it across the bed to change into for dinner. "You've made that abundantly clear. It's a waste if you ask me. I won't be here forever, you know. I don't know how you think you'll make a living without me. You certainly don't know how to talk to people. You have no personality. All you've got is your face and that body. If you don't learn how to use them, you'll starve to death inside of a week."

Meggan turned away. She did have a personality. She had plenty to offer a man besides her appearance. But if the woman who raised her couldn't see it, it wasn't likely anyone else would either.

As usual, Gloria didn't realize she had hurt Meggan's feelings. "It doesn't do any good to take yourself so seriously all the time," she went on. "You should have a little fun when the opportunity presents itself. Like with that Shane Casey fellow. If I was twenty years younger—all right, thirty—you can bet he'd know I was interested."

Meggan pursed her lips, determined not to rise to Gloria's bait. She had been interested in the cowboy, but what good would it do her? Gloria would have her on the train headed to Seattle in a few days, and who knew where to after that. She wanted more than a passing conversation with a man she met in a stagecoach.

She wanted a life.

She pinned an opal brooch to her lapel while she waited for Gloria to change. The brooch was her favorite.

TERESA SLACK

She loved how it brought out the light in her green eyes. Alice had given it to her for her sixteenth birthday. Meggan convinced herself Alice bought the brooch, though more than likely, she had lifted it from the jewelry store after she saw Meggan admiring it. Meggan wouldn't dwell on how the brooch came to be on her lapel. If she did, she wouldn't enjoy any gift the two women had given her over the years.

Downstairs in the hotel restaurant, she surreptitiously watched the other diners. Willow Wood seemed to have its share of wealthy merchants, businessmen, farmers, ranchers, and everyday citizens. Gloria was watching, too—probably deciding who presented the easiest mark with the biggest payday, even though they wouldn't be in town long enough to make use of the knowledge.

"This is a nice restaurant," Meggan said, hoping to distract her. "I'm surprised it's so well appointed for such a small town."

"Not so small." Gloria leaned over the table and kept her voice down. "I noticed some nice homes on our way here. You heard Shane talking about those women who gave him a scholarship. They must be swimming in money. I doubt they're the only ones. There's wealth in this frontier town."

Meggan groaned inwardly. Naturally, Gloria would notice nice houses and successful women and men in well-cut suits—anything that offered an opportunity to enrich herself.

She ignored Gloria's observations. "I noticed a lovely brick church at the bottom of the hill opposite the stage stop. It reminds me of the one I used to attend in Lawrence with Grandma Elsie."

Gloria's lip curled in distaste. "What made you think of Kansas?" She didn't like it when Meggan talked about Grandma Elsie or mentioned the past.

"You did," Meggan reminded her. "You were the one flashing around Harold Watkins' poster on the stage, your very first conquest."

Gloria stabbed a piece of roast beef. Her fork scraped noisily against the plate. "Harold Watkins is a ghost of the past. We needn't speak of him ever again."

"I wasn't speaking of him. You were." Meggan kept her voice intentionally calm. After two weeks of listening to the older woman's braggadocio stories to everyone they met, she enjoyed annoying her. "All the talk of Kansas reminded me of Grandma Elsie. She would love it here. It's so quiet and peaceful. The type of place where a person can settle down."

"What are you talking about, Meggan?"

"I'm talking about Willow Wood. Going to a real church and making friends. Swapping recipes and talking about husbands and children and flowers and sewing circles. You just said I should learn to interact with a man. To catch a husband."

Gloria nearly choked on her tea. "I never said anything about a husband."

"Well, maybe I want one. I'm twenty-one, Granny. Maybe I don't want to go to Seattle."

Gloria's eyes darkened, reminding Meggan for a moment of Alice. Dread wrapped around her stomach like a tight fist. She wouldn't give in to the memories. She wasn't a child anymore. Alice couldn't hurt her. Neither could Gloria. Not physically anyway.

"You don't have a choice, no matter how old you are," Gloria said, her voice low and menacing. Meggan never stood up to her, never openly defied her, and she didn't like it.

"As soon as I rest a few days, we're going to Seattle to meet our contacts. We didn't come all this way to throw away our hard work in some little drink-water town with nothing to offer."

"Maybe it doesn't have anything to offer you, but I like it. I could get a job," she said hopefully. "I could work as a clerk at the factory Shane told us about. Or a...a seamstress at one of the shops."

Gloria laughed. "Oh, darling, you can barely thread a needle."

She dabbed her mouth with her napkin and slipped back into the matronly persona Meggan knew so well. "Once we conclude our business in Seattle, we'll have enough money to go wherever you want. What do you think about San Francisco? I can introduce you to high society men who can give you the life you deserve."

An image of the dusty cowboy on the stage flitted across Meggan's mind. She didn't want to be kept by a man of high society. She wanted a husband who loved her, one to work with side by side as they built a life together. But she was encouraged Gloria was actually talking about settling down, even if it was in San Francisco.

Meggan had noticed the gray pallor around Gloria's mouth and eyes the last few months. Her age was showing. Since Alice died, she promised each job would be the last. Maybe this time it was true. Maybe she finally realized she was too old for subterfuge and staying up all night and tracking felons across the Midwest.

"Are you feeling all right? You look tired."

Gloria sighed and pushed away the plate she had barely touched. Meggan's concern flared anew. Gloria always had a healthy appetite.

"I am tired," the older woman admitted. "All this travel. A necessary part of our profession, but that stagecoach ride took the strength clean out of me."

As they gathered their things and headed upstairs to their suite, Meggan's gaze strayed out the large windows to the darkened streets of Willow Wood. Could she dare hope her life would ever change? She hated to think it would only happen once Gloria became too infirm to make their decisions. Gloria was the closest thing Meggan had to a family.

But she wanted more. A future. A life of her own. Maybe one with a tall, intelligent, dark-headed cowboy with rich brown eyes, a chiseled jaw, and an easy smile. As she followed Gloria through the dining room and across the hotel lobby, she reminded herself not to get her hopes up. Every time she did it ended in heartache.

Download a digital copy or grab the paperback from your favorite online retailer to keep reading *A Cowboy for Meggan*.

Reader Bonus

The story that started it all:

A Promise for Josie:

A Willow Wood Prequel

After a broken promise and a broken heart, is love worth the risk?

Abandoned at the altar on her wedding day, Josie Segal doubts she'll ever find true love. When a tall stranger on his way south to build his own ranch rides into Josie's life, her dreams of love and adventure are reawakened. Can she move beyond the pain and fear of broken promises to trust Owen Dutton, and her own heart?

Sign up for my newsletter and receive a link to download **A Promise for Josie—A Willow Wood Brides Prequel.** Stay up to date on upcoming releases in the exciting Willow Wood Brides series, among other books and series in the works. You'll also be among the first to learn of promos, giveaways, and contests.

I love hearing from readers. Email me at teresa@teresaslack.com anytime with your thoughts or questions about the stories.

About the Author

Teresa Slack loves reading, writing, and falling in love. Creating clean and wholesome western romances where rugged cowboys still sweep independent women off their feet was an easy choice for her.

She writes from her home in the beautiful southern Ohio hills, which she shares with her husband and rescue dog and rescue cat. Any errors and typos she blames on the cat randomly running across her keyboard.